THE SHAPE OF YOU

Praise for Georgia Beers

Blend

"You know a book is good, first when you don't want to put it down. Second, you know it's damn good when you're reading it and thinking, I'm totally going to read this one again. Great read and is absolutely a 5-star romance."—*Front Porch Romance Book Reviews*

Right Here, Right Now

"The angst was written well, but not overpoweringly so, just enough for you to have the heart sinking moment of 'will they make it,' and then you realize they have to because they are made for each other."—*Les Reveur*

What Matters Most

"There's so much more going on, from the way they flirt to how they each learn who the other really is, the way their feelings come about to how the conflict is resolved and where the relationship is at by the end of the book. All the right romantic elements are there, packaged in a way that kept me interested, surprised, and often smiling."—*The Lesbian Review*

A Little Bit of Spice

"As always with Ms Beers's novels, this is well written and edited, well paced and flowing. Definitely one for the reread pile…in fact, one of my favourites from this author." —*The Lesbian Reading Room*

Lambda Literary Award Winner *Fresh Tracks*

"Georgia Beers pens romances with sparks."—*Just About Write*

"[T]he focus switches each chapter to a different character, allowing for a measured pace and deep, sincere exploration of

each protagonist's thoughts. Beers gives a welcome expansion to the romance genre with her clear, sympathetic writing."
—*Curve magazine*

Finding Home

"Georgia Beers has proven in her popular novels such as *Too Close to Touch* and *Fresh Tracks* that she has a special way of building romance with suspense that puts the reader on the edge of their seat. *Finding Home*, though more character driven than suspense, will equally keep the reader engaged at each page turn with its sweet romance."—*Lambda Literary Review*

Mine

"From the eye-catching cover, appropriately named title, to the last word, Georgia Beers's *Mine* is captivating, thought-provoking, and satisfying. Like a deep red, smooth-tasting, and expensive merlot, *Mine* goes down easy even though Beers explores tough topics."—*Story Circle Book Reviews*

"Beers does a fine job of capturing the essence of grief in an authentic way. *Mine* is touching, life-affirming, and sweet."
—*Lesbian News Book Review*

Too Close to Touch

"This is such a well-written book. The pacing is perfect, the romance is great, the character work strong, and damn, but is the sex writing ever fantastic."—*The Lesbian Review*

"In her third novel, Georgia Beers delivers an immensely satisfying story. Beers knows how to generate sexual tension so taut it could be cut with a knife…Beers weaves a tale of yearning, love, lust, and conflict resolution. She has constructed a believable plot, with strong characters in a charming setting."—*Just About Write*

By the Author

Turning the Page

Thy Neighbor's Wife

Too Close to Touch

Fresh Tracks

Mine

Finding Home

Starting from Scratch

96 Hours

Slices of Life

Snow Globe

Olive Oil & White Bread

Zero Visibility

A Little Bit of Spice

Rescued Heart

Run to You

Dare to Stay

What Matters Most

Right Here, Right Now

Blend

The Shape of You

Visit us at www.boldstrokesbooks.com

THE SHAPE OF YOU

by
Georgia Beers

2018

THE SHAPE OF YOU
© 2018 By Georgia Beers. All Rights Reserved.

ISBN 13: 978-1-63555-217-1

This Trade Paperback Original Is Published By
Bold Strokes Books, Inc.
P.O. Box 249
Valley Falls, NY 12185

First Edition: August 2018

Credits
Editor: Lynda Sandoval
Production Design: Stacia Seaman
Cover Design by Ann McMan

Acknowledgments

I've always been athletic. I've also always been a little bit lazy. But I turned over a new leaf over the past year, for a variety of reasons, and one of the things I decided to focus on was getting fit. So, I hired a trainer, I geared up to hate every session, and I wasn't terribly optimistic about seeing results. Turns out, I was wrong, wrong, wrong. I have become both stronger and healthier. Plus, I was shocked to find that I actually enjoy going to the gym. Madness! They say art imitates life, and for me, that's true a lot. I tend to take whatever new thing I've discovered in my world and craft it into a book. Fitness training sparked the idea for this one, and I hope you love it.

I want to thank Wayne Haygood, a knowledgeable, big-hearted guy who started out as my trainer and has become my friend. Wayne showed me that exercise and fitness is not only good for the body, but also good for the soul. He helped me to find my lost confidence and to be proud of the woman I've become. It was a gift, what he taught me, and I will be forever grateful to him.

Thank you to everybody at Bold Strokes Books, especially to Radclyffe and Sandy Lowe, for always making the book publishing process smooth and easy. I hope they know how much this writer appreciates that!

To my editor extraordinaire, Lynda Sandoval, who does her best (and trust me, it's not always easy) to teach me while simultaneously making me look good. I am so keeping her.

My pack of writing support has become so large, it's too much to list everybody individually. Therefore, to my writer friends who cheer me on when I'm having a good writing day and who understand and commiserate with me when I'm feeling like a miserable failure, I say thank you. They know who they are, and there are days I wouldn't make it through without them, without their love, understanding, and support. They're a vital part of my life and my career, and we're all in this together.

To my family, who always supports me, no matter what. Even after doing this for nearly twenty years (!), my parents still tell me they're proud of me and remind me whenever they haven't received the latest book. I'm a really lucky girl, and I know it.

And last, but never, ever least, to you, my readers. Thank you for your encouragement and support through the years. This career can be crazy and unpredictable at times, but the one steady thing is you. Not for the first time, I share this deal with you: I'll keep writing if you keep reading. Thank you from the bottom of my heart.

Chapter One

S on of a billy goat!"
A small, mustard-colored bead rolled off the table and onto the hardwood floor, then bounced several times, the sound of the clicks the only way Spencer Thompson had to keep track of where it went. She set down her round nose pliers and did her best to follow the bead until it settled silently on the area rug somewhere near the chrome and glass coffee table. On her hands and knees, half under the table, Spencer was startled by the slamming of the door and jumped, banging her head with a loud whack.

"What in the world are you doing?" Marti Daniels tossed her attaché onto the couch and looked down at Spencer with an amused grin.

Spencer rubbed the back of her blond head with one hand and held up the small, yellow glass bauble with the other, in pain but victorious. "Lost a bead." She hauled herself to her feet and sat back in the uncomfortable chair at the tiny workspace she'd set up in the corner of Marti's town house.

"You should be more careful; those beads will go everywhere. I thought that's what the board thingy was for. So you don't lose beads." Marti spoke on her way to the kitchen, which was visible to Spencer, as was everything else on the first floor in the open-concept living space.

"It is, but I can't get it to lie flat in this small space." Spencer said it quietly, moving the bead board here and there as she did every time she lost a bead and tried to readjust her setup. She was pretty certain Marti wasn't really listening as she poured herself a glass of wine; she tended to get lost in her own head, tuning everybody else out. The fact was, there wasn't enough room for Spencer to work in that space, but it was all Marti had been willing to relinquish. Spencer's table was small—maybe two and a half feet square—and she had a myriad of tools and supplies stacked precariously high. Her workspace in her own house was much more comfortable and spacious, and she could spread out. Not for the first time that night, she considered packing up her stuff and just going home.

Marti flopped onto the black leather couch and kicked off her pumps, crossed her feet at the ankles on the coffee table, and blew out a very loud breath. "Man, what a day."

"Yeah?" Spencer squinted at the wire in her hand as she bent it with the pliers. At home, she had a freestanding magnifying glass to help her see, but not here. Moving her head at different angles to adjust her view, blinking rapidly and squinting, she finally managed to attach the lobster claw clasp.

"God. That Dawson case is going to be the death of me yet." Marti then launched into details of the case she was working on at her law firm, her biggest since being made partner a couple months ago.

Spencer listened with one ear, as a lot of what Marti said tended to be a reiteration from the previous night's recap of the previous day. Spencer nodded and uh-huh'd in all the right places as Marti droned on, but her focus was on the necklace she was crafting. Her mother's birthday was in November, and for as long as Spencer could remember, her mother had always complained about how ugly her birthstone was. November technically had two official birthstones: topaz and citrine. And while topaz came in a range of colors from blue to yellow to red to pink, to Spencer's mom, November's birthstone had always been the unimpressive, mustardy-goldish-orange color of citrine. When Spencer started making jewelry as a hobby, she'd vowed to make her mother something featuring citrine that would change her opinion of her birthstone. Now she held the necklace up, a finished product, and smiled. It was of average length—not a choker, but not a long necklace either. She'd alternated the citrine-colored beads with some gunmetal ones with an iridescent finish. It was unique and subtle, and Spencer knew her mother would love it. She turned so Marti could see it.

"Nice," Marti said, then continued with her recap of a contract case one of the other attorneys was working on without missing a beat.

Spencer sighed quietly and turned back to her supplies. Everything was portable here, but at home, there was a vast array and she missed it. Beads and balls in every imaginable shape, size, and color. Wires of different thicknesses. Tools for a variety of adjustments. Sitting at her crafting table in front of all her materials was about the only place in the world where Spencer felt confident, felt like she had everything under control and was the mistress of her own universe.

"Did you get my email?" Marti asked, yanking Spencer back to the town house. "I sent you a link."

"I haven't checked it in a while," Spencer said, putting things away in their individual spots. Truth was, she'd been focused on the necklace for the better part of three hours, but she wasn't about to tell Marti that. Marti thought her hobby was a waste of time.

"Well, it starts next week, so make sure you're ready." With that Marti got up and grabbed her attaché. She crossed the room, put a finger under Spencer's chin, and tilted her head up for a quick peck on the lips. "I'll be in my office for a couple hours. Got some things to go over."

Spencer nodded, watched her go. Marti Daniels was very attractive—tall with dark hair and eyes. Focused. Intelligent. Driven. Confident. Her surety was what had drawn Spencer in the first place. Marti always knew what she wanted and she always got it. That had been intoxicating for a while. Now?

Spencer didn't like to think about now.

With another sigh, she turned off the desk lamp on her table and stood. She crossed to the kitchen, deciding that Marti's glass of wine looked good, and poured herself one of her own. Back on the couch, she pulled out her own laptop to check her email and see what Marti had been talking about.

The subject line read simply, *Starts Monday*.

The body was typical Marti—short and to the point. *You're all registered. Enjoy!*

Brow furrowed, Spencer clicked on the link, which brought her to the website of a local gym and the headline of *Be Your Best Bride*. Her gaze went to the description.

Wedding day getting too close? Worried about fitting into the perfect dress? Want to wow your groom and all your guests? We can help! Join us for this twelve-week group class and get yourself in the best shape of your life! Our own Kara Laughlin will guide you through a mix of yoga, weight training, and cardio to get you fit, fabulous, and sexy so you can be your best bride!

Spencer sat there, blinking. She couldn't really be too surprised, because she'd seen an ad for the class and had commented on it to Marti. Spencer could use some exercise. She was a little soft in some places; she knew that. But Marti signing her up for the class without even running it by her first made something else painfully clear to Spencer: Marti also thought she could use some exercise.

With a hard swallow, Spencer clicked on the link that took her to the bio of Kara Laughlin. If she was going to actually take this class, she at least wanted to know what she was in for.

The information was not comforting.

Kara Laughlin was tall, blond, and imposing, all sinewy muscle and few curves. The full-length shot of her in skintight workout pants, arms folded over a red sports bra, staring intimidatingly into the camera filled Spencer with the inexplicable urge to hide behind something large. The close-up of just her face showed a woman with intensity, sharp features, and demanding eyes. Spencer had a sudden image of herself on her back on the ground, struggling to do crunches, while Kara Laughlin and her Zero Body Fat frame stood over her shouting angrily at her to work harder! Push harder! Move her lazy fat ass!

Spencer was already terrified of her.

She was about to slam the laptop shut when she noticed a clause at the bottom of the description, right next to the—in Spencer's opinion—exorbitant price: *cost refundable if canceled with a week's notice. Cancellations with less than seven days until class starts are not refundable.*

"Well, that seems ridiculous," Spencer muttered. And now she was stuck. Because it was Thursday and the class began on Monday and there was no way she'd throw away that much of Marti's money just like that, just because she was beyond intimidated. Apparently, it was important to her fiancée that she attend this class and get herself into better shape, so Spencer would attempt to do so, Fitness Nazi or no Fitness Nazi.

She scanned the rest of the details, punched the start time into her iPhone, and then zipped through the rest of her email, which was mostly ads from stores. Spencer nibbled on the inside of her cheek as she deleted most of them, but held on to a couple from stores she frequented that were having sales. She was going to need some workout apparel if she was going to do this.

With a soft click, she closed her laptop and set it on the coffee table, then picked up her wine and sipped. She enjoyed the quiet like this. No television. No music. Just…silence. A wiggle of her butt helped her burrow a bit further down into the couch cushions. While she would never have spent as much money on one piece of furniture as Marti had on this couch, Spencer couldn't argue against its comfort. She sometimes thought she liked the couch better than Marti's bed, had fallen asleep there more than once.

Not for the first time, she wished she had a dog. This would be the perfect time for snuggling. She'd always wanted one, ever since she was young, but her mother was allergic. And then there'd been college, and then she'd lived with two roommates in her first apartment. Then she'd fallen in love and moved in with Stephanie, who didn't like dogs (which probably should've been Spencer's first clue). By the time she had her own place and had begun thinking about getting one, she'd started dating Marti, who always said they'd get one together when the time was right. Which seemed to be never. But how great would it be to cuddle up right now with a four-legged furball that she could kiss all over and hug and love? That would love her back unconditionally, no matter what kind of shape she was in?

Spencer sighed, then chuckled to herself as she realized that she'd been doing an awful lot of sighing lately. Doing her best to shake off the feeling of restlessness that seemed to envelop her the past few weeks, she grabbed the *People* magazine that had come in Marti's mail today, Katy Perry smiling back at her from the cover. Turning sideways so her head was perched on the arm of the couch, Spencer settled in and began to read.

The next time she was aware of anything, the lights were off and there was a thick fleece blanket covering her as she lay on the couch. A glance at her watch told her it was nearly 2:00 a.m. The *People* magazine was back on the coffee table next to her wineglass, which was still half full. Marti must have covered her up and turned the lights off. Spencer tried not to think about the fact that, rather than wake her up and lead her to bed, Marti had left her on the couch.

Another sigh emanated from her lungs as she turned onto her side and pulled the blanket up over her shoulder.

It was fine. The couch was much more comfortable than the bed lately anyway.

Spencer closed her eyes and willed herself back to sleep.

CHAPTER TWO

R eally, Nick?" Rebecca McCall stared at her best friend as he handed his menu back to the waiter.

"What?" he replied, the mischievous expression on his face telling her he knew exactly what she was talking about.

"Heart attack on a plate. That's what you just ordered." Her voice was unintentionally harsh and she grimaced as soon as she heard herself. "Sorry. I'm just frustrated with work. And I worry about you."

"I know you do." It was the truth. Nick Scarfano wasn't always as big as he was now. Sure, he'd played football in high school more than fifteen years ago and had bulked up as much as the next guy. He'd even played a bit in college. Since then, though, he'd given up on most sports, but not on the way he'd always eaten when playing sports. He was a big guy now. Too big. He knew it. And Rebecca knew it. While she always managed to make him feel a little bit guilty, she also knew he still looked forward to the double cheeseburger and fries that would soon be set in front of him. She'd been trying to change his eating habits for the better part of a decade, and she'd been mostly unsuccessful. He tapped his straw on the table and removed the wrapper, popped it into his Coke. "What's up with work?" he asked before sipping.

Rebecca took a slug of her water as she glanced out the window next to their table and watched the lunch rush go by. "Kara Laughlin somehow managed to come down with mono."

"That's good, right? You hate her."

Rebecca snorted a laugh. Leave it to Nick to see the bright side of somebody else's misery. "I dislike her intensely."

Nick held up his hands. "Oh. Excuse the fuck out of me. You *dislike* her. My bad. So, why are you bummed out that she's sick? Mono should keep her out of the gym—i.e., out of your hair—for quite a while."

"It would be awesome except I have to cover her stupid bridal class."

Nick shook his head with a shrug, telling her he needed further explanation.

Rebecca sat back in her chair. "It's this ridiculous fitness class she thought up. For brides-to-be to get themselves in shape for their upcoming weddings."

"Why is that bad?"

Leaning forward on the table, Rebecca got serious. "It's not bad in general. What's bad is the way she's marketed it. She's basically saying you have to be as skinny and fit as possible in order for your wedding to be awesome. The ad says things like 'want to wow your groom?' As if being thin is the only way you can do that. She's a fitness instructor, yet she's constantly perpetuating body image issues for women." Rebecca had tried to make Kara see how the ad came across, but she refused to. And as one of the most senior fitness instructors at BodyFit, she was rarely questioned. It drove Rebecca crazy. "This is the fourth time she's run this class, and it's been pretty successful, so they keep letting her do it again."

The waiter came, carrying a tray loaded down with food. He set Rebecca's salmon salad in front of her, then slid the giant plate of grease and fat in front of Nick. He looked up at her and grinned like an eight-year-old in a toy store. She shook her head but said nothing more about his choice of lunch, and they were quiet for several moments as they ate.

Nick swallowed a bite, wiped his mouth with a napkin, and said, "You know, instead of being angry, you could maybe use this as an opportunity to run the class the way you think it should be run. I mean, do you *have* to follow her plan?"

Rebecca furrowed her brow. "I honestly don't know." She'd

been so busy being annoyed all morning that Nick's suggestion hadn't occurred to her.

"And who would know if you didn't?" He popped three fries into his mouth at once.

"I suppose I could tweak it a bit." Rebecca chewed some salad, her brain beginning to whir. "I'd have to step carefully. A lot of the clients come due to word of mouth from their friends who've already attended a previous class. I couldn't change it completely."

"But you could change the attitude around it." Nick pointed his fork at her.

She held his gaze.

"It's not a bad idea, is it?" he asked, proud of himself.

Rebecca grinned at him. "It's not." She had known Nick since their junior year of high school. They were probably the two people least likely to maintain a friendship of anybody in their very large school, but here they were, thirty-five now, and nobody knew her better than Nick. She trusted him implicitly, as much as her own family, and he rarely steered her wrong. "But some of the clients who sign up are…difficult." She wrinkled her nose.

"Bridezillas?"

She groaned. "You have no idea."

"Change the attitude," he said again. "If anybody can do it, you can. You know your shit."

Rebecca was still thinking about Nick's words two hours later as she finished up with a client. Kara would hate it if Rebecca messed with her class, but she couldn't really complain if she altered the mindset of it a little bit. Could she? And would it matter? Kara might have been high up on the seniority list at the gym, but Rebecca held her own. She hadn't been there as long, but she got great feedback from her clients and lots of referrals. And not for nothing, Nick was right: she knew her shit. She'd studied—and continued to study. She wasn't there to make her clients skinny. She was there to get them *healthy*. There was a massive difference.

It was Friday afternoon, which meant the gym was pretty sparsely populated. No classes were held after one o'clock because too few people showed up. Thus, the spinning room was dark, the yoga rooms were empty, and only a few diehard bodybuilders were groaning up a storm and clanging down free weights one floor below.

Rebecca sat at her desk in the open space that ran along a wall of windows overlooking the weights section below. The gym was set up in two stories. The second story—the main one—housed the front desk, the trainers' desk spaces, the day care center, the spinning room, and all the cardio equipment. The first floor contained the locker rooms, the yoga rooms, all the weight machines, and the free weights, and part of the second floor opened so that the free weight section of the first floor had a high ceiling.

From her desk, Rebecca could look down and see the free weights and some of the weight machines, and a lot of the time after a long shift, she liked to just sit and watch. Decompress from her day. The clients who knew what they were doing with the free weights were something to behold, and they often captured Rebecca's attention for moments at a time. The flexing of muscles as they worked had always fascinated her. The bodybuilding men who were enormous, as well as the experienced women who weren't necessarily bodybuilding but were in amazing shape, both caught and held her attention. She watched technique and form and found herself impressed more often than not.

"Hi, Rebecca." The words yanked her back to reality. "Have you had an awesome day? I have." Bobby Pine stopped pushing the wheeled cart full of dirty towels and held out a fist for Rebecca to bump.

"It's been okay, Bob," she responded with a grin, as she touched her fist to his and they exploded them together. "You working late?"

He nodded. "I'm gonna make it a great evening." Bobby was tall and gangly, all limbs. The lenses of his glasses were very thick and made his brown eyes seem much bigger than they were. He'd been hired by the gym's owner about eight months earlier, part of an outreach program for intellectually disabled adults. He emptied the garbage, washed and dried the towels, mopped the floors, and did odd jobs around the facility. He was easily the friendliest, most cheerful person Rebecca had ever met.

"You do that," she said to him, as he resumed his path toward the laundry room, humming a tune as he went.

Pecking at a couple of keys on her keyboard, Rebecca called up the list of participants for the Be Your Best Bride class, which would start on Monday. Five of them total, so not a huge class.

Change the attitude.

She heard Nick's words again. Maybe a smaller class would make that change a bit easier.

A few more pecks and she pulled up her boss's email, along with Kara Laughlin's "curriculum," as she called it. It wasn't bad—Kara might have had a questionable outlook on body image, but she knew fitness pretty well—but there were a few tweaks Rebecca would've made had she been designing the program herself. With a little half shrug, she decided she'd make them anyway, so she copied and pasted the outline, then edited it with her own ideas. They would change as the class progressed; she knew that. It was natural. That was another of her issues with Kara's stance. Rebecca was a big proponent of changing with your client rather than "sticking to the script," so to speak, no matter what.

A large shout and the clang of dropped free weights startled Rebecca from her concentration and she looked down to see a couple of very large men laughing and high-fiving. *Somebody hit a new goal.* She grinned, totally understanding that feeling.

"Remember that?" The question came from Sherry Vincent, fellow trainer and yoga instructor, who stood next to Rebecca's desk and gazed down at the weightlifters. "From when you first got into fitness? Remember when you lifted a weight you never thought you'd be able to? What a rush it was?"

"God, yes," Rebecca said quietly. And she did remember. The exhilaration. The high. The sense of accomplishment.

"We thought we could do anything after that." Sherry blinked rapidly, then turned her gaze to Rebecca. "Well, I did."

"Oh, me, too."

"You're taking Kara's bride class, I hear." Sherry propped her foot up on a chair and tightened the laces on her cross-trainer.

Rebecca made no effort to contain the sigh. Sherry understood. "Yes, I am."

"Good."

A laugh barked out of Rebecca. "As in, better you than me?"

"No." Sherry looked at her then, tilted her head as if surprised Rebecca didn't get what she was saying. "As in, you can put your own spin on it."

Brow furrowed, Rebecca said, "You're the second person to say that to me today. Did I miss a memo?"

"We all know Kara knows what she's doing when it comes to fitness. We also all know that she's rigid and annoying and has questionable...*opinions* on what it means to be in shape. It would just be nice to see this class be something positive instead of debatable."

Sherry was in her late forties and was their main yoga instructor and one of the spin instructors, but she'd been a personal trainer for years before that. An injury to her back—as well as the birth of her children—had shifted her focus a bit, and she'd studied feverishly to get certified in yoga. Her classes were always full, people from all over the city jockeying for a spot on her hardwood floor several times a week. She'd been a sort of mentor for Rebecca when she'd taken a position at the gym, and her opinions were very important.

Pen in hand, Rebecca pointed to a few things on the computer screen.

"I was thinking of changing this to this. I want to eliminate this altogether..."

"Ugh, yes. Useless, that move," Sherry agreed.

"Then I thought I'd add these and this."

They spent the next twenty minutes going over the tweaks and alterations Rebecca had in mind, Sherry giving suggestions and approvals as they went. By the time they were done, the program was the same, but different. Exactly what Rebecca was going for.

They high-fived and Rebecca thanked Sherry for her help.

"Those girls are going to be so happy with this class. You wait."

For the first time since being told she was taking over the group, Rebecca was actually looking forward to it.

CHAPTER THREE

S pencer held up her hand, flat so her palm faced down, and watched her fingers tremble uncontrollably. She couldn't remember the last time she'd been this nervous. She'd actually had a terrifying dream about the Fitness Nazi the night before, complete with tons of shouting and failed attempts at pull-ups and weights Spencer couldn't even move, let alone lift, and she'd ended up bursting into tears. She'd awoken in a cold sweat, her heart hammering in her chest. Now, with a groan of frustration, she dropped her hand down into her lap and stared out the windshield of her car at the gathering storm clouds that felt much like the inside of her head. It was late July and very humid—too humid to be sitting in her car without it running. Maybe the forecast rain would cool things down a bit, but it was more likely that it would make things worse. Stickier. Thicker. Even less comfortable, if that was possible.

She knew that if she turned the ignition back on, she could flick on the A/C and be cooler. She also knew if she turned the ignition back on, the chances of her slamming the car into gear and fleeing the gym parking lot were that much higher.

A glance at her watch told her the class would start in twelve minutes.

Just enough time to sit in her own sweat and work herself into more of a nervous frenzy.

"All right. Enough." Spencer said the words out loud into the silence of the car. "Come on, Spence. Suck it up." With that, she tugged the car door handle and got out, grabbed her bag from the back seat, and walked toward the BodyFit building, which suddenly looked like some large and ominous brick behemoth that was about to swallow her whole.

The locker room buzzed with conversation and laughter, punctuated by the whir of blow dryers and the whoosh of running showers, all underscored by a Lady Gaga song piped in through the speakers in the ceiling. Spencer had read someplace that Monday was the busiest day at gyms everywhere, people vowing to start the week right with a class or a workout. By Thursday, things tapered off, and Fridays were dead. Since this class was Monday, Wednesday, and Friday, she supposed she'd find out how true that assumption was.

Never having been comfortable taking her clothes off in front of others, Spencer had given herself time to go home after work and change, so she was pretty much ready for class. She wore a pair of gray sweatpants, a baggy Adidas T-shirt in navy blue, and bright pink Nikes she'd purchased over the weekend specifically for this class. Her blond hair was pulled into a ponytail, and as she tucked her bag into a locker along with her purse, she pulled out the empty pink water bottle. The ad had said to wear comfortable workout clothes and bring a water bottle, and Spencer was nothing if not a direction-follower.

As she closed her locker and clicked the lock, she picked up a snippet of conversation from the row behind her.

"You're in that class, too? I'm super excited. I'm so fat right now and I don't want to have to alter my dress," one woman said.

"Oh my God, right? My thighs. Seriously. When's your wedding date?" another asked.

"November thirteenth."

"Mine's in November, too!"

As their voices began to fade, Spencer turned to get a glimpse. Both were wearing skintight nylon black shorts and fitted tank tops, one in bright orange and the other in bright yellow. Neither of them could have been larger than a size small.

Spencer shook her head and, for the twenty-seventh time,

wondered if she should just bail. Run, hop in her car, and go home. Would Marti even know? Would she care?

But Marti was the one who had wanted her to come, so apparently, she *did* care.

Spencer picked up her water bottle, filled it at the sink, and headed for Yoga Room #3, where she'd finally meet the Fitness Nazi in person.

I hope she doesn't make me cry.

It sounded silly in her head, and Spencer knew it stemmed from her dream, but still.

Sucking in a deep, fortifying breath, she pushed the door open.

Yoga Room #3 was a large, square room with mirrors on two sides, windows on one, and the door and a storage closet on the fourth. The floor was light-colored hardwood, just like a school gymnasium, and a large and complicated-looking sound system was set up in one corner. The two women from the locker room were talking together, and it looked liked they'd joined a third.

They didn't hold Spencer's attention for long, though, because it was snagged by the woman at the front of the room. *Wow.* "Why don't you guys grab a few mats out of that closet back there and have a seat here in front of me." She pointed toward the storage area in the back.

Before Spencer could move, a voice said quietly behind her, "That's not the chick on the website."

Spencer turned to meet the soft blue eyes of a woman much shorter and plumper than she was.

"Hi. I'm Lucy." The woman held out her hand.

"Spencer. Nice to meet you." They shook, and by unspoken agreement, walked to the storage area to grab mats.

"I don't know about you, but that woman on the website totally freaked me out." Lucy handed Spencer a rolled-up mat, then grabbed one for herself.

"Oh, God, me too!" Spencer said in hushed tones. "I had a nightmare."

Lucy's laugh was big and brash and Spencer liked it immediately, but they had no more time for discussion as they sat, because the woman stood in front of them and commanded their attention without saying a thing.

She was stunning. It was an assessment Spencer came to instantly. She wasn't tall—maybe five-five—but she seemed it. And she wasn't a walking muscle like the Fitness Nazi had seemed to be. She was just...fit. Lean and strong-looking, but still feminine and soft. She wore form-fitting black workout pants and black-and-purple Nikes. Her T-shirt also clung to her body, but not in a look-how-tight-my-shirt-is kind of way. More like a this-shirt-was-made-for-this-body kind of way, and Spencer appreciated it. The woman's hair was dark and barely skimmed her shoulders, and she kept both sides tucked behind her ears. And her eyes...God, when Spencer saw the blue of them, the way they stood out, she couldn't look away. She was mesmerized, and her brain suddenly threw her images of the very naughty things she'd like to do with this woman. Spencer felt herself blush, felt the instant rush of heat to her face, wondered if anybody else noticed. She hoped not. She was in a brides class, for God's sake.

"Okay," their gorgeous instructor said, as she stood before them. "Welcome to the Be Your Best Bride class. As you can see, I am not Kara Laughlin. Unfortunately, she's ill and I'll be running the class. I hope that isn't a problem for anybody." She paused, gave them time to protest before continuing. "I'll tell you a little about myself, and then you'll introduce yourselves. We're going to be together three times a week for the next twelve weeks, so we should get to know each other a bit." She smiled and Spencer felt a little flutter in her belly. *Oh, yeah. Serious crush vibes happening here.* "My name is Rebecca McCall and I've been a fitness instructor for almost ten years now. I've been at BodyFit for about five." She took a few steps one way, then turned and did the same in the other direction. Slowly, meandering, as if the words she was saying were scrawled on the floor and she was finding them as she went. "I don't believe in whipping you into shape." Rebecca stopped then and made eye contact with each of the five women. She held Spencer's as she said, "I believe in controlled, planned workouts that shape the entire body, that make your heart strong and your body strong."

The woman from the locker room, the one in the orange top, shot her hand into the air and asked, "What if I want to focus on a certain body part? Like, I want my hips to be smaller before my wedding day."

Spencer watched as Rebecca McCall seemed to stare for a beat before responding. "Okay, so there's no such thing as spot-toning. You can't work on one thing without working on others. What we do will tone all of you."

"But we'll lose weight, right?" Yellow Shirt asked, jumping in, obviously not satisfied with Rebecca's response.

"You might. You might not." Rebecca held up a hand as Orange Shirt opened her mouth. "Muscle weighs more than fat. So, while you will be in better shape at the end of our twelve weeks, you may not weigh any less. You won't mind, though. I promise you. Weight is only a number. I want you to throw your scales away. Or at least stay off them. Fitness is about how you *feel*." Orange Shirt looked skeptical, but that seemed to pacify her, at least for the time being, and Rebecca went on. "How about we go around, introduce ourselves, and tell a little bit about why we're here and what we hope to achieve?"

Orange Shirt, of course, shot her hand up and started speaking, her dark ponytail bouncing as she turned her head from side to side to look at each of them. "Hi, I'm Brittany Hughes. I'm getting married on November thirteenth to my awesome fiancé, Brian."

Brian and Brittany. Well, that's ridiculously cute.

"My best friend, Ally, took this class, but with the other teacher, and she said it kicked her ass until she was able to fit into a dress two sizes smaller than she originally thought."

Yellow Shirt gave a happy little gasp as the third woman in a blue shirt clapped with her fingers only.

"So, as I already said, I'd like to slim down these *ballooning* hips and leave Brian speechless when I walk down the aisle."

"Oh, my God," Yellow Shirt scoffed. "Your hips are so not ballooning." She waved a dismissive hand at Brittany. "Hi. I'm Bella Templeton. I am also getting married in November to my wonderful fiancé, Dylan. We've been together for five years now, so it's about time we had a wedding." Spencer watched as Bella rolled her eyes good-naturedly, then toyed with a chunk of her blond bob. "I've been feeling pretty out of shape lately, so, like Brittany here…" She laid a hand on Brittany's shoulder as if they were old friends. "I'd like to fit into my dress without having to fast for three days first, and I'd like to make Dylan's eyes bug out of his head." Bella then dissolved into a fit of girlish giggles.

Spencer was pretty sure she noticed Rebecca trying not to roll her eyes.

On Spencer's left, Lucy spoke next. "I'm Lucy Schubert-soon-to-be-Schwartz. From one German name to another." She laughed that big sound again and Spencer smiled next to her. "I've always been a little chubby, and while I don't really expect that to change, I'd like to make an effort to get myself a little healthier. For my wedding, yes, but for life, too." A sheepish expression suddenly settled on her face and she glanced down at her folded hands in her lap.

"I guess I'm next," Spencer said. "My name is Spencer Thompson. We don't have an exact date because it's just going to be a courthouse thing. But we've talked about January, so a bit later than you guys." She tossed a glance toward Brittany and Bella. "My fiancée signed me up for a gym membership and this class and surprised me. I guess she thinks I need to get into better shape before we get married, so…here I am." Any other words she might have had evaporated in her head when she looked up at Rebecca and saw a flash of—what was it? Disbelief? Disappointment? Sympathy?— cross her features.

"I'm Willow Becker," said the last woman in the room, and Spencer was grateful to escape the focus. Willow was a brunette, her long hair in a braid down her back. "I'm getting married in early December, and my fiancé has no idea I'm here." She gave Spencer a friendly bump with her shoulder. "Just wanted to do something good for myself."

Rebecca seemed very pleased with Willow's words, and for a quick few seconds, Spencer found herself to be inexplicably jealous.

"Thank you, and I'm really glad you're all here." Rebecca

started up the slow pacing again. "Here's the plan. We're going to use a combination of cardio, weights, and other exercises to give you an entire body workout. You'll be here three days a week for the next twelve weeks, so that gives us plenty of time. Now." She held up a finger. "You may not all be doing the same things. We'll start out together, but as we progress, I'll be watching each of you and deciding what works best for your individual needs. For example, some of you may need more core work while others may need to build muscle. You'll all gain strength, though, regardless. And you'll all be making your heart stronger, which is the most important aspect of exercise." Rebecca tapped her own chest with a finger. "Keeping that ticker in good shape so you have a long life with the person you're about to marry." A half grin tugged at one corner of her mouth and then she clapped once. "Okay. Let's see what you've got. Follow me."

Not quite two hours later, Spencer stood in her own shower at home, letting the scalding water pound on her shoulders. She was exhausted and already a little bit sore. Her muscles were likely to be screaming tomorrow. Rebecca McCall had put them through the wringer, testing each of her five clients to see where their strengths and weaknesses lay. After an hour with the Be Your Best Bride class, Spencer was pretty sure she had zero strengths. Not a single one. Only weaknesses.

She had just finished drying herself off when her phone rang and the screen said it was a call from Jennifer Kowalski, Spencer's coworker and friend for the past few years. Pretty sure she was still sweating, Spencer fell backward onto her bed naked and spread her arms and legs out in an attempt to cool off. She hit the answer button on her phone.

"Hey."

"And?" Jennifer asked, getting right to it. "How'd it go?"

Spencer groaned.

"That good, huh?"

"I think I might be dead."

"You're not. How was the Fitness Nazi? Everything you hoped for and more?"

"No, it wasn't even her. She got sick or something, so this other woman took over the class. Super hot, but also super tough."

"Yeah? That's good, though, right?"

Spencer told Jennifer about the other people in the class, the speech Rebecca had given. "Then she wanted to see what kind of shape we were all in."

"Fun times."

"Yeah, not at all. She put me on this thing that's not quite a treadmill, but not really an elliptical, and it took every ounce of concentration I had to keep myself pushing the pedal thingies forward instead of backward. I felt like an idiot. I mean, seriously, how hard is it to go forward?"

Jennifer's laughter came through the phone. "Did you fall off?"

"Shockingly, no."

"Then you did good. Bet you burned some calories."

"I guess. I wasn't on it for that long because then we had to lift some weights and do push-ups and a plank, which almost killed me, and the hour I was there felt like seven. And I think the instructor hates me."

"She does not. She's supposed to be hard on you. It's her job. And here's the good news: that was the hardest it will be. From here on out, you'll only get stronger."

Spencer scoffed. "Of course you say that. You've been working out since you were, like, six."

"Who else is in the class?"

"There are five of us, total. Me, a couple of girls that seem nice, and a couple who seem like mean girls."

"You always manage to find the mean girls, Spence."

Spencer could hear the humor in Jennifer's tone. "They find me."

"You go back on Wednesday?"

"If I decide to, yes."

Jennifer paused for a second or two, then said, "You know what I think?"

"No, but I bet you're going to tell me."

"Damn right I am. I think you should go back. I think you

should go to every one of those classes. For you. Not for Marti. For you." When they'd spoken over the weekend, Jennifer had made it clear what she thought of Marti signing Spencer up for the class without asking her first. Her opinion had included several swear words, and most of them began with *F.* "It never hurts to be fit, Spence. To be strong."

"I know." Spencer blew out a breath. "The reality is, I may not be able to move by Wednesday."

Jennifer chuckled. "At least think about it. I think it'd be good for you."

"I promise I will think about it."

They spoke about a few more mundane topics, then hung up, knowing they'd see each other at work the next day and could pick things up then. Spencer dropped the phone and returned to what she'd been doing before she answered: nothing. As she lay sprawled on the bed and finally started to feel cooler, she flashed back to Rebecca McCall. To her face, her eyes, her hands. Spencer had watched her a lot, had felt utterly drawn to her. *Just a crush*, she'd told herself the entire time. *Just a little crush.* Besides, once they'd introduced themselves, Rebecca had barely looked at her. Well, not in her eyes, anyway. She'd focused on Spencer's legs, her arms, her torso. Whatever she'd been testing and evaluating. Apparently, Spencer's face didn't make the cut.

"Fine with me," she mumbled into her empty bedroom. "It'll be less embarrassing every time I can't do something if I don't have to look her in the eye."

At least she didn't have to worry about it for two days.

❖

"Good work, Ty," Rebecca said to her client, who'd just finished up his final reps of the day. "I see a lot of improvement."

Ty nodded, and his face broke into a grin of satisfaction. "Thanks. Feels good. Thursday?"

Rebecca nodded. "See you then." Ty headed for the locker room as Rebecca put away the equipment they'd used for his session. It was seven o'clock on Tuesday evening, and the yoga class had just finished up, judging by the number of yoga-clothes-clad women filing down the hall toward the stairs as Rebecca waited for an opening in the flow of people.

"Hey." Sherry was the last one, a white towel draped over her shoulders.

"Hi." Rebecca walked next to her, both on their way to their offices. "Good class?"

"Full."

"Not unusual."

Their desks butted up to each other and Sherry flopped down into her chair. "Long day for me. You?"

Rebecca tilted her head back and forth. "Not too bad. I had a cancellation, so ended up with a free hour."

Sherry sat forward suddenly, forearms on the desk as Rebecca drank from her water bottle. "Hey, how did the bride class go? I haven't seen you since. Any bridezillas?"

"Not really." Rebecca thought back to the previous night's class. "A couple with that make-me-skinny attitude, but the other three seemed fine. Although there was one…" Rebecca sighed and shook her head. "Her fiancée signed her up for the class."

Sherry furrowed her brow. "After they'd talked about it?"

"I don't think so. She said she surprised her."

"She? Her fiancée's a she?"

"Yes! Which makes it worse, if you ask me."

"Oh, women body-shaming other women. My favorite."

"Right? Who does that to somebody they love?"

"Does she need it?" Sherry's grimace and slight hesitation told Rebecca it wasn't a question she'd ask just any staff member at the gym.

Rebecca called Spencer's face up in her mind's eye, her body. She was beautiful. She really was. Rebecca couldn't deny that. There was something…magnetic about her. "No, not really. I mean, she could use a bit of toning. She's not terribly strong and her stamina could use some work, but she's not unhealthy. She just doesn't move enough."

"Like eighty percent of the rest of the country."

"Exactly."

"So, she plays on your team. She cute?" Sherry raised one eyebrow in a lame attempt to look mischievous.

"I am not answering that," Rebecca said, with a laugh. *She is. Very.*

Sherry tossed her a wink and a wave. "See you tomorrow."

Rebecca watched her go, then turned her gaze to the windows by her desk. BodyFit was fairly populated but would start to clear out in the next hour, folks who made their after-work or after-dinner stops finishing up their workouts. As she watched the bustle of activity below her, Rebecca reflected on Sherry's question.

Spencer Thompson *was* cute, though that wasn't really the word Rebecca would use. She was more…pretty. Femininely attractive. Her blond hair had some curl to it, even in a ponytail, and her blue eyes were big, softly expressive. Physically, she'd caught Rebecca's eye immediately. Unfortunately, she came across as a bit passive, a characteristic that tended to drive Rebecca a little nuts, considering her family history, and that lost Spencer points. Big ones. She also had a bit of a self-deprecating sense of humor that Rebecca had gotten a tiny glimpse of, and an odd sense of protection had come along with it. Rebecca didn't like Spencer mocking herself. She wasn't sure what to do with that and tried to shake it away, move her thoughts to other things.

Later, at home, Spencer was still taking up a small amount of space in the back of Rebecca's mind. Unsure why—and needing it to stop—Rebecca decided to combat it by checking the two dating sites she'd signed up on, thanks to prodding by both Sherry and Nick—and Nick's wife, Michelle, who was gentler than Nick in her approach, but still.

Rebecca hadn't signed on in a few days, and as she sat down and opened her laptop, Veruca Salt hopped up into her lap for some attention and scratches on her white kitty head.

"Ready, Ruke?" Rebecca asked. "You know how much we love being subjected to entirely new levels of ego-bruising. Yay for dating sites!"

Veruca yawned widely, then began kneading Rebecca's thighs—a painful process given the thin workout pants she still wore.

"Okay, what have we got?" The first site had three matches and a message waiting for her. "Look at that, Ruke, three matches and three profiles with no pictures. Delete, delete, delete." Rebecca and Michelle had had endless debates about this, Michelle being of the you-could-be-deleting-your-soul-mate-just-because-you-can't-see-her argument. Rebecca was of the I-need-there-to-be-at-least-some-kind-of-physical-attraction-first argument.

The message was riddled with misspellings and grammatical errors, and that was all Rebecca needed to delete that as well.

"Am I too harsh, Veruca? Too judgmental?" Rebecca pressed her lips together in a thin line as she signed out of one site, signed in to the other, and had much the same luck. There was one woman, though, who'd messaged her a couple days ago. Her profile photo was pleasing—light brown hair, big brown eyes, a nice smile. Her profile said she was a first-grade teacher and was looking for somebody to hang with, maybe more.

Rebecca didn't respond to the message but didn't delete her either.

She poured herself a glass of the cucumber water in the fridge, then took it into the living room where she flopped onto her couch and picked up her Kindle. As Veruca Salt made herself a new bed on her stomach, Rebecca discovered that she wasn't really in the mood to read, her mind wandering. Kindle returned to the coffee table, she ran her fingers along the white softness of her cat.

"I'm not really looking for a relationship, Ruke. Right? I mean, a date here and there would be nice. Somebody to go to a movie with or out to dinner? But I don't need a *relationship*." Body humming with her purrs, the cat looked at Rebecca, gave a very slow blink of her huge green eyes. "Besides, those sites make me feel awful about myself." It was true. More than once, she'd found a profile and photo that intrigued her, sent a message, and never heard anything back. Rebecca was not a woman who needed a shot of confidence; she did just fine in that department. But unanswered messages, she found, would often mess with her head. Start a barrage of questions that were very unlike her. *Did she see my photo and find me unattractive and delete me?* Which was fair enough, as she'd done the same thing multiple times, so she couldn't really complain about that. Still. More questions. *Is my profile lacking somehow? Am I unappealing and just don't realize it? What's wrong with me that she isn't responding?* All these questions would swirl in her mind until she literally had to talk to her own reflection in the mirror, remind herself that she *was* attractive, she *was* intelligent, she *was* worthy...things she'd never had to focus on before.

It was exhausting.

And just like she did every time she checked the dating sites, she silently cursed Sherry and Nick and Michelle for talking her into signing up. Then she cursed herself for *letting* them talk her into signing up.

Absently, she wondered if Spencer Thompson had found her fiancée through a dating site...

With a groan and a shake of her head, she stretched for the TV remote and clicked it on. She needed something to pull her mind out of the dating sinkhole it was being sucked toward.

CHAPTER FOUR

A ll ready for day two?" Lucy asked Spencer as they passed each
other in the locker room. Lucy was cheerful and bubbly and
dressed in a pair of loose-fitting red nylon shorts and a black tank
top.

"I am," Spencer replied, pasting on a smile. "Not dreading it
at all."

Which was, of course, a giant lie, because she'd been dreading
it all day long, since the moment Marti had left the house that
morning. Her parting words, "this is going to be so good for you,"
followed by a squeeze and a kiss on the cheek, only served to remind
Spencer about the class. She'd conveniently put it out of her mind,
but it came screeching back in then and had poked at her for the next
eight hours.

"Meet you out there," Lucy said, and bounced out of the locker
room.

Spencer was running late. It couldn't be helped; an issue had
cropped up at the real estate office where she worked and the agent
in the middle of it needed her help in a big way. Things had been
resolved but had Spencer leaving the office twenty minutes later
than she'd intended.

With a frustrated groan, she changed into her workout clothes,
pulled her hair back, tied on her Nikes, and hurried out to the gym.
She found Rebecca easily—her form-fitting top was bright royal
blue today. The other members of her class were all on recumbent

bikes, Rebecca leaning on the last empty one. Spencer tried hard not to notice her figure, the gentle curves in all the right places, soft-looking skin showing at her throat, her calves. She failed, of course, sexy thoughts running rampant through her head. Rebecca turned then, and that intense, blue-eyed gaze fell on Spencer, causing butterflies to take flight in her stomach.

"There you are," Rebecca said, her tone making it clear she noticed Spencer's tardiness and wasn't thrilled about it.

"Sorry." Spencer flushed and watched as those sexy thoughts in her head evaporated like morning fog on a pond. "Work."

Rebecca stepped away from the bike, gestured at it with a small flourish. "Your chariot awaits."

Spencer sat down and stretched her legs beyond straight in an attempt to reach the pedals.

"Slide your seat forward."

Craning her neck this way and that, Spencer had trouble locating the correct lever until Rebecca sighed and leaned very close to Spencer. They made eye contact and continued it as Rebecca reached between Spencer's legs. Spencer held her breath, totally mesmerized by Rebecca's eyes. Yeah, the sexy thoughts were back.

"Slide forward," Rebecca quietly ordered.

Spencer did so and suddenly, their faces were mere inches apart. Spencer's focus dropped to Rebecca's mouth; she couldn't help it. There was a moment. A beat. It held...

Rebecca stood quickly, almost jerked away from Spencer, who blinked in surprise. "Warm up. Fifteen minutes at level five." Then she was gone, scurrying away from Spencer as if she'd been shoved in that direction.

"So glad I could piss off the teacher on my second day," Spencer muttered, then poked buttons on the bike's touch screen until she'd set it correctly.

She liked biking. She decided that immediately. She could feel her lower body working right away. Her quads, her calves, even her ass all got in on the action. At the same time, she could let her mind wander. Or watch TV, she saw, as the touch screen had a small square that looked to be showing a scene from *Grey's Anatomy*. Whatever she chose to do, it was an almost relaxing way to get some activity, which was an odd thing to think about exercise, but it was true.

To her left, Brittany, Bella, and Willow had all stopped pedaling and were chattering about their respective stats. Spencer squinted at her own screen, saw that it measured distance, calories burned, and average speed, among other things.

"I was going, like, seventeen miles an hour there for a bit," Bella said. A glance at her screen told Spencer she was going eleven miles per hour.

Lucy must have seen her grimace because she tapped her on the shoulder and said quietly, "Don't listen to them. Doesn't matter." Her face was glistening with a sheen of sweat and her breathing was rapid, and it occurred to Spencer that maybe Lucy was as new to this gym thing as she was. She sent a nod Lucy's way but picked up her own pace anyway.

An hour later, she and Lucy were both in the locker room, sweating and flushed. Spencer dropped down to the bench, elbows on her knees, and let her head hang down as she did her best to catch her breath and bring her racing heart down to normal levels.

"Wow," Lucy said, spinning the dial on her lock. "That was something, huh?"

Spencer was glad the other three women from their class were in another aisle of the room. To her, they only amplified how out of shape she was. Lucy seemed to see it differently.

"I'm really liking this so far. I think it's going to help my body and my mind, you know?"

Spencer looked up at her.

"I mean, I'm never going to be a size four," she went on. "And that's fine. I accepted that a long, long time ago, believe me. I'm just me. You know? But now I'll be me, stronger." Her smile was contagious, and Spencer grinned back at her. "You just have to compete with yourself. Nobody else."

Spencer nodded, understanding the concept. But knowing that and putting it into practice would be easier said than done for her. "I think I'm competing with Rebecca's expectations," she said, with a slight scoff.

Lucy wrinkled her nose. "What do you mean?"

"I don't think she likes me."

It was Lucy's turn to scoff. "Nah." She waved a dismissive hand. "She's just tough."

Maybe Lucy was right. *Maybe it's just me.* It wasn't like Rebecca wasn't hard on all of them; she was. It just felt...harder... to Spencer. Rebecca didn't say anything, it was her attitude, almost an aura of disappointment when she was around Spencer. Was she being paranoid? It was possible. Though after the eye contact on the bike, Rebecca didn't look at her again for the rest of the session. Well, she looked at her—it would be difficult not to and still do her job—but she hadn't looked her in the eye. Again. Spencer was big on eye contact, so having somebody avoid it on purpose was punishingly obvious to her.

Lucy bid her goodbye and Spencer took her time gathering her things. Having no desire to take a shower in a public place, she didn't bother changing her clothes. She'd just go home and shower there. The locker rooms were on the first floor, the main entrance to BodyFit on the second, so Spencer had to come upstairs in order to then go down the front stairs and out the door. As she passed the smoothie bar and approached the front desk, she noticed Rebecca leaning on the counter and talking to a middle-aged woman with short red hair. The woman must have said something funny because Rebecca threw her head back and laughed, a shockingly feminine and contagious sound. Spencer found herself smiling as she passed. Rebecca spared her a glance, but quickly turned back to the redhead without another word.

See? Not just me.

Spencer shook her head, picked up her pace, and pushed her way out of the gym. The atmosphere felt suddenly heavy and thick, oppressive. Spencer wanted to be out of there. She *needed* to be out of there.

❖

"Who was that?" Sherry asked, then sucked on the fat green straw in her smoothie.

Rebecca watched Spencer's back as she exited the building, all the while feeling Sherry's eyes on her. "Nobody."

"Wait." Sherry said that one word in such a way that Rebecca had no choice but to turn and meet her gaze. "Is that the one? The one whose fiancée made her go to class?"

Rebecca nodded. "That's her."

"She's pretty," Sherry said. "Not terribly out of shape from what I can see."

"No. She's not." Rebecca had to agree with that.

Sherry made a show now of craning her neck to see out the window into the parking lot. "And drives a hot little car from what I can tell."

"That's nice." Rebecca pushed herself off the counter, ready to finish up some things at her desk before heading home.

"Becks."

Damn it. Sherry's tone stopped her in her tracks. She was the only adult who could still do that. She was also the only person on the planet besides Nick who was allowed to use a shortened version of her name. Rebecca turned back to face her mentor.

"Don't you be extra rough on that girl."

"I won't," Rebecca said as she walked away, trying not to sound defensive, but pretty sure she failed.

"I've met you," Sherry called after her. "I *know* you."

It was a little bit of an issue Rebecca had. Being a tiny speck… judgmental when it came to this subject. She knew it, but that didn't mean she wanted to discuss it, even with Sherry, who knew her history. Rebecca had spent most of her teen years watching her mother do everything her father said, barely thinking for herself. It didn't matter that she seemed perfectly fine in that life; Rebecca hated to watch it. She wanted to shout at her mother, "Speak up! Say something! Stand up for yourself!" But none of those things ever happened, and Rebecca, despite her deep love for her mother, thought of her as weak. Because of that, she made an immediate assessment of anybody who behaved in a similar way. Whether or not she spent any time getting to know them, she formed an opinion about them. An often unfavorable one.

Had she done that with Spencer Thompson?

Rebecca snorted as she sat down at her desk. Of course she had. Instantly. Spencer was only in the bride class because her fiancée said she should be. That told Rebecca all she needed to know about Spencer's self-worth (she had very little), her backbone (or lack thereof), her level of self-esteem (low). Rebecca had labeled Spencer weak before she even realized it, but it was pretty clear Spencer Thompson was exactly that.

Wasn't she?

"You judge too fast and too harshly."

Sherry's voice startled Rebecca enough to make her jump. "For God's sake," she ground out, hand pressed to her chest.

Sherry gathered her things from her desk. "You do. You always have, and we both know it." Keys jangling in her hand, she said, "I have to go pick up my kids." She kissed Rebecca on the top of her head and added, "Give the girl a chance before you write her off. Everybody deserves a chance, you know? You don't even know her story." With a half shrug and her signature grin, she left.

Rebecca blew out a breath and tried to push Sherry's words out of her head for the time being.

Bobby Pine and his perpetual smile helped with that chore. "I'm having an awesome day, Rebecca. How about you?" He held out his closed fist as he walked by and Rebecca dutifully bumped it.

"I'm doing okay, Bob."

"You can do better than okay!" He turned to her and walked backward, shot his fist up in the air like a cheerleader, then turned around and kept walking.

❖

"Hey, I need a favor." Jennifer stopped in front of Spencer's desk.

"Sure," Spencer said, as she gathered her purse and gym bag together and tried to force herself not to bail on the gym.

"Oh, you've got class again tonight. I forgot." Jennifer grinned. "Happy Hour after? A couple of us are heading to Mack's."

"Maybe." Marti had texted that she'd be working late that Friday night, and Spencer was pretty sure she'd be ready for a drink after her workout. "What favor do you need?"

Jennifer sighed. "Can you run my open house on Carlson Street on Sunday? It's just a two to four. I double-booked myself like an idiot."

"No problem." Open houses were easy. Spencer had run dozens of them in the years she'd been with the firm. "Text me the details."

"You're the best," Jennifer said, clapping her hands together once. "Now go have fun working those muscles."

"Yeah, fun isn't a word I associate with this class."

"No? It should be. I love working out." Jennifer rubbed Spencer's upper arm as she passed. "Just give it time. You'll grow to really like it."

Spencer didn't see that happening, but she smiled at Jennifer anyway, not wanting to burst the bubble of friendly support she'd created. The fact was, Spencer dreaded this class. Not because of the exercise—she actually liked the feeling she had afterward; the soreness in her muscles made her feel accomplished—but because of the instructor and the mean girls. Lucy was a bright spot, though, so Spencer tried to focus on her, on her sunny disposition that could light up just about any room.

Twenty minutes later, Spencer was dressed for physical activity and pedaling away on the recumbent bike to warm up. Rebecca strolled down the line of her brides-to-be, chatting with Willow, then asking Lucy what she did for a living (kindergarten teacher, was Lucy's answer). When she reached Spencer's bike, Spencer did her best to be friendly and open, even smiling at her. But Rebecca didn't see the smile because she didn't look at her face. Only the screen on her bike.

"You can push harder than that." Rebecca tapped the bike's level up two, then turned and walked back the way she'd come.

Spencer rolled her eyes.

Fifteen minutes after that, Spencer and Brittany were on leg press machines. Rebecca watched Brittany, complimented her on her form and speed.

"Good work. Really good work. Five more."

She then turned her attention to Spencer, who was doing exactly the same thing at exactly the same speed as Brittany.

"Slow it down," Rebecca said, her tone stern and her eyes on Spencer's legs. "Controlled movements."

"Okay," Spencer said, and consciously slowed down the press.

"Wait. Stop." Rebecca held up a hand. "Rack 'em."

Spencer obeyed, let the weights reach their resting spot.

Rebecca reached down, pulled out the pin, and pushed it back in at a lower spot. "You can lift more than that. You aren't big on challenging yourself, are you?" She didn't say it in a light or joking manner. She was dead serious, even sounding a bit irritated to Spencer, who clenched her teeth together to keep from saying something snarky back. Something like *Oh, I don't know. Working with* you *has presented quite a challenge.* But she'd been raised to be polite. *If you don't have something nice to say, don't say anything at all.* Her mother's words. Spencer kept quiet, a little surprised when she actually lifted the new weight.

Half an hour later, all five brides-to-be were finishing up their session stretched out on foam mats, in plank positions, lined up on the floor like piano keys and holding themselves up on their toes and forearms. "Super Freak" was blasting over the speakers as Rebecca strolled in front of them, her phone in her hand, running her timer for sixty seconds, encouraging them by talking about core strength and how important it was to their overall health. While Spencer was admittedly pleased that this activity was hard for every single one of them, she was not pleased by Rebecca's barking at her when her midsection dropped down to the floor about thirty seconds in.

"No. Get that ass in the air. Come on."

Spencer felt a toe tap at her hip and she ground her teeth, pretty sure Rebecca hadn't singled out anybody else. She milked a couple more seconds of rest before pushing herself back up, every muscle in her body shaking with tremors. A drop of sweat ran from her hairline down her forehead and to the tip of her nose, then dripped off onto her clasped hands.

The timer sounded, and all five women dropped to the ground with groans of relief. Next to her, she heard Lucy mutter, "Goddamn."

"Agreed," Spencer muttered, lungs heaving.

"Did she kick you?" Lucy asked, keeping her voice low.

"It wasn't really a kick," Spencer said honestly. "But yeah, she poked at me with her foot."

Lucy shook her head but didn't comment any further.

"Good job, ladies. I'll see you on Monday. Have a great weekend." Rebecca turned and left the area, calling out to a man who waved at her from a treadmill. "How's it going, Phil?"

Spencer, still lying on the foam mat and trying to catch her breath, watched Rebecca climb the stairs to the cardio equipment.

"You coming?" Lucy said from above her, standing now.

Spencer turned her head, looked up at her. "I'm just gonna lie here a bit longer."

Lucy's grin lit up her whole face. "I get that. I have to scoot, though. See you Monday." She scurried toward the locker room. The other three girls had also headed in, but Spencer was content to just stay on her stomach for a bit longer.

BodyFit wasn't busy at all, only a small handful of people milling around the equipment, mostly muscular men lifting the free weights, diehard bodybuilders. Spencer watched one guy curl a dumbbell that was bigger than her head. Not for the first time, she was amazed by how strong men were.

As Spencer slowly got herself to her feet, she saw Rebecca and the guy named Phil coming down the stairs, chatting away. Rebecca led him to a nearby area that had long straps with handles on the ends fastened to the wall. He must have said something funny because Rebecca laughed. Not a fake laugh. Not a polite laugh. A full-on laugh. It was fun and contagious enough to make Spencer smile at the sound.

"Not at all," Rebecca said. "We're going to challenge you, yes. But this will be fun." She stressed the word, put a hand on

Phil's shoulder. "Working out should be hard, but not stressful. Not something you dread. I want you to enjoy it. Okay?"

Spencer simply blinked at the words. At the relaxed, approachable expression on Rebecca's face. It was one she hadn't seen before. The encouraging words were ones she hadn't heard before. And she found herself annoyingly jealous of Phil.

Feeling her anger beginning to simmer, Spencer made a face as she wiped down her mat and put it away. Without looking at Rebecca again, she stalked into the locker room.

❖

"You got Phil tonight?" Sherry asked from behind the front counter as Rebecca approached.

Rebecca smiled. "I do."

"You love him."

"I do." Joining Sherry behind the counter, Rebecca searched the shelves underneath. "I think I left my notebook back here. I've got a new circuit I want to try with him and can't remember it all." She bent down, moving folders and bottles and other people's crap out of her way. A tap on her back made her move to stand, but she whacked her head on the counter first. "Son of a bitch," she muttered as she stood, rubbing the back of her head, surprised to see Spencer Thompson standing on the other side of the counter. Her face was still flushed from her workout and still had a slight glisten from perspiration, but her sandy brows were furrowed into a V above her nose and her eyes were not their usual inviting blue. They were cool. Frosty. She had her bag slung over her shoulder, which she hefted as she met Rebecca's eyes.

"I just wanted to let you know I won't be back to class." Her tone was quiet, but firm, not even remotely resembling the timid, shy tone Rebecca was used to hearing from her.

"Oh?"

"No. Frankly, I'm tired of the way you treat me, the way you single me out for constant criticism. I saw you with your client downstairs. Phil. And I heard you tell him how working out should be a challenge but also fun. And I realized that I am not having any fun here. *You* are not trying to make it fun. You make it hard and stressful, and I get enough of that on my own. I don't need it here. This class isn't for me." With that, she hefted her bag again, turned, and stalked out the door, Rebecca and Sherry both watching her go.

"Wow," Sherry said. "Kitty's got claws."

"You did not just say that." Rebecca shook her head, trying to laugh at Sherry's remark but finding herself stunned into inaction by Spencer's words, by the chill in her eyes, which had turned to sparks as she spoke. "I should do something."

"Are you asking me?"

Rebecca sighed, resigned. "No. I have her number. I'll call her and apologize, see if I can talk her into coming back."

Sherry looked at her for a beat, then finally asked, "Was she right?"

Rebecca found that she couldn't meet Sherry's eyes. Shame was funny like that. She didn't like what Spencer had said, mostly because it was true. Thanks to her own baggage that had nothing at all to do with Spencer, she'd been unintentionally unprofessional, and she was not proud of it. "Yeah, she kind of was."

"Kind of?"

"Not kind of. Was."

"Yeah, you need to fix it, then. Leslie won't be happy if we get bad reviews from her, and it'll be worse if she mentions you by name."

Rebecca hadn't even had time to think about that possibility. Leslie Baker owned BodyFit and prided herself on her friendly staff. Bad reviews made her get all twitchy, which was never good. Plus, Rebecca would not enjoy being called out for being a bitch, which was exactly how she'd been acting. At the same time, the idea of eating a big slice of humble pie was utterly unappetizing. Her face must have said so because Sherry gave a humorless chuckle.

"You did this to yourself, babe." With a gentle squeeze of Rebecca's shoulder, she grabbed up her belongings. "See you Monday."

Rebecca shook herself free of her frozen state, knowing she'd left Phil too long. With renewed vigor, she dug around and found her missing notebook, then headed back downstairs. Phil was awesome and fun to work with and she always enjoyed their hour-long personal training sessions, but tonight, she was preoccupied.

Tonight, her mind was filled with images of a pretty blonde who no longer held the title of weak and passive. Instead, she was now kind of tough. Stronger than originally thought. Assertive. A little bit of a badass. And wrapped around Rebecca's embarrassment and irritation with herself, there was intrigue. Spencer Thompson had shifted Rebecca's perception of her in a matter of thirty seconds.

Impressive.

She turned back to Phil, watching his form as he did squats. "Go down a little farther on that."

"That's what she said," Phil ground out through clenched teeth, making Rebecca laugh. But only for a moment, and then she was back to thinking about Spencer and how she really owed the woman an apology.

I need to fix this.

CHAPTER FIVE

God, it was hot.

Spencer didn't love the heat but also didn't complain about it the way Marti did. To Spencer, complaining was useless. It wasn't going to change anything, so why bother fretting over something you couldn't control? But Marti didn't see it that way and whined incessantly about the humidity, despite the fact that her house had central air.

They'd spent all day together yesterday, and Spencer didn't like to admit that she often looked forward to time on her own. It had been a nice day. Very pleasant. They'd done a little shopping, had lunch in a lovely new café downtown (though sat inside rather than "sweat like farm animals," as Marti had so eloquently put it, at an outside table for two), then watched a few episodes of *Scandal* on Netflix before adjourning to the bedroom, where Marti went to sleep instantly and Spencer had lain awake for another ninety minutes.

A typical Saturday for them, and now Spencer had some time on her own while she ran the open house for Jennifer. She found the correct place—the For Sale sign was a dead giveaway—and pulled into the driveway. The neighborhood was adorable, all small bungalows and one-story homes that were well kept and tidy. She expected a sizeable turnout today. Jennifer would have a sale on her hands in no time.

Leaving the air-conditioning of her car and stepping into the heat of that Sunday afternoon was jarring. Spencer took a moment just to breathe, the air feeling thick and heavy, like she was breathing through cheesecloth. She started to sweat almost immediately, so she popped her trunk and hauled out her signs as quickly as she could. The house had central air and she wanted to get inside, make sure it was comfortable for visitors.

She'd left a sign at the corner of the street to help people find the open house. Now she walked toward the street to the section of grass between the sidewalk and the road and propped a sign there. Then she took the smaller rectangular placard that read *Open House 2–4* and slid it onto the top of the For Sale sign. A nod of approval and she went back to her car and bent in to grab her bag. In it was paperwork, sell sheets detailing the house's features, and Jennifer's business cards. She pulled it out, slammed the car door, and heard a familiar voice.

"Spencer? I thought that was you."

Spencer turned to meet the blue-eyed gaze of Rebecca McCall.

Fudging son of a barn cat! Not somebody she expected to simply run into on a Sunday afternoon. There was a beat of hesitation while Spencer shook off the feeling of her worlds colliding. "Rebecca. Hi." Rebecca wore a pair of black shorts, a green racer-back tank that left her shoulders visible, and flip-flops. "What are you doing here?"

Rebecca reached up and tucked her hair behind her ear, then gazed off somewhere past Spencer. With a jerk of her thumb over her shoulder, she said, "I live next door."

Spencer shifted her gaze to take in the house behind her. It was small and neat, slate gray siding with bright white trim. Two pots of beautiful pink impatiens stood on either side of the front steps. A white Honda Accord was parked in the driveway. "Oh," Spencer said, as she wasn't sure what else to offer, especially given how they'd parted on Friday. Honestly, Spencer had expected never to see Rebecca McCall again, and that was okay with her.

"Listen, I know you're busy, but…" Rebecca wet her lips, and it occurred to Spencer that maybe she was battling nerves. "I don't know if you got my voicemail message…" She let her voice trail off, and Spencer realized she, typically, hadn't checked her voicemail in a couple days. Mostly because nobody ever left her voicemails.

"You left me a voicemail message?"

"I did. Yesterday."

"Do people still do that?" The question slipped out before Spencer had time to think about it, and she watched as Rebecca looked away, her face tinting pink. She'd embarrassed her, which shouldn't have bothered her, but did. She softened her tone. "No, I haven't listened to it yet. I'm sorry."

Rebecca's throat moved as she swallowed. "Okay, well, I wanted...I owe you an apology."

That was a surprise, and Spencer was sure it showed on her face.

"I was terribly unprofessional. You were right. I wasn't treating you like I should, and I wasn't helping you enjoy your workouts. That's totally on me."

Spencer watched her face, looked for sincerity. Found it.

"I'd like you to give me another chance. Come back to class. I promise it'll be different." She lifted herself up on the balls of her feet, then dropped back down, chewed on her bottom lip as she waited for a response.

"I..." What to do here? While Spencer knew she hadn't really given the class a chance because Rebecca had made it so difficult, she'd been relieved to call it quits. But now...Rebecca looked so genuinely sorry. Spencer wasn't stupid, however. She knew that Rebecca could simply just be doing damage control, trying to save her reputation, trying to keep BodyFit from getting a bad review (which Spencer had no intention of posting, but still...). Her face, though.

"Please?" Rebecca's expression was softer, gentler than Spencer had seen up until now, and it made her waver.

A car pulled up out front, and that took care of Spencer's wavering, as time had run out on her. "Okay," she said quickly and with a wave of her hand. "Fine. I'll give it another shot." She wasn't about to stand there and argue, so she took the easiest path. Spencer didn't count on how Rebecca's face would light up. Or how warm that would make her feel.

"Great. That's...that's fantastic. Thank you." Rebecca took a step backward. Another. Her face held the same expression as a kid who has just been told there's a snow day. "I'll see you tomorrow, then?"

Spencer nodded as the car began to empty and a young couple looked up at the house. "Yes. Yes, fine."

Rebecca continued to grin, gave Spencer a little wave, then turned and went back to her own yard.

Having correctly predicted the popularity of the neighborhood, Spencer was kept busy pretty much for the entire two hours of the open house, as potential buyers tromped through almost nonstop. There were a few who were obviously there just to look—it wasn't unusual for people to use open houses to get ideas for decorating their own homes—but there were also a couple of serious contenders.

By the time she'd fastened the lockbox back onto the front doorknob and was heading to her car, Spencer was way overstimulated. That wasn't going to change when she stopped by her parents' house, so she sat in the driver's seat for a good ten minutes to decompress. She sent a text to Jennifer, told her about the success of the day and that she'd send information on the potential buyers once she got home. Tucking her phone back into her purse, she ventured a glance to her left. She was in no way up for dealing with Rebecca again but found herself feeling a mix of relief and disappointment when she noticed the Accord that had been parked in Rebecca's driveway was now gone.

Yeah, that was for the best.

Ninety minutes later, she was seated at the dining room table in her parents' house, having been talked into staying for dinner by her younger brother, Travis.

"And I got to push the huge cart today with all the stuff on it," he was saying as he shoveled food into his mouth.

"Heavy stuff?" Spencer asked.

"Yeah. Dog food and cat litter and stuff like that. I really had to use my muscles." He held up an arm and flexed. "Feel."

Spencer squeezed his biceps, then dutifully widened her eyes and made all the right sounds of being impressed by his manly strength. It made him beam with pride, something Spencer always loved to see. "So, the job's working out?" she asked him, but it was more directed at her parents.

Travis nodded as he forked half of a rather large salt potato into his mouth.

"Honey, small bites," Spencer's mother said gently. "You don't want to choke."

Travis nodded again and spat the potato out onto his plate, then cut it in half.

Spencer tried not to grin as her mother just sighed and shook her head. "Yes, the pet store owner is very patient with him," she told Spencer. "Seems to be good so far."

"Tomorrow is adoption day," Travis said, his blue eyes sparkling with excitement.

"Yeah? What does that mean?" Spencer loved when Travis was this animated about something. Life could be hard at times for an intellectually disabled thirty-year-old, and finding a job that held his interest, even harder. Travis had been through many since he'd been old enough and educated enough to give it a shot. He always started strong, but his mind would wander and he had a terrible time concentrating.

Travis started to talk with his mouth full, but caught the look his mom shot him. After he'd made a show of swallowing, he said, "The animal shelter brings in some dogs and we put them in pens around the store. People can come and look at them and play with them and maybe adopt them."

"And do you get to play with them?" Spencer asked.

Travis nodded vigorously.

"That sounds awesome."

"It is." Travis shoveled more food into his mouth. "I love adoption days."

Spencer stabbed a piece of meat with her fork and looked at her mother. "Anybody hear from Mary Beth lately?" Her older sister led a busy life and it was rare that their paths crossed unless they made them.

"I called her last week," her mother said. "Everything is fine. Work is busy. Life is busy. Still dating Brent. Trent? Troy?"

"Bryce," Spencer supplied, with a grin.

"Yes. Him."

"I should shoot her a text," Spencer said, more to herself than to her mom.

"So, what's new with you, honey?" Spencer's father asked. Greg Thompson was a quiet man with a big presence. He rarely raised his voice—Spencer suspected that came from having a son like Travis, as shouting at him didn't help anything at all. Made things worse, in fact. Instead, Greg had a gentle, soothing tone pretty much all the time. Spencer felt safe and comfortable with him, always, and knew others felt the same way.

"Not a lot," Spencer said, chewing a bite of grilled chicken. "I started a class at the gym, quit it, and am going back tomorrow." Her chuckle held little humor, as she was now beginning to regret agreeing to giving Rebecca McCall a second chance.

"Oh?" her mother asked. Margie Thompson was a small woman, petite. Spencer got her blond waves from her mom, as well as her ability to adjust to almost any situation. "What's the class?"

"It's called Be Your Best Bride. We're all getting married fairly soon and we all want to get in better shape for it."

"That sounds great. How'd you find it?" Her mother was listening, while also keeping an eye on Travis. It was a skill she'd mastered over the years.

"I didn't. Marti did. She signed me up."

There were several beats of silence around the table before her father broke it.

"Marti signed you up? For a fitness class? Did she run it by you first?"

Spencer cleared her throat. "No, but it's fine. I could stand to be in better shape." Wishing she hadn't said anything, she pulled a Travis and stuffed a too-big salt potato into her mouth so she wouldn't have to speak.

Her parents didn't love Marti. They liked her just fine, but Spencer knew Marti wasn't their ideal partner for her. It had nothing to do with Spencer's sexuality and everything to do with Marti. Her parents loved Spencer and respected her, so they never badmouthed

Marti or said mean things. Mostly, when Marti did or said something of which they didn't approve, they simply got quiet. Spencer had suspected it for a while, but it became crystal clear when she'd told them Marti thought they should get married. The silence had been deafening.

"I just think she…could treat you better," her father had said, when Spencer had questioned his lack of input. "And I don't think you're happy. I don't think you've been happy since you and Chelsea broke up."

Spencer wanted to argue. She wanted to explain to her father just how wrong he was, how mistaken. Except that he wasn't.

"Anyway, I didn't like the instructor, so I ended up quitting the class." Spencer talked now to take the focus off *how* she'd gotten into the class. "As it turns out, she lives next door to the open house I ran for Jennifer today, and she saw me and came over to apologize."

"Well, that earns her points," her mother said.

"I guess it does. She asked me to give her another chance, and people were starting to show up for the open house, so I said yes just to move things along."

"And now?" asked her father.

Spencer sighed, wiped her mouth with a napkin. "I wish I hadn't said I'd go back, but…I gave her my word, so I will."

Greg Thompson gave one nod of satisfaction. "Good girl. Why were you running an open house for Jennifer?"

With a shrug, Spencer said, "She asked me to. She double-booked herself today."

"I don't understand why you don't finish up getting your license. You could sell houses easily. You know that business inside and out."

"I know." They'd had this discussion more than once, and Spencer was in no mood to do it again. To prevent it, she turned to her brother. "Hey, buddy, do they have cats at adoption day, too?"

"Uh-huh," Travis said excitedly, and the discussion about cats went on for a long time, just as Spencer had hoped.

❖

"That is a crazy weird coincidence." Nick's eyes never left the TV over the bar as he spoke, then took a swig of his Heineken.

"Right?" Rebecca's gaze was on the same thing, and she sipped her club soda with lime. This was how she and Nick did golf. And football. And baseball. And hockey. And occasionally soccer. Well. How Nick did sports and how Rebecca got to spend time with him. They carried on entire conversations barely looking at each other. "I glanced out the window and thought the woman looked familiar, but then she turned around and bam! It was totally her. So weird."

"It's good that you apologized." Nick did look at her then, his brown eyes saying more than his words.

"I just didn't want her giving the gym a bad review someplace."

Nick arched one eyebrow at her, something Rebecca thought only women did.

"Fine," Rebecca said on a sigh. "I may have owed her an apology."

"Damn right you did." Nick turned back to the TV.

"Shut up."

They fell silent for a bit. Nick, because he was watching the TV. Rebecca, because she knew Nick was right and she was embarrassed. She *had* owed Spencer an apology. She'd been unnecessarily hard on her simply because she didn't understand why somebody as wonderful-seeming as Spencer wouldn't put her foot down. Who lets their partner sign them up for a fitness class without talking to them about it? To Rebecca, that was the epitome of "you're not good enough, let me help you improve." And Spencer was going to marry this woman? This person who *obviously* didn't see what she had. And why did it bother Rebecca so much? She'd never seen Spencer before. Probably wouldn't see her again once class was over and she ran off to marry somebody who thought she needed to be in better shape. Ah, well. It was none of her business. Seemed like she had to keep reminding herself of that, which she wasn't thrilled about.

With a quiet sigh, she tried to focus on the TV. Which was hard because: golf.

"How do you watch this?" she asked Nick.

"You ask me that every time you meet me here" was his response, his eyes never leaving the screen.

"I know, but I don't get it."

"Well, see that guy?" Nick pointed at the TV. "And see that little ball? He's trying to hit that little ball into the hole with the stick he has—ow!"

"You're such a dick," Rebecca said, with a laugh, after punching him in the arm.

An enormous plate of chicken wings was set in front of him then, steaming and slathered in reddish-brown barbecue sauce, three little pods of blue cheese tucked neatly next to them (Nick had ordered extra).

"Aw, yeah," he said, drawing out the words, using the same voice he'd use if he was in the front row at a strip joint.

"I think you've got some drool on your chin."

"You're just jealous." Nick picked up a wing, dipped it into the first pod of blue cheese, stuck the entire wing into his mouth except the end where his fingers were, and pulled out a nearly clean bone. Pointing the bone at the dish, he said, "Eat."

Rebecca liked chicken wings, just not three dozen of them. She grabbed one, avoided the blue cheese and nibbled at it, wiping her mouth after every other bite. "You gonna eat that?" she asked, pointing at the celery.

Nick snorted, as she knew he would. "Have at it."

Rebecca chewed and glanced around. The bar was busier than she'd expected. She assumed that, in August, people were most likely poolside or at the beach or in the movie theater. But Turtle's had air-conditioning, food, booze, and sports on TV. Rebecca decided that made for a pretty tempting hangout on a day that was blazingly hot. She'd felt sorry for Spencer earlier, who was wearing a very pretty suit in the August afternoon humidity. It was light blue and seemed to be made of fairly substantial material, maybe cotton or a cotton/poly blend of some kind...

Rebecca literally shook her head, like she was trying to loosen something inside. The fact of the matter was, she was annoyed that she'd paid attention to so many details about Spencer Thompson.

Yeah, I think she's pretty. So what?

While it felt good to admit that to herself, it didn't help her feel any less irritated. Because being attracted to somebody like Spencer—who was also off-limits—was never a good thing.

Wait. Am I attracted to her?

She bumped Nick with her shoulder. "Hey. Do you think there's a difference between finding somebody attractive and actually being attracted to them?"

Nick did turn and look at her then, thick, dark eyebrows furrowed. "What?"

Rebecca shifted on her stool to face him. "Like, if you see a girl and you think she's pretty, does that mean you want to sleep with her? That you're attracted to her? Or can you think a girl's pretty, but it stops there because she's not your type or whatever?"

Nick looked at her like she'd grown a third eye in the middle of her forehead. "Beckster. Come on. I'm a guy. Every pretty girl is my type."

Rebecca chuckled. "Yeah, that was a stupid question, huh?"

"Ridiculous."

Nick turned back to the TV. Rebecca wrinkled her nose and picked up a celery stick to munch on. Enough of this silliness. She forced thoughts of Spencer Thompson out of her head.

Because she would see her tomorrow, and she intended to have her shit together by then.

She *needed* to.

CHAPTER SIX

Mondays were busy. Always. Rebecca had come in at 5:30 that morning for a private session with a client who preferred to get his workout in before he hit the office. Rebecca liked that way of thinking, understood it, didn't even mind that *she* had to get up that early. The only time it was hard for her was when she also had a late appointment. Like today. The brides class was at six, so she'd be here until after seven. Nearly fourteen hours to her workday.

The good news was this: because Mondays were so busy, they flew by, and that helped her not to dwell on any sense of fatigue. She didn't have a chance to. She'd slept well, gotten in a full eight hours, so she was doing all right. A glance at the clock told her it was 5:45. Almost time for her brides.

And Spencer.

She'd done her best to keep her thoughts on other subjects all day, but Spencer had a strange talent for worming her way into Rebecca's brain, to the point where Rebecca felt like Spencer was shadowing her all day, hanging out in the background, watching every move she made. She knew it all boiled down to nervous anticipation. Spencer had said she'd come back, but would she really? Did she simply say she would to get Rebecca off her back, when she actually had zero intention of showing up? Rebecca knew it was a definite possibility. In fact, that was exactly something she herself might have done if the roles were reversed.

Doing her best to shove her nerves into dark corners in her

brain, Rebecca popped the last section of a tangerine into her mouth just as she noticed Mr. Shanahan settling himself into the seat of one of the recumbent bikes. He sat there and stared at the screen as if unsure what to do next.

"Hey there, Mr. S. How are you today?" Rebecca moved in front of the bike so he could see her. He was an elderly man of eighty-four and had suffered a minor stroke several weeks ago. That meant that there were times when he got confused, wasn't quite sure what to do next.

He looked up at her, his rheumy blue eyes soft, the left side of his face just a bit slack. "Hello, Ms. McCall. I'm okay. You?"

"Rebecca," she said, with a smile. "Ms. McCall is my mother."

That earned her a grin from him and a playfully dismissive wave of his hand.

"Can I help you with the settings on this?"

He inhaled, then blew it out in obvious frustration. "I always think I've got it and then I sit down and I'm completely lost." He frowned.

"It's okay. These things can be more complicated than necessary. First, let's get your feet onto the pedals." She bent down and helped him slide each foot onto the large, black pedals and then she tightened the straps so they wouldn't slide off. Standing beside him, she pointed to things on the screen. "Okay. You're supposed to take it easy, if I remember correctly. Right?"

Mr. Shanahan grunted in apparent irritation. "I guess so."

"Well, we don't want you keeling over from pushing harder than you should. That would be bad for all of us."

That got her a chuckle.

"So we're just going to go at a nice, easy pace." She set the bike at a reasonably low level of resistance, then pointed to a number at the bottom of the screen. "This is your time, so you can see how long you've been riding."

With a nod, Mr. Shanahan started to pedal.

"Good?" Rebecca asked.

He nodded again. "Feels fine."

"Terrific. Pedal away. And don't overdo it." She rested a hand on his shoulder and watched as he rode.

"Thank you for helping a decrepit old man, Ms. McCall. Much appreciated."

"Please. You are far from decrepit." She stepped away and back behind him so he couldn't see her, but she stayed and watched for several moments, making sure he had the hang of it, that he wasn't off balance or pushing harder than he should. In her many years in the fitness industry, one thing Rebecca had discovered was that clients—overwhelmingly male clients—often pretended to be fine with a move or a weight or a stretch because they didn't want to seem weak in front of a woman. So they'd strain too hard or push too far to keep from failing in front of her. She'd had several clients with whom she'd had gentle discussions on the subject. The last thing she wanted was somebody to get hurt on her watch, so she stood where she could observe Mr. Shanahan for a bit, make sure he was safe. It was her job. More than that, it was her passion. She couldn't imagine doing anything else.

❖

Spencer was surprised. She could admit it. She was also unexpectedly touched—that one was harder to accept. In her mind, Rebecca McCall was a sort of ice queen. A hardass. Little bit of a bitch. But none of those things applied to the scene Spencer watched from the drinking fountain as she filled her water bottle.

No, what she saw was Rebecca being gentle. Patient and kind. She helped the old man get his sneakered feet onto the bike pedals, then strapped them in for him. Then she calmly helped him set the bike to the right resistance, pointed out different things he might want to keep track of. But most surprising was how she stepped away. The old man evidently thought she was gone, as he focused hard on what he was doing. But Rebecca wasn't gone. She hovered a few feet behind him, arms folded across her chest, and watched. Just watched. Made sure he was doing okay.

Yeah, Spencer was surprised.

"Are you...done?" came a voice from behind her.

Spencer flinched and then looked down at her overflowing water bottle. "Darn it!" She let go of the button and dumped out some of the excess. Glancing at the person behind her, a man who was obviously waiting to get some water for himself, she grimaced in apology. "Sorry."

He smiled. "No problem. I was worried you might drown."

Spencer grinned back and indicated the fountain with a dramatic flourish of her arm. "All yours, my man."

Heading down to the designated area where the brides always met, Spencer found Lucy where she stood with the other three women, but also a bit apart. Apparently, cliques didn't end with high school.

"Hey there," Lucy said with her usual perkiness, bouncing to the beat of the Matchbox Twenty song that played over the speakers; apparently it was a day for the '90s channel on the gym's Sirius radio.

They talked for a minute or two before Rebecca arrived and laid out the plan for the session. When her eyes met Spencer's, she gave a hesitant smile. Spencer returned it; she couldn't seem to help herself. Seeing Rebecca smile was a nice change, not to mention getting actual eye contact.

Maybe things would be different now.

Half an hour later, all five women were lined up on the floor, not for planks this time, but for push-ups. An exercise Spencer despised, as she'd never been able to do more than two.

"Keep your back straight," Rebecca said, her voice alarmingly close. Spencer realized she was kneeling next to her. "Lower this." Spencer felt a warm hand on the small of her back, gentle pressure telling her what exactly to bring down.

Spencer obeyed. Did a push-up. Grunted.

"Elbows closer to your sides."

Spencer obeyed again, grunted louder. "That makes it harder," she complained.

"Yes, it does," Rebecca replied, but her tone was light, friendly. Almost playful. It confused Spencer, who did one more push-up. "Good!"

Spencer dropped her body to the floor, lungs heaving. "Sugar and spice," she said, in lieu of a curse. "That's it. That's all I've got."

"Sugar and spice?" Rebecca repeated, amused. "Don't you mean 'holy shit,' or something?"

"Yes."

Rebecca grinned. "I'm sensing a challenge." Then she moved on down the line.

"We'll get this," Bella said, and it took a moment for Spencer to realize she was looking right at her, had directed the comment her way. Spencer smiled at her, gave her a thumbs-up from where she lay sprawled flat on the floor like a stingray out of water. Spencer watched as Rebecca helped each woman with her form. At one point, she glanced back at Spencer and gave her another smile.

What is happening?

Rebecca had evaluated each of them, noted the strengths and weaknesses of each individual woman, and made a plan for her. "For our last circuit, we're working upper body. Arms, shoulders, back." Pointing, she directed each bride to a specific place in the gym. Some were at equipment. Brittany was at the straps fastened to the wall that Spencer had noticed the previous week. Spencer was sent to the free weights with the instruction to grab a seven-and-a-half-pound dumbbell and Rebecca would be right over.

As she sat with her dumbbell and waited, Spencer watched the men around her. They were lifting what were, to Spencer, extraordinary amounts of weight, barbells loaded with two and three plates, dumbbells three times the size of the one Spencer had set by her feet. One muscle-bound man to her left had his earbuds in and a barbell at his feet, each end with two heavy-looking plates. He grabbed the bar and stood, bringing the weight with him, then set it back down loudly. Up. Down-crash. Up. Down-crash. He repeated this eight times. At the fifth time, Spencer covered her ears.

Not hearing Rebecca's approach, she was startled to find her standing close, watching the man with a disapproving expression on her face.

"That's really loud," Spencer said quietly.

"I hate when he does that. It's so obnoxious and totally unnecessary." Rebecca shook her head as if shaking herself back to the task at hand. "Okay. Kickbacks. These are for your triceps."

"Oh, good," Spencer said, with a laugh. "Mine could use some help. I call these my Nana Arms." She lifted an arm as if to flex her bicep, but wiggled her whole arm instead, the loose muscle and skin underneath flapping in the breeze.

"Most women could use help in this area." Rebecca picked up the dumbbell from near Spencer's feet and took it to one of the several benches in that area. She put her left knee and left hand onto the bench. The dumbbell in her right hand, she let her arm hang down toward the floor. "Okay. You're going to start like this. Then bring the weight up." She bent her elbow until her upper arm was parallel to her back. "Then extend out." Straightening her arm, she lifted the weight back toward her rear end. "Then back." She repeated the process. "Slow, controlled movements. That's the key here. None of this." She whipped the weight back, using her whole body to do so.

Spencer grinned.

"Slow and controlled." Rebecca stood and handed the weight to Spencer. "We'll start with eight on each side."

Spencer mimicked the movement, the first couple reps easy, then becoming harder rather quickly.

"You should feel that here." Rebecca touched a finger to Spencer's triceps.

"You mean the fire that's burning through my muscles like lava? I should feel that?"

"Exactly that."

"Then I'm good."

Rebecca chuckled, then seemed to grow serious. "Listen, Spencer." She paused, as if gathering her thoughts, and Spencer was glad to have the weight in her hand, something to concentrate on rather than feeling awkward. "I'm really glad you came back. Again, I apologize for last week, and I appreciate you giving me another chance."

Spencer nodded, unsure of what words to say. She wanted to ask what she'd done to cause Rebecca's initial dislike of her, but it didn't seem like the time or place. Instead, she offered a friendly smile, and that seemed to alleviate any discomfort either of them felt.

When Spencer finished the first set, Rebecca said, "Rest for one minute, then do another set. Both arms. Rest for one minute, then do a third. I'll be back by then."

"Yes, ma'am." Spencer watched Rebecca walk back toward where Brittany was pulling on the wall straps and realized she was seeing her in a new light. It was kind of amazing how easily that had happened. Just from Rebecca being nice, friendly instead of standoffish and cold. Today, she wore tight nylon workout pants and a light blue racer-back tank that was also fitted. It showed off her body nicely, and for the first time, Spencer found herself looking. *Really* looking. Rebecca was trim and fit, unsurprisingly. But she was also feminine. She had curves. Hips and breasts and a round ass that Spencer had trouble pulling her gaze from, wondered what it would feel like to have it in her hands…

Okay. Enough of that. Marti. Marti. Marti.

She shook her head and turned her focus back to the exercise at hand, doing her best to keep her movements slow, to concentrate on her form, which Rebecca had told them endlessly today was very important.

Rebecca returned as Spencer started her third set. After three reps, her arm started to quake.

"It's okay to rest," Rebecca told her, and Spencer immediately set the weight down in relief. "Just don't wait too long. Give yourself a few seconds, then get back to it. You can rest as many times as you need to, just finish the reps. You'll be surprised how quickly you improve."

"Will I? That seems to be a tall order right now." Spencer

picked the weight back up, did three more reps before dropping it again.

"I promise. If you do the work, we're gonna get you results." Her smile was reassuring. "Finish up, and meet us over in the corner."

This time when she walked away, Spencer forced herself *not* to watch.

"What happened to her?" Lucy whispered in the locker room ten minutes later. "Was she body snatched by aliens? Visited by three ghosts?"

Spencer shook her head. "I have no idea." She popped her lock open, then sat down to take off her Nikes and sweaty socks. "But I like it. It's nice." That was the truth.

"Me, too. I hope it's not a fluke of some kind."

"Yeah."

Spencer was well aware that this might, in fact, be just that: a fluke. Maybe Rebecca had been in a great mood today, and that was the only reason she'd been as nice as she had. But her apology— her *second* apology—told Spencer that maybe she really *had* had a change of heart. Either way, Spencer would take it. It had been a good workout, and for the first time since the class had begun, Spencer started to think about what it would be like to be in better shape. More importantly, how would it feel?

"What are you up to tonight?" Lucy asked, tugging her back to the present. "Anything fun?"

"On a Monday? Doubtful. I'm going over to Marti's, I think."

"Ethan likes to go out on Mondays. Monday Misadventures, he calls it. It's a thing he has." Lucy giggled. "It sounds silly, but I love it. One time, we went bowling. Another, to a new ice cream place. Last week, it was a wine bar. He's always got a new place picked out, and I never know what it is until we get there."

"I don't think that sounds silly at all," Spencer said. "I think it sounds amazing." Marti would never do something like that. She was routine, almost rigid. Spencer predicted she'd get to Marti's, Marti would come home from work some time around eight. Maybe later. Spencer would have eaten dinner alone. They'd chat about work, maybe a few other things, then they'd go to bed. Predictable. They had become so very predictable.

"I can't wait to see what tonight is." Lucy's smile was wide, her excitement palpable.

"I expect a full report," Spencer called as Lucy shouldered her bag and headed out of the locker room. With a sigh, she went back to her own stuff. Yeah, envy was big right now, sitting on her shoulders like some sort of raven.

She didn't like feeling that way.

Doing her best to shake it off, she drove to Marti's. As expected, nobody was home, so she went in and scoped out the contents of the fridge before texting Marti.

ETA on coming home?

She set the phone on the counter, pulled out a jar of sauce and a box of pasta.

"But first, vino," she said, to the empty kitchen.

Her first sip of a lovely Gewurztraminer was in her mouth when her phone dinged, indicating a text.

Probably not until late. Big case. Ordered some Chinese.

Spencer's wave of disappointment was short-lived, instantly replaced by happy anticipation of a night alone. That had been happening more and more lately, and she'd been trying to ignore it. Shouldn't she be excited for her partner—no, her fiancée—to come home? Shouldn't she look forward to spending time with her rather than be happy to be alone?

The pasta and jar of sauce tucked back in the cupboard, Spencer pulled eggs out of the fridge instead. As she was beating a couple with a fork, thoughts flew around her head, fast and furious.

She loved Marti. Didn't she? They'd been together for nearly two years. They knew each other well. Rather, Spencer knew Marti well. If they were forced to play *The Newlywed Game* and were asked questions about each other, Spencer would beat Marti easily. That was only because Marti wasn't good with detail and she wasn't a romantic at heart. Not like Spencer, who could lose an entire weekend watching the Hallmark Channel's cheesy romance movies and loving every second of it. Marti was pragmatic. Logical. And her job as an attorney had taught her to tuck her own emotions into a box and leave them at the door. Depositions and trials were no place for feelings, she liked to say.

Did she wish Marti had a tiny bit of a romantic side? Of course. But that just wasn't her and that was okay. Spencer gave a firm nod as she scrambled eggs in a frying pan, then sprinkled some grated cheddar onto them.

I could do a lot worse than Marti. I'm lucky to have her.

She took a large gulp of her wine and tried not to wonder who she was hoping to convince.

❖

Well. That was good. Sort of.

Rebecca stowed her things in her own locker in the staff locker room—a separate, secure room away from the public locker room—before heading for the showers. It felt better, anyway. It was much more pleasant to be nice to Spencer Thompson, to treat her like any other client rather than let her own judgments seep in. There was a thing she hadn't counted on, though: liking Spencer a bit too much.

What was it about her anyway?

She cranked the water as hot as she could get it and let it beat a rhythm against her shoulders, trying her best to focus on all the work she'd done today, all the bending and stretching with clients, as well as her own workout she'd snuck in after lunch. But the more she tried not to think about Spencer, the more she thought about Spencer.

She drew people. Rebecca could see that. People liked Spencer immediately. Lucy adored her. Even the other three (that Rebecca had dubbed "the clique") seemed to be warming to her little by little. There was something about Spencer that made people feel relaxed with her. Comfortable. Rebecca was no exception.

She was kind. Even when she'd told Rebecca she was quitting

last Friday, she'd been almost...professional about it. She was angry, that had been obvious, but she'd said her piece and walked away. No raised voices. No name-calling. No swearing.

That last thought made Rebecca chuckle beneath the spray of water. What had Spencer said? Sugar and spice? Yeah, Rebecca was going to get an F-bomb out of her if it was the last thing she did. Then her mind began to wander to the physical attributes of Spencer Thompson. And that was dangerous.

Spencer was in much better shape than she gave herself credit for. She was a bit...soft, yes. Untoned, as most people were. But she had great potential. And her blue eyes were kind. Inviting. She had lovely hands. Feminine and pretty. Her wavy hair was beautiful, just waiting for fingers to dig in—

"Stop it!" Rebecca hissed the command at herself, eyes squeezed shut, fists balled tightly until her nails left red crescents in her palms.

Spencer was engaged.

She was getting married in a few months.

She was *so* off-limits. You couldn't get much more off-limits than Spencer Thompson was. Rebecca needed to remember that and derail this train of thought completely. Right now. Before it became a problem. Well, a bigger problem. She made a mental note to back off again, just a little, when it came to Spencer. She didn't like that idea, but at this point, the way her thoughts were going, it was necessary.

Once she'd toweled off and dressed, Rebecca gathered her things and headed upstairs. It had become quiet, as it was getting late and the gym closed shortly. She waved to the college-age kid behind the desk, who was most likely doing an internship for his sports medicine degree, and drove herself home, determined.

When she had fed Veruca Salt, who meowed her dissatisfaction over eating at this late hour—even though she ate around this very time more often than not—Rebecca settled onto her couch, clicked on the TV to Lifetime, and pulled her computer onto her lap. She didn't tell a lot of people that she was a Lifetime movie addict, but she was. She loved them, their lame plots, their ultra-cheesy titles. And once in a while, she'd hit pay dirt and stumble across a really good one. Mostly, she had it on for background noise. Being somebody who worked in a gym for anywhere from seven to fourteen or fifteen hours a day, she was used to the constant hum of activity. Being in her house alone with no sound weirded her out a little bit.

Rebecca set the remote down and waited for Veruca Salt to make herself comfortable alongside her, then she signed on to one of the dating sites. Not bothering to look at her new matches, she scrolled and clicked until she found the friendly looking brown-haired girl whose name was Beth. She had two other photos, which Rebecca checked out, then read her profile again. She was into yoga, hiking, rowing (so active, which earned her points). She was a nurse and thirty-seven, two years older than Rebecca.

"Okay, Ruke, here goes nothing."

This was good.

This was a surefire way to yank her thoughts back to where they were supposed to be instead of where they'd cause nothing but trouble.

This was good.

CHAPTER SEVEN

Y ou know," Marti said as she poured them each a cup of coffee on Wednesday morning, "you've barely packed anything. I mean, I kind of thought you'd be in by now. Or at least moving some stuff over." Her tone was matter-of-fact, as if she was working very hard to make sure it didn't seem like this was a subject that bothered her.

Spencer knew better.

"I know. I'll get there. Just been really busy with work and the gym and stuff." It was a lame excuse. Just as lame as it had been the first time she'd used it. Marti was right; Spencer had barely packed a thing at her house. She wasn't worried about how quickly it would sell. It was adorable, in a fantastic neighborhood, and had a modern kitchen and a newly remodeled bathroom, thanks to Spencer's dad. And there was the added bonus that she worked for a real estate firm. No, selling would be a breeze, so she hadn't even begun to take the steps necessary to do so.

Most of her day at work was spent replaying the conversation in her head, short as it had been.

Analyzing why was not something Spencer wanted to get into…even though part of her knew she should. Marti had wanted her to move in ages ago. It made sense. Marti's place was much bigger, everything was new so there was nothing to update or change. Spencer thought of the painting she'd done in her own small house, painstakingly picking out paint chips at Home Depot (or Homo Depot, as Marti called it). Then she taped them up on the walls and looked at them for days and days before narrowing them down. Once she'd done that, she'd gone back to Home Depot and bought three or four tiny sample cans, brought them home, painted a swatch of wall, and looked at those for days and days more. Only after all of that did she decide on a color and paint the room. She'd gone through that process five times, for five different rooms, and she'd been thrilled with the results.

That house was all Spencer. And she loved it.

Marti's house was beautiful, all open concept and big spaces. It was also a bit...cool. The walls were all creamy ivory, and Marti liked them that way. The kitchen, with its dark wood cabinets and deep slate countertops, was gorgeous, but also a little cold. Spencer often racked her brain to come up with ways to warm the place up, make it feel more like a home and less like the model house in a new housing tract.

Try as she might to not think about the subject, to push it away, it hung out in the back of her head like a soccer player waiting to be put in, bouncing around in excitement, its energy too palpable to ignore completely.

Spencer had never looked forward to the bride class at the gym before, so realizing she was doing just that helped a bit. *I guess there's a first time for everything.* Seeing Rebecca in her new, friendly and approachable persona was something she found herself anticipating with an unexpected sliver of optimism. Seeing Rebecca in her workout clothes was another (though she tried not to get distracted by that).

"Hey, how was your day?" Lucy asked when she and Spencer were standing at what had become their usual lockers. She was in her underwear and cheerful and bouncy as always. Spencer wondered if there was a person on the planet who wouldn't like Lucy instantly.

"It wasn't bad," Spencer said truthfully, then stopped with her hands on her bag and looked at her friend. "I don't even know what you do. Do I?"

"I teach kindergarten," Lucy said, and nothing made more sense than that.

"Oh, right. I remember now. Only a couple more weeks of summer left."

"Don't remind me."

Out in the gym, the five of them stretched, moves they now knew how to do on their own, so they didn't have to wait for Rebecca to give them the go-ahead. Bella and Willow were talking about a cake decorating class. Brittany was on the other side of them, obviously listening and looking for a spot to jump in. Which she did.

"What do you think of class so far?" Lucy asked Spencer quietly as they each did a hamstring stretch. "I'm loving it. I already feel better."

Spencer furrowed her brow. "You know what? I haven't really thought about it, though I can tell you that I couldn't straighten my arms all the way yesterday. I felt like a T. rex."

Lucy's laugh was musical. "That's good, though. Don't you feel accomplished when that happens?"

"That's a good way to look at it. I've been trying to think like that." Spencer had done her best to focus on that. To enjoy the exercise rather than dread it.

"Hello, ladies." Rebecca appeared in front of them dressed in her usual black workout pants. Today's top was a deep purple T-shirt, the gray and purple Sauconys on her feet completing the outfit. Her dark hair was sleek, tucked behind her ears, and her gorgeous blue eyes were… Spencer couldn't tell because Rebecca didn't look at her.

It stayed that way for most of the class. Spencer did catch a glance from Rebecca from across the gym while she was on the lat pull-down machine, and Rebecca was helping Lucy on the leg press. But that was about it.

They finished up with sixty-second planks.

"Jiminy Cricket, I hate these things," she muttered, then lasted twenty-five seconds before having to drop to her belly and rest.

"Nope," she heard Rebecca say from above her. "Get up. You can do this."

There was no poke with her toe, and her tone, though just as firm as last time, didn't hold the same disdain. Spencer groaned and pushed herself to her toes and forearms.

"Fifteen more seconds," Rebecca announced as Lucy dropped.

Spencer had no idea how the other girls were doing, as she was on an end with Lucy to her left. Her arms quaked, her stomach muscles burned like they were on fire, and she dropped. Rebecca's timer went off no more than five seconds later.

"All right. All right. Not bad." All five of the women were panting, a couple groaned. "Planks are notoriously hard because we tend to forget to concentrate on strengthening our core. But core strength is essential for good posture, to avoid back problems, stuff like that. So we're going to keep working on it, and Friday, I'll have some new moves for you."

More groaning, but Rebecca just grinned.

Spencer rolled over onto her back, breath still ragged. Lucy followed suit.

"See you on Friday," Rebecca said, by way of dismissing them.

Spencer watched as Rebecca walked away and headed up the stairs, not looking back. The PA was playing something by Rihanna, the first time Spencer had paid any attention to the music today. That was unusual, but she'd been too busy watching Rebecca. Watching Rebecca barely watching her.

So, we're back to that, are we?

With a sigh, Spencer sat up. Lucy did the same, then stood and held out her hand. Spencer took it and Lucy pulled her to her feet. "You okay?" Lucy asked, squinting a bit at her.

Spencer shot her a half grin that took too much effort. "I am."

"Good. You got really quiet once we started. I was wondering if you didn't feel well."

With a shake of her head, Spencer said, "I'm fine. Just got some things on my mind." Which wasn't a lie. Together, they hit the locker room.

It bothered Spencer more than she cared to admit, Rebecca's odd shift in demeanor. She'd enjoyed Monday. She'd enjoyed having some of Rebecca's attention focused on her. Maybe she shouldn't have. Maybe this was better because…yeah, Spencer didn't want to go there.

When she and Lucy were both dressed, Lucy pulled out her phone and gave it a quick glance. Turning to Spencer, she said, "Hey, I've got an hour or so before I have to be home to meet Ethan. Want to grab a cup of coffee or something?"

Spencer glimpsed the clock on the wall. It was a little after seven. Marti might be home. She probably wasn't, but even if she was, that didn't mean Spencer couldn't go out with a friend for a bit. "Coffee sounds great." She gave Lucy a big smile and packed up her stuff.

Fifteen minutes later, they sat at a little table for two in Grounded, a coffee shop not far from the gym, a latte in front of each of them. They took tandem sips.

"Mmm," Lucy said. "I love Starbucks, but this place comes pretty darn close."

"Agreed. Though I'm a fan of Starbucks's chai latte, and I haven't come across another place yet that does it quite as well."

They sipped again before Lucy said, "You said earlier that you didn't know what I did. I realized the same thing. What do you do?"

"Oh, I work for a real estate firm."

"You're a Realtor?"

"I'm not, though I only have to take the test to get my license."

"What do you do there?" Lucy's big eyes focused on her, and it occurred to Spencer that she'd forgotten how nice it was to have somebody's full attention.

"I'm the admin. I set up appointments, take info on new houses, deal with clients. Sometimes I cover open houses for agents. I do my best to keep them organized."

"Are they bad about that?"

"You'd be surprised." Spencer chuckled. "How long have you taught kindergarten?"

"Three years." Lucy's face changed then, went from its usual pleasant expression to one that was bigger, if that made sense. Excited. Filled with joy. "I've only been teaching for six years now and I started with third grade. Then, three years ago, one of the kindergarten teachers retired and the administration asked me if I'd be interested in making a switch." She gazed dreamily out the window next to their table. "Oh, my goodness, Spence, these kids." She shook her head, the love for her job as obvious as if it had been written across her forehead. "It's such an amazing age. They're learning and curious and they have questions. And they're so full of love." Her words trailed off and she refocused her gaze on Spencer. "I never want to do anything else."

"Wow," Spencer commented, simultaneously thrilled for Lucy's happiness and envious that she didn't feel quite the same way about her own job. "That sounds amazing. Those kids are lucky to have you as their teacher."

"I don't know about that." Lucy blushed a pretty pink. "I do know that I'm lucky to have a job I love." She sipped her latte. "Do you love yours?"

Spencer also sipped, then took a moment to really think about the question. "I don't necessarily love being an admin, but I do love the real estate field. I find it really interesting in that it's always changing and updating. I love keeping up with trends, researching what's hot and what used to be hot, but isn't anymore."

"Do you watch *House Hunters*? You probably don't. I imagine it would drive you crazy."

"I *do* watch and it *does* drive me crazy!" They both laughed. "Why don't any of those people understand that if you don't like the color of the walls, there's this fancy new invention called paint?" Lucy shook her head, her shoulders still shaking with her laughter.

"Right? Also, what the hell do these people do for a living that their budget is always half a million dollars or more?"

"And they're all, like, thirty!" They went back and forth a couple more times before exhausting the subject. When their merriment died down again, Lucy said, "So, I'm pretty sure when you mentioned your fiancée on the first day of class, you said she. I assume you're gay? Or bisexual?" At Spencer's nod, she added, "Tell me about your fiancée."

"Marti?" Spencer asked, taken a bit off guard by the request. "Oh, she's…she's a lawyer. She just made partner a few months ago."

"And how long have you been together?"

"Not quite two years."

Lucy nodded. "Big wedding?"

Spencer inhaled, let it out slowly, and studied her coffee. "We're not really having a wedding. We're just going to go to the courthouse, quick and easy." When she looked up at Lucy's confused expression, she elaborated, doing her best to keep her tone light. "Marti isn't big on fancy celebrations and stuff. Thinks they're a waste of money."

"And what do you think?"

"I think…" Spencer glanced out the window, as if the words she was searching for would come wandering down the sidewalk. "I always thought a big, fancy, gorgeous wedding would be amazing. All the people I love there. My dad walking me down the aisle. My bride's dad walking her." Spencer looked back at Lucy, slightly embarrassed. "Sounds like a Hallmark movie, huh?"

"I think it sounds amazing."

Spencer let out a dreamy little sigh. "Doesn't it?"

"And Marti knows that's the kind of wedding you'd like?"

Spencer shrugged, not quite ready to delve into the details of the answer, and stayed quiet. Lucy seemed to study her, and Spencer wanted to squirm in her chair. "What?"

Lucy shook her head. "Nothing." She sipped her coffee, then seemed to collect herself. Her phone pinged, giving them both something else to focus on. "There's my guy," Lucy said, and the way her face changed—softened, a tender smile appearing—hit Spencer with a dose of envy that felt like she'd been slapped in the face. "Gotta go." Lucy tipped her cup up and finished her latte, then stood.

Spencer stayed in her seat. "I've got a bit more, so I'm going to hang for a little while. But I had a nice time. Thanks for inviting me out."

"Thanks for coming." Lucy surprised her then by leaning down and hugging her tightly. "See you on Friday."

Spencer watched her go, the spring in Lucy's step obvious, her face nearly glowing. Try as she might, Spencer couldn't remember the last time she'd dropped everything to go meet Marti. In fact, she couldn't remember the last time Marti had texted her from someplace and wanted Spencer to meet her.

Shifting her focus to the others in the coffee shop, she sat at her table and did some people watching. In the corner was a middle-aged man sitting alone and reading a book, the title of which she couldn't make out. *College professor*, she thought. Across from him were two women somewhere in their late thirties drinking glasses of wine rather than coffee, both with big smiles, taking turns leaning toward each other. *Old friends who don't see each other as often as they'd like.* The next table over from Spencer's, which she hadn't been able to see when Lucy was in her seat, was occupied by a young man and woman. Both in their twenties or early thirties. Both looking nervous. She toyed with her mug. He looked everywhere but at her. *Internet date. First-timers.*

It was a game Spencer enjoyed, one she played often when she had time to kill. It had started when she was a kid, whenever they went somewhere either as a family or just her, her mother, and Travis. Her brother had taken a lot of concentration, and young Spencer rarely had the full attention of her parents. She could be in mid-sentence and then one or both of them would simply turn away to say something to Travis or they'd simply leave while she was talking, having to chase her brother down or snatch something from his hands (or mouth) that he shouldn't have. She'd grown up never getting 100 percent of the focus, so she began finding ways to amuse herself. Thus, the Who Are They and Why Are They Here game, which had carried into her adult life. She did it during open houses as people inspected the goods for sale. She did it in restaurants when Marti went on and on about a case she'd talked about half a dozen times before. And she still did it when she was out in public with her family. She was used to not being listened to; no big deal really. So, she used the game to prevent boredom. She used the game to amuse herself.

Tonight, she was using the game to avoid two things: going home and thinking about Rebecca.

It was only working on one of them.

❖

Rebecca McCall was a self-assured woman. Being confident had never been an issue for her. Not in elementary school. Not in junior high or high school. Not even in college. She'd always known what she'd wanted and how best to get it, and it never occurred to her that she couldn't do something.

No, confidence had never been an issue.

Until today.

She sat in a booth at Casey's Lunch Box, a cute little diner on the west side of town, and fiddled with the white mug that all diners seemed to use for coffee, its ceramic thick and heavy. She spun it slowly in a circle on the red Formica table and tried her very best not to stare out the window looking for any woman who even remotely resembled Beth, her match on the dating site.

Beth had seemed quite receptive to Rebecca's lunch date suggestion, and Rebecca wondered if she thought of the safety nets involved the same way Rebecca had. One, lunch was a good bet because it limited their time. Not like dinner or drinks after work. Two, it was the middle of the day, so there would likely be no alcohol involved, which was better for both of them. (*Or was it?* Rebecca was now thinking, second-guessing the decision because a shot of tequila might help calm her nerves at the moment.) And three—though this one was only for Rebecca—Casey's was a good twenty-minute drive from the gym, so she was reasonably sure she wouldn't accidentally run into one of her colleagues, who would then have a million questions about why she was sitting alone in a diner that took her half her lunch hour to get to, with no lunch in front of her.

They were supposed to meet at noon, she and Beth, but a glance at her watch told Rebecca it was now 12:15 and still no sign of her. Not in a hurry to humiliate herself, Rebecca decided she'd give it until 12:30 and then she was out of there. If Beth thought it odd that Rebecca hadn't offered up her phone number for texting, she hid it well, and she didn't offer hers either. Therefore, the only way they had to contact one another was through the dating site.

Something could have come up. Rebecca was willing to give Beth the benefit of the doubt. Maybe her car broke down. Maybe she had a meeting at work. Maybe she got sick. Any number of reasons that did not involve "decided she didn't want to meet with me after all" were possibilities.

At 12:25, Rebecca pulled her wallet out of her small bag and took out four dollars to tip the waitress who'd refilled her coffee cup three times in the thirty-five minutes she had been here…the coffee that now threatened to burst her bladder if she didn't hit a ladies' room. Beth was obviously not coming, and Rebecca didn't want to admit how disappointed she was. She was about to stand up when somebody flopped down into the booth across the table from her, startling her enough to cause a slight intake of breath. She looked up, expecting to see a very late Beth.

Instead, she was greeted by a very pretty Spencer Thompson.

"Hey. I thought that was you when I came in." Spencer smiled at her as she set down her napkin-wrapped silverware and a cup with the straw sticking out, then set her placard with the number 16 on it next to the cup.

"What are you doing here?" The question was out of Rebecca's mouth before she could take a second to think about how it might sound. Accusatory and a titch rude. That was how it sounded. She managed not to wince at her own tone.

"I was going to ask you the same thing," Spencer replied, not missing a beat. "They don't have food near the gym?" Her soft smile took any sting out of the words that might have seeped in. "My office is across the street. I eat lunch here a lot."

Doesn't that just fucking figure? Rebecca tried not to notice how appealing Spencer was in her work clothes. She was so used to seeing her client in workout pants and sweaty T-shirts, her hair in a ponytail, that this alternate version of Spencer was unexpected. Only able to see her from the waist up, Rebecca took in the black-and-white pinstriped top with silver buttons and how it was open at Spencer's throat, revealing a chunky silver necklace that accented a visible collarbone. Her blond hair was down, the waves even more prominent out of the ponytail, and it was longer than Rebecca had originally thought, cascading past her shoulders to skim the tops of Spencer's unexpectedly ample br— *For God's sake! Stop that!*

Rebecca squeezed her eyes shut and willed her brain to be quiet.

"Are you waiting for somebody?" Spencer asked, her tone innocently inquisitive and not at all like she knew what Rebecca had been thinking.

"I was. She didn't show." Rebecca hadn't meant to say that either. God, what was wrong with her?

"A date?" Spencer asked just above a whisper, leaning forward conspiratorially.

"No," Rebecca snapped. Her shoulders dropped in defeat and she sighed. "Yes."

Spencer nodded as if she understood completely. She sat back as the waitress arrived with a grilled cheese and tomato sandwich and chips on a white plate that matched Rebecca's coffee mug. When the waitress took the numbered placard and left, Spencer asked, "A set-up? Or online?"

"Online."

"Do you think she peeked in, saw you, and left?"

Rebecca stared at her, blinking, then her brow furrowed, but before she could snap off a retort, Spencer held up her hand, a big grin on her face.

"I'm kidding. I'm kidding. Please, like anybody would see you and walk away. No. Not happening." She gave a small snort, then took a bite of her sandwich. She chewed as she looked out the window, suddenly seeming at a loss for words.

Rebecca sipped the last of her coffee—even though she was certain her bladder had zero room left—and stared back at her. The silence lasted for several beats before Spencer apparently located words again, cocked her head, and surprised Rebecca by asking, "What's your deal with me?"

Brow furrowed, Rebecca asked, "What do you mean?" even though she was pretty sure she knew exactly what Spencer meant. She did her best to maintain eye contact instead of looking away guiltily, which was really what she wanted to do. Spencer's eyes were a deep blue, subtly but darkly lined, and accented by thick, mascaraed lashes that only made the blue more intense.

Spencer looked at her for several seconds, as if trying to decide on the best approach. "I mean, what's the deal? I start the bride class and you obviously can't stand me. Which was weird because you'd only just met me. That goes on for an entire week, making me miserable, so I quit. You apologize to me, which seemed pretty sincere."

"It was."

"So I come back and you're awesome. Friendly. Helpful. Made the class fun."

Rebecca couldn't help the soft smile that appeared on her face at the words.

"Then yesterday, you stepped back again. Not all the way, thank God, but back enough for me to notice the difference. So, what's the deal?"

There were a few different options in front of Rebecca at that moment. She could tell the truth, ask why Spencer was okay with somebody who supposedly loved her pretty much telling her she needed to be in better shape for her wedding, tell her she was having trouble getting beyond that because she watched her mother do the same thing throughout her married life and it was brutal, and she didn't want Spencer to be sentenced to the same existence. She could lie, make up a story to satisfy the woman who sat across from her, looking so inquisitively attractive. Or she could feign confusion, pretend she had no idea what Spencer was talking about. A bevy of choices laid out for her choosing.

She chose the last one.

"I'm not sure I understand." Rebecca furrowed her brow, shook her head, did her best to look puzzled. "I don't think I treated you any differently from Monday to yesterday." She shrugged, sipped her coffee, did her best not to fidget in her seat while Spencer studied her intently. A long beat passed. Two. Three. Rebecca swallowed.

"Okay."

Okay? Rebecca's eyebrows shot up before she could stop them, she was so surprised by Spencer's reply. Spencer picked up her cup, sipped from the straw, popped a chip into her mouth, and looked at Rebecca.

"Good," Rebecca said with one firm nod. *She doesn't believe me.* Rebecca was sure of it. It was right there on Spencer's face. Searching for a way to not immediately cut the conversation short, but not to drag it out any longer either, she said, "I think you're doing great, and in another week or two, you're really going to see results."

"Thanks." Spencer continued to eat her lunch but didn't say any more.

Rebecca took that as a good time to leave. "Well, it was nice running into you, but I should get back to work."

"Sure." Spencer took a bite of her sandwich and watched Rebecca gather her things. Rebecca could feel her eyes. As she stood, Spencer said, "Sorry about your date. Her loss."

Which made Rebecca feel even worse as she practically fled the diner for the safety—and solitude—of her car. Once inside the car, she let out a huge breath of relief and weirdly felt like she'd just run a couple of miles. Heart pounding, breath ragged, blood rushing. This was all so unlike her.

"What the hell is happening to you?" she whispered to her reflection in the rearview mirror. It had no answer for her.

Jamming her key into the ignition, she sped back to the gym. A place where she was comfortable and actually felt like she knew what she was doing. Because God knew she wasn't feeling that way anyplace else today.

She spent the rest of the day distracted, doing her best to focus on her clients and mostly failing. The strangest part was that she wasn't distracted by Beth's no-show, as she'd expected to be. No, she was distracted by blue eyes she couldn't stop seeing in her mind and the question she'd answered with a lie.

What is *my deal with Spencer?*

Pretending she didn't know the correct response only worked for so long, especially since she'd see Spencer the next day.

CHAPTER EIGHT

R ead 'em and weep, gentleman. And lady." Dwayne Blair slapped
down his cards, revealing a full house. "Read 'em and weep."

Groans went around the table as the other three guys and
Rebecca threw their cards down in feigned disgust.

"Are you cheating somehow?" asked Kevin Lippman, sandy
brow furrowed.

Dwayne's brown eyes widened behind his glasses as he gasped,
his handsome face an expression of horror. "How dare you?"

"I don't know, man," said Nick, as he reached for his beer.
"You used to suck at this game and now you're cleaning us out. It's
suspicious."

"Damn right it is." Dave Goldstein jumped in and played along.
"Rebecca?"

"Totally suspicious," Rebecca said.

"Fuck all y'all," Dwayne said, scraping the chips from the pot
toward his chest. "You're just jealous."

They all laughed as the deal moved to Dave. Rebecca loved
poker nights. Not because she enjoyed poker (she didn't), but
because she'd been hanging out with this group of men for nearly
nine years. They were Nick's friends—Kevin, from high school;
Dwayne and Dave from college—but Nick had always included
Rebecca in their gatherings, and because he did, so did the others.
Rebecca was simply one of the guys. They pulled no punches with
her, didn't tread carefully or watch their mouths because there was a

lady present. Rebecca loved that about them. They all knew she was gay, and over the years she had bitched or raved about her women just as the guys had. Except now she was the only one left who was single.

"Quick," said Dwayne. "Fuck, marry, or kill. The women of *Buffy*. Go."

"Fuck Buffy, marry Anya, kill Willow." Nick looked to Rebecca with one arched eyebrow as if daring her to call him on killing off the lesbian.

Rebecca just scoffed at him. "Seriously, dude? Fuck *Faith*, marry Willow, kill Dawn."

Grunts and nods of agreement went around the table.

"Oh, Dawn!" Nick smacked his forehead. "Okay. Willow can live another day. Dawn buys it."

Rebecca chuckled as their conversation was interrupted by Nick's wife, Michelle, her arms loaded with munchies. Rebecca was the first one up to help. "Here. Let me." She took a container of French onion dip and two bags of chips from Michelle's hands.

"There she goes, flirting with my wife again," Nick said playfully.

"Maybe she'll teach her a thing or two," Dave said, winking in the direction of the women.

"Maybe she'll teach *Nick* a thing or two," Michelle responded, dissolving the room into hoots and hollers. Nick shook his head as his face turned a very deep red. Michelle blew him a kiss. "Love you, honey."

Nick opened his arms and pushed his chair back. When Michelle had set down the plates of jalapeño poppers, pizza rolls, and a veggie plate for Rebecca, she stepped to him and sat on his knee, gave him a quick peck on the lips.

"So," Nick said, then waited until he had the attention of his friends, all of whom had turned their focus to the food. "We have a little announcement." When everybody was chewing, but quiet and looking in his direction, he shifted his gaze to Michelle.

Rebecca watched with a mix of both love for her friends and envy of their relationship. Nick and Michelle were perfect together, his yang to her yin. They fit seamlessly and she loved being around them, envy be damned. Their bond made her feel good.

Michelle was small, no more than five-three, but she had a big personality. Her light brown hair was in a ponytail and Nick playfully tugged at it now. She gave him one subtle nod and he turned to his pals. "We're pregnant!"

A beat of silence went by before the basement rec room burst into sound. Whoops, claps, exclamations of happy surprise. Rebecca jumped up from her chair and caught Michelle in a bear hug. Nick stood, shaking hands with his buddies, receiving slaps on the back. When his eyes met Rebecca's, she smiled and her heart filled with affection for this man, her best friend in the world. She wrapped her arms around Nick's neck and he hugged her tightly enough to lift her off the ground.

"I'm so happy for you, Nicky," she said softly in his ear. His arms tightened in response.

"If it's a boy, you're naming it after me, right?" Kevin asked.

"No, I think Dwayne is a much better name. Kevin sounds like a wimp." Dwayne dodged a smack from Kevin.

The celebration went on for several more minutes, and Nick even cracked open a bottle of champagne. Rebecca was not a big drinker, but she made an exception and accepted the plastic flute to toast. Then it was back to the card game.

"Any luck on the dating site, Rebecca?" Dwayne asked some time later, rubbing a hand over his bald head as he studied his cards.

Rebecca lifted one shoulder in a half shrug. "Meh. It's really kind of disheartening."

"My advice is to stick with it," Kevin said. "I met Maria on a dating site." Rebecca had met his wife; she was super nice, and they seemed to complement each other well.

"What about that one chick?" Nick asked. "Didn't you have a lunch date set up?"

"Yeah, that was today." Rebecca wasn't at all self-conscious about talking to these guys about her dating life. After all the time they'd spent together over the years, they knew as much about her as she did about them. With a grimace she told them, "She didn't show."

"Seriously? No text or anything?" Dwayne sounded irritated for her, and she appreciated that.

"We hadn't gotten far enough to exchange numbers yet. I'm always hesitant about that."

"Understandable," Dwayne said. "Lotta crazies out there."

"You must've been bummed," Nick said, and gave her shoulder a squeeze with his meaty hand before discarding.

"I was until…" This time she did hesitate, but only for a second. "Spencer showed up."

"Spencer…?" Dwayne looked at her questioningly.

"Oh! That's the chick from the bridal class, right?" Dave said and pointed at Dwayne. "The one whose girlfriend signed her up 'cause she's too fat for the wedding, remember?"

"Right, right, right," Dwayne said with a nod.

"She's not fat," Rebecca said, feeling a need to defend Spencer…and then was irritated by it.

"She showed up to lunch?" Nick asked, obviously confused.

"Apparently, her office is across the street, and she eats there a lot."

"Well, that's a weird coincidence." It was the second time in a week Nick had made that comment regarding her and Spencer. He wasn't wrong.

"She saw me before I saw her and just…plopped herself down at my booth." Rebecca remembered Spencer's soft smile and kind eyes, how pretty she'd looked.

"And you had lunch together?" Dave was dividing his focus between his cards and Rebecca.

"No, I'd already been there for half an hour. I needed to get back to work." Rebecca laid down a card, drew another. "So, just a quick chat."

"How'd she look?" Dwayne asked. "You said she's not fat?"

God, men were so blunt.

"Does she even need to be at the gym?" Dave asked.

"No, she's not fat, Dwayne, and everybody needs to be at the gym, Dave." Rebecca rolled her eyes but did her best to keep a grin on her face.

"You should ask her out," Nick said, not looking at her. "You keep running into her. Maybe it's for a reason."

Nods and murmurs of agreement went around the table before Rebecca cut them off with, "You guys. She's engaged. I'm not asking her out and she wouldn't say yes anyway."

"Then don't ask her out," Kevin said. "Just…tap that."

Rebecca blinked at him in disbelief.

"Yeah," Dave agreed. "She'd probably appreciate one last booty call before settling down with the same person for the rest of her life."

"I agree with that," Dwayne piped in.

"You'd just be doing her a favor, you know?" Nick added, rearranging his cards in his hand.

"Seriously? You guys are horrible people." Rebecca shook her head as she folded her hand. Smothered smiles and quiet chuckles around the table told her they weren't actually serious, and even though she knew that, she felt a rush of relief anyway. Then she picked up a chip and threw it at Dwayne, who was across the table from her. He caught it in one hand, and his chuckle grew into a laugh as he popped it into his mouth. Soon the whole table was laughing. "Horrible. You're all horrible."

"You wouldn't have us any other way, Becky," Dave said, with a wink.

"Call me that again and you'll be playing cards with a black eye," she warned him, then winked back at him.

These guys.

Her heart swelled with affection for each of them, and before she had a chance to tamp it down, she found herself wondering what Spencer would think of them.

With a literal shake of her head—a hard one—she focused in on her cards with laser precision.

Yeah. No more of *that*.

❖

Friday had been surprisingly quiet at work. Usually a day when phones rang off the hook—calls from folks wanting to set up last-minute open houses; never a good idea, as there was no time to advertise—things stayed relatively calm. Spencer preferred it to be busy and bustling, as that always made the day go by faster. It also kept her mind off things she had no desire to dwell on. Like moving in with Marti. Like how tired her mother had sounded on the phone last night. Like Rebecca McCall's deer-in-the-headlights expression yesterday when Spencer had sat down in her booth.

Those subjects took turns racing through her mind like bikes on a motocross course, jumping and skidding and banging into the side of her skull until she ended up with a steady, throbbing headache and an almost irresistible desire to skip out on bride class tonight.

But no. She wouldn't give Rebecca the satisfaction.

If Rebecca really didn't see that she treated Spencer differently than the other women—differently in general, really—then there was nothing Spencer could do about it. And even if she did see that and simply didn't want to own up to it, there was still nothing Spencer could do about it. And why did it matter anyway?

That was the big question, the one that plagued her more than she cared to admit: *Why does it matter?*

"It doesn't," Spencer said out loud just as Jennifer walked through the front doors.

"It doesn't what?" she asked, crossing to her desk. The office was a large open space, with Spencer's desk poised near the door so anybody entering would go to her first. Beyond her were eight more desks, butted against each other in pairs and arranged like islands in the large, sunny room. Jennifer's was one of those closest to Spencer's.

"Nothing," Spencer said with a shake of her head.

"Class tonight?"

"Yes, unfortunately."

"Don't you like it? I mean, I know it's probably hard work…"

Spencer shrugged. "It's fine. I'm just tired." Not a total lie, but not the complete truth. It was pretty clear that she and Rebecca weren't friends, and that was just fine. Who knew, maybe Rebecca had a thing about being friends with clients. Spencer had a similar unwritten rule: no socializing with work clients if she could help it. That only led to trouble…people expecting special treatment, better dates for open houses, priority listing, etc. No, it was fine. She understood. She was simply a client. Better that it stayed that way.

Ninety minutes later, Spencer was stretching along with the other four members of the class, as Rebecca walked around them, observing, correcting, moving limbs slightly here and there. She looked very sleek in her tight-fitting black workout pants and matching black tank with the low-cut back, strips of fabric crisscrossing the exposed skin there. Spencer pretended not to notice.

"Here," Rebecca said, squatting down beside Lucy, who was on Spencer's immediate left. "Straighten this leg more." She tapped Lucy's thigh. "Good. Then bend this one." She helped Lucy steady herself with a hand on her back until Lucy found the exact right position. "There you go."

"Oh, ow. Yeah, I can feel that."

Rebecca turned to Spencer and swallowed; Spencer saw her throat move. "You as well. Straighten that leg more." She pointed at Spencer's left leg and Spencer did as she was told. "Now, angle that one a bit more." Again, she pointed. Spencer obeyed with a nod. "Feel that?"

Spencer nodded, not looking at her.

"Good." And then Rebecca was in front of the row of them. "As I told you Wednesday, today we're going to work our core strength. Core strength is super important, and a lot of people forget about it. To most people, core exercises mean sit-ups or crunches, but it's so much more than that." She went on to reiterate things she'd already mentioned, benefits of having a strong core, but Spencer was only half listening. Instead, she found herself looking one floor up to the windowed wall of the spinning room. She could feel the thumping bass line coming from the music up there and saw several people pedaling away to nowhere.

It intrigued her, but she had no idea why.

"Okay, let's get started."

Rebecca's clap snatched Spencer back to the present, and she followed the other girls to an unoccupied corner of the gym.

Ten minutes after that, Spencer was on her third set of a core exercise that she'd missed the name of but that was brutalizing her abdominal muscles. She was on her back on the floor and held an inflated ball the size of a beach ball between her ankles. She lifted her legs and arms so she could transfer the ball to her hands, then lowered her limbs. Then raised them again to repeat the move what felt like 150 more times.

Rebecca approached and stood over her. "Keep your back down against the mat. Don't arch it." Spencer made the adjustment, and Rebecca moved on to where Brittany was doing the same exercise. Spencer turned her head and followed Rebecca's retreat, watched as she stopped next to Brittany and put a hand on her stomach. "Don't arch your back," Spencer heard her say.

Her abs were burning, but Spencer forced herself to finish the set. After the last rep, she let her feet drop to the floor, the ball rolling away from her as she gasped for breath.

"Oh, my God, I'm going to feel this tomorrow," Lucy said from a few feet away, where she was doing some kind of twisting maneuver.

"Right?" Spencer said, with a chuckle. She watched the move for a moment before her gaze was again drawn above to the bicycles.

Class ended with planks. Again. The bane of Spencer's existence.

Once more lined up like eighteen-wheelers in a parking lot, the five of them held themselves up on toes and forearms as Rebecca held a timer and strolled back and forth in front of them. Spencer was always amazed by how easy it was to get into plank position and how quickly she started to sweat, quake, and struggle for breath.

Just as Rebecca informed them that thirty seconds were down, Spencer dropped to the floor, a rivulet of sweat rolling from her hairline down her cheek.

"Get up. You can do this." No poke with a toe, but Spencer got back up. A quick glance to her right showed Willow flopping to her belly.

"Fifteen more seconds." Rebecca stopped her pacing and stood in front of Spencer, who barely noticed as every muscle in her body tightened to keep from collapsing. "Five."

Spencer's arms were shaking so badly, and she squeezed her eyes shut, willing those five seconds—which felt like five minutes at this point—to pass. Finally, the beeper went off and those of them who weren't already down dropped to the floor with groans of exhaustion.

"Dare I say you guys are getting better at this?" Rebecca's voice seemed to hold the tiniest hint of pride. "Planks are very difficult, and the only thing that makes you better at them is practice. Work that core." When Spencer glanced up from where she'd had her forehead pressed to the floor, Rebecca was looking at her. "Have a great weekend. See you Monday." And she left them.

"Holy shit." Lucy's voice was muffled, as she was still lying face down.

Spencer chuckled. "You okay?"

"I may not ever be able to move again."

"That was a pretty rough session." Spencer could already feel the burning soreness in her torso, but she also felt something else. Something new.

"Rough? I think I murdered my abs."

Spencer pushed herself to her feet, then reached her hand down. "Come on."

Lucy looked up, blinked pathetically, then gave a dramatic sigh. "*Fine*." She grabbed Spencer's hand and allowed herself to be pulled to her feet.

"I think we deserve smoothies as a reward for surviving class today. Yes?"

Lucy gave a nod. "If I can make it to the locker room and

change my clothes, then yes. I will have a smoothie with you. It's a long shot, though."

Spencer picked up Lucy's water bottle and handed it to her. "Drink," she ordered as she mopped her own sweaty face with a towel.

"Bossy." Then Lucy tipped the bottle up and drank greedily.

They managed to change without incident, albeit a tiny bit slower than usual. Spencer was acutely aware of the muscles around her ribs, tight and a bit sore to the touch, as if they'd recently been installed and she was just getting used to them being there. Lucy was right: she was going to feel this tomorrow.

Lucy slammed her locker. "Ready?"

With a nod, Spencer gathered up her things and they headed up to the smoothie bar where Brittany and Bella already sat. They nodded their hellos but were already deep in conversation. Spencer and Lucy took a couple of seats down the counter a bit. The bar was situated so they could look down over a metal pipe railing to the workout areas below.

"Fruit or chocolate?" Lucy asked her.

"I'm thinking the mixed berry."

A young girl whose name tag said she was Kelly stopped in front of them. "Protein added to that?" Her brown eyes were big and round, her smile revealing a mouthful of what seemed like a few too many teeth.

"Um…?" Spencer looked to Lucy.

"We just did core work," Lucy told Kelly.

Kelly tipped her head from side to side. "Not necessary, can't hurt. If you were lifting, you'd want some protein."

Spencer shrugged. "I like can't hurt. Protein, please."

"I'll take the chocolate peanut butter," Lucy said. "No extra protein. 'Cause peanut butter."

Kelly nodded and got to work.

"What do you think about spinning?" Spencer asked her friend.

Lucy followed Spencer's gaze to the hallway where a line of very sweaty people was filing down like so many train cars. "No way. I don't bike."

Spencer turned to her, squinted at her. "Why not?"

"My butt's too big."

Kelly slid Lucy's smoothie in front of her and Lucy clenched the straw between her teeth, took a sip.

"What?" Spencer said with a laugh.

"I'm serious. Those seats are tiny. Skinny. My butt swallows them. Plus," she lowered her voice, "my lady parts don't enjoy biking."

Spencer laughed again, louder this time as Kelly gave her the mixed berry smoothie and offered, "That's only the first time or two. They get used to it."

"The lady parts?" Spencer asked.

Kelly nodded as they gave her their money and Spencer looked to Lucy, who shrugged.

"I guess I didn't stay with it long enough."

"Lucky for your lady parts."

"Damn right."

They drank their smoothies (Spencer's was unexpectedly delicious) and chatted about this and that. The entire time, Spencer found herself surreptitiously watching to catch a glimpse of Rebecca. Once Lucy finished and bid Spencer goodbye, she was able to concentrate fully on spying, scooting her stool a bit closer so she had a better view. She generally hated all the mirrors, as they made it so she couldn't escape the view of her mushy body, but she suddenly realized a benefit to them: she could find Rebecca no matter where she was. It was a Friday night and the gym was sparsely populated. Rebecca was working with the same guy as last time—Paul? Phil?—and from what Spencer could see, she was just as cheerful and fun as she'd been the night Spencer had quit class.

Okay. It's fine.

Spencer nodded to herself as she sucked the last of her smoothie up through the straw and turned away from the handful of exercisers left. Rebecca had some inexplicable issue with her that kept them from being anything beyond trainer and client, and that was fine. Spencer needed to accept that. She didn't like that accepting it was hard, but she was a grown woman. She obviously didn't understand, but she'd been rejected before, so this wasn't something new to her.

It's fine.

She left the gym and headed into her weekend with a bit of a new outlook: the gym was now going to be for her. Not Marti. Not Rebecca. Spencer.

It was the most relaxed she'd felt in quite some time.

CHAPTER NINE

S pencer was pretty sure she was dying.

She gasped for breath. Her heart hammered in her chest so intensely, if it exploded and burst completely out of her body, she wouldn't have been shocked. Her muscles burned and she was covered in sweat.

Yeah, this might be the end.

"Don't you let up," said the far-too-cheerful voice over the speaker system. "If you have to ease up on the pace, that's okay, but don't you stop. You're in the home stretch."

Spencer couldn't look at her, this woman at the front of the room, pedaling as if she was totally relaxed and seeming to be barely winded. Meanwhile, Spencer was pedaling like a madwoman, was pretty sure her lungs were about to burst, and couldn't remember the last time she'd sweated this much. The class was an eclectic mix of people. Men and women. Twentysomethings and a man who looked to be seventy. People in excellent shape and people not. Spencer had chosen a bike in the back row, not wanting people to be able to see her if she did something silly. Like fall off. She also wanted to be able to slip out if necessary.

"And…ease up. Drop down a couple of gears. You did it."

Spencer did as she was told, had never been so happy to do anything as she was to move that little black lever on the bike that had tried to kill her.

"Let's cool it down," the instructor said, and Spencer hated her a teeny bit less. But not much.

The cooldown was like heaven compared to the rest of the class. Nice, easy pedaling. She followed the instructions, lifted her arms over her head, stretched, leaned to the left, then to the right, pedaling slowly and steadily the whole time as Lady Gaga sang to them about her bad romance. Then they all slid off their bikes to stretch their legs. Spencer held tightly to the handlebars of her bike, understanding that her legs giving out on her was a distinct possibility.

Once the stretching was done and the instructor—Sherry?—congratulated them on a ride well done, the music turned off and the low buzz of conversation began. One by one, the riders filed out the door until only Sherry and Spencer were left. It had taken that long for Spencer's breathing to dial back to normal levels. She grabbed the spray bottle on the windowsill next to her and pumped some of the cleaner onto her seat and handlebars, then wiped with her towel.

"Was this your first class?" the instructor asked, and her close proximity startled Spencer, who flinched and then recovered quickly.

"It was, yes."

"What did you think?" Sherry's smile was friendly, and up close, she looked less like an evil witch who was trying to kill Spencer and more like a regular person. Plus, it did look like she might have sweated a *little*, which made her seem slightly more human and less like a robot. Slightly.

"Brutal," Spencer said, with a chuckle. "I couldn't keep the pace."

"You stayed pedaling the entire time, though. That's impressive for your first class."

"It is?"

Sherry nodded. "Absolutely. You stuck it out. Good for you. I hope you come back." With that, she left the room and Spencer was alone.

Well, that was nice, she thought as she waited a minute or two before leaving so as not to seem like she was stalking Sherry. Her legs felt rubbery, but they managed to hold her upright as she slowly walked down the hall that led to the trainers' desks.

Rebecca was sitting at hers.

Spencer's steps faltered. *Why is she here on a Saturday?* was her first question, which was quickly answered by the realization that Rebecca might very well have clients on Saturdays as well as during the week. Rebecca hadn't seen her yet, and now a tall, lanky man approached from the opposite side as Spencer. He looked to be in his thirties and was pushing a metal wire cart filled with what looked to be used towels.

"Hey, Rebecca," he said, with almost excessive glee. His glasses were thick, and as he reached out and performed a complicated handshake with Rebecca, Spencer immediately saw traces of Travis.

"Bobby, my man," Rebecca said. "How's it going?"

"It's going great." Bobby threw both arms up in the air like Rocky. "I'm gonna make this the best Saturday ever."

"I have all the faith in you," Rebecca said, and Spencer noted the way she actually looked at him, like she was paying attention and not just humoring the intellectually disabled guy. She'd seen more than her share of people treat Travis like a toddler, or worse, dismiss him altogether. Rebecca seemed genuinely fond of this man.

"Make it the best day, okay?" Bobby said to her, as he leaned over the cart and began pushing it toward Spencer. Rebecca followed him with her gaze, which landed on Spencer and stayed there. "Hi there," Bobby said to her as he pushed his cart past. "You have a great Saturday, okay?"

"I'll do my best," Spencer said, smiling at him. She watched him as he pushed the cart in the direction she'd come from, then turned back to see Rebecca almost smiling at her.

"You're here on a weekend," she said.

"So are you," Spencer countered.

"I have a client."

"I went to spin class."

Rebecca's expression seemed to shift, to lighten a bit. "Yeah? Sherry's? She's tough. What did you think?"

"I think I died and you're actually talking to my ghost. My body is still on the bike. Slumped over. Dead." Spencer jerked a thumb over her shoulder.

Rebecca's shoulders moved in gentle laughter. "I see."

Spencer shrugged as she resumed walking. As she passed Rebecca's desk, she heard the question, "But how do you feel now?"

Spencer stopped and turned back to face Rebecca, was surprised to see her face the picture of genuine curiosity, so she thought about it, then answered honestly. "Accomplished. Proud of myself."

"Good." Rebecca nodded. "That's really good. That's what you want. That's excellent."

Their gazes held. Rebecca fiddled with a pen while Spencer spun her water bottle in her hands. It felt like a long time before Spencer finally forced herself to move. With a quick wave, she said, "Well. See you Monday."

"Yeah. Definitely. Have a great weekend."

Once in the locker room, Spencer just stood there with her forehead pressed against the metal. *What the hell was that?* Why was she unable to simply walk past Rebecca and not give her the time of day? God, Rebecca made her feel... Spencer fumbled for the right words. What *did* Rebecca make her feel?

"No," she said aloud. Standing upright suddenly, as if the locker had zapped her with an electric shock, she spun the dial on her lock and quickly gathered her things.

No, that was not a question she wanted the answer to.

Slinging her gym bag over her shoulder, Spencer exited the locker room, then the gym, keeping her eyes straight ahead and making sure she didn't face Rebecca again.

"Have a good one," said the young girl at the front desk.

Spencer lifted a hand in a quick wave, but didn't look at her. She just kept walking, picked up her pace as if making a clandestine escape and the front door was her finish line. The front door meant safety and freedom.

She pushed herself through the door and exhaled a breath of relief.

❖

Rebecca only had two clients that Saturday morning. One was a regular and one was making up for a missed session during the week. She didn't mind working on weekends if it was in the morning and she could be done and still have some of her Saturday left.

Seeing Spencer had thrown her off a little bit. Not only was it unexpected, like she was out of context, but she looked… Rebecca shook her head now, just as she'd done several times during her session with Serena Carter, her make-up client, trying to rid herself of the picture of Spencer after a spin class. Black yoga pants, a close-fitting turquoise T-shirt, and a sunny yellow hat, her blond hair in a ponytail and sticking through the hole in the back. But it was more than the clothes. It was her face, all flushed and glistening. It was her eyes, which seemed to hold a glimmer of satisfaction, maybe even a little pride. It was her bare forearms (*Seriously, Rebecca? Forearms?*) and her feminine hands and…

She must have groaned aloud because Serena looked up at her from the bench where she was doing flies. "Am I doing them wrong?"

"No, no. Sorry. Just, um, clearing my throat." Rebecca forced a smile onto her face. "You're doing them perfectly. Five more."

Later, as she was walking out toward the front door, done for the day, Sherry skidded up alongside her so they could walk together.

"Big plans today?" she asked.

Rebecca wrinkled her nose. "Not really. Gonna go hang with Nick and Michelle for a bit, but it's just casual."

"You playing Aunt Rebecca already?" Sherry asked knowingly.

"Absolutely."

They pushed through the front doors and Sherry said, "Your little blond cream puff was in my spin class this morning."

Rebecca shot her a look of irritation. "She's not my cream puff. And I saw her."

"She did really well. Looked like she was going to keel over at any moment, but stuck it out. You tell her to come?"

"Nope." Their cars were parked next to each other and they each stopped at their respective driver's side doors. With a shake of her head, Rebecca said, "I don't really talk to her outside of the bride class."

Sherry stared at her for a beat over the roof of her car. Finally, she said simply, "Mm-hmm." Then opened her door and got in.

Poking the inside of her cheek with her tongue, Rebecca kept her eyes on Sherry's car for a moment before getting into her own. She hated that look. The one that said Sherry knew something she didn't. Or worse, Sherry knew something Rebecca was trying to hide. Whichever, it made Rebecca feel exposed. Vulnerable. She didn't like either of those feelings.

Shoving her keys into the ignition, Rebecca started her car and headed home. She was looking forward to spending some time with the Scarfanos. More than that, she was anxious to stop thinking about Spencer Thompson.

She's a pushover. A very attractive pushover. A very attractive, off-limits pushover. Jesus, Rebecca, get your shit together.

This was her mantra for the rest of the day.

❖

"Mom, seriously." Marti forked a bite of steak into her mouth and chewed.

Spencer also ate, but kept herself quiet. She was never any kind of match for Cookie Daniels, so she tended to take the high road more often than not and let Marti do all the talking.

"If you would just let me pay..." Cookie's voice trailed off on the sentence she'd begun about seven hundred times since Marti had informed her of her engagement to Spencer several months ago.

"I don't want you to pay," Marti said, her standard response. Spencer stopped noticing that Marti continually said "I" rather than "we."

"But you could have something big. A celebration." Cookie's voice bordered on whiny. She was a beautiful woman...in an artificial kind of way. Bottle blond, acrylic fingernails, Botox injections in her forehead and collagen in her cheeks, a deep bronze tan all year round. In fact, she was a walking stereotype. When Spencer tried to conjure up an image in her mind of a wealthy socialite and widow,

Marti's mom fit the picture to a T, right down to the silly first name. She could be a *Real Housewife*. She'd fit right in. Cookie loved her daughter very much; Spencer knew that. But it was pretty obvious she was more concerned about image than much else in life. The Daniels family was very wealthy, and when Marti's father had passed away five years earlier, his wife was left with more money than God and assets that, had Spencer been in her shoes, she'd never in a million years be able to decide what to do with.

"I've told you a hundred times, I don't want to invite people." Marti had patience, there was no denying that. Her voice stayed calm. If she was irritated with the conversation, she didn't show it. It was one of the things that made her so good at her job: it was nearly impossible to tell how she was feeling if she didn't want you to know. "I want a quick and no-nonsense thing at the courthouse. No guests. No fuss. Simplicity at its finest. Right, honey?"

"Hmm?" It took Spencer a beat to realize the question was directed at her. She was so used to not being included in conversations about money or business—and lately, about her own marriage—that she tended to zone out when at dinner with Cookie Daniels. "Oh. Right."

Cookie sighed, the loud, put-upon sigh of a woman used to getting her way, but having trouble doing so now. "I wanted to invite the Carsons. And the Mangiones. And the Harringtons…they invited me to their daughter's wedding."

"Well, you can't." Marti wiped her mouth with her napkin, then set it on the table, indicating she was finished. A glance at her plate told Spencer she'd eaten half her steak, none of her asparagus, and a few bites of her potatoes. In contrast, Spencer's plate was almost clean. She shrugged internally. When she had nothing to contribute to the conversation, what else was there to do but eat her dinner?

"I just don't understand it." Cookie also put her napkin down. Her plate also still held a good portion of her dinner. "You have such a healthy appetite, Spencer."

Spencer smiled and nodded. It wasn't the first time Cookie had said that to her. And it wasn't a compliment. "It was very good," Spencer said. "Thank you."

Later that night, they were at Marti's house, going through their usual routines. Marti was already in bed, in her glasses, reading a book from her favorite genre of true crime. Spencer removed her makeup and washed her face. There was a full-length mirror on the back of the bathroom door. With a glance at Marti to see that she was immersed in reading, Spencer closed the door quietly, then stripped off her pajamas.

Standing naked in front of her own reflection was never something she'd enjoyed doing. Ever. She did her best to be gentle with herself, to look with possibility rather than disdain, but it wasn't easy. Being critical was easy. Still, she took a deep breath, focused, and tried to look with an open mind. It took effort, but she made herself stand there and look anyway. It wasn't a bad body, really. Her thighs were a bit bigger than she'd like. A little soft. But she wondered if that was actually the smallest bit of muscle definition in her quads she was seeing. Probably not. Was that even possible? It had only been a few weeks. But maybe…

Suddenly, Rebecca's voice was echoing in her head.

Fitness is about how you feel.

Spencer turned so she could see her naked behind. Her ass and hips had always been problem areas for her, but she also knew that spin class would target both of those things as well as her legs and her heart. And while her quads were beginning to poke at her with a bit of soreness that would most likely blossom in the morning, the pain was good.

She narrowed her eyes when the thought hit. *The pain is good? Really?*

But it was. It meant she'd succeeded. It meant she'd go again.

Hit with a weirdly unexpected surge of confidence, Spencer stared at herself for another moment or two before putting her pajamas back on and heading to bed, realizing just how tired she was. As she slid under the covers, Marti closed her book and took her glasses off, set both on the nightstand. With a flick of the switch, the lights went off and Marti rolled toward her.

Thankful for the darkness so Marti couldn't see her expression, Spencer suppressed a sigh. She wasn't really in the mood—she rarely was anymore, if she was being honest—but their sex life had become so depressingly sporadic that she didn't dare brush it off. She took Marti's weight, moved her legs so Marti could settle between them, and when Marti's mouth closed over hers, Spencer kissed her back.

When had this started? This play-along thing. This "go through the motions, it'll be over soon" mentality. Was it recent? How recent?

Marti pushed Spencer's shirt up, took a nipple into her mouth, sucked gently, Spencer laid a hand on the back of her head. Marti wasn't a bad lover, really. She was considerate if not passionate. She took her time, focused. Spencer closed her eyes, willed herself to relax, to melt into the sensations, to try to enjoy herself, even if she could predict Marti's every move.

As their sex life had tapered down to a couple times a month, then once a month, then hardly ever, something else had become a regular occurrence: Spencer knew in a matter of minutes whether she'd get there or not, whether she'd climax or end up doing a bit of...performing in order to finish things up. Tonight, she'd be performing, which seemed to be the norm now.

Most of the time, Spencer tried not to think about it, tried not to analyze when, why, all those questions that she probably *should* be asking herself. And she always did her best to banish the thoughts and worries from her head, to just concentrate on feeling. On where Marti was touching her. On which body parts were experiencing what sensations. But she knew how it went: tell somebody not to think about pink elephants and suddenly, their mind was full of them.

It helped that Marti rarely changed up her act. Some kissing, a few minutes on each breast, fingers sliding through (sometimes) heated and wet flesh, done. And as Spencer cranked up her acting skills, the guilt settled in like an old friend, making itself comfortable next to her, because seriously? Was this how her sex life was going to be? For the rest of her life? Shouldn't she fix it? Attempt to fix it? Spencer closed her eyes tightly, tried to focus.

She couldn't pinpoint when exactly it happened. She hadn't

wished for it. She didn't see it coming. But suddenly, in her mind, it wasn't Marti on top of her, kissing her, sliding fingers between her legs.

It was Rebecca McCall.

What in the world?

The internal battle was fierce. It was confusing. Rebecca pushed inside Spencer, coaxing a moan from her. She moved in and out, slowly at first, causing that delicious slow burn deep in Spencer's body. *Stop this. Stop it now.* The commands from her own brain were weak, and Spencer kept her eyes closed, squeezed shut, in fact, not wanting to give in, but not wanting to let go, as her arousal surged higher and higher, crested, tightened every muscle in her body until she felt like she might simply shatter into pieces like a broken water glass. And just as the orgasm began rushing in, she opened her eyes, saw not Marti's brown ones, but Rebecca's beautifully intense blue ones looking at her, looking deep *into* her with such a blatant and raw sexiness, and Spencer gasped in shock, shoved, pushed herself free and rolled away.

"What the hell, Spencer?" Marti fumbled at the nightstand, clicked on a bedside lamp, her voice full of surprised confusion. "Did I hurt you?"

Spencer got out of the bed as if propelled by some unseen force, stood next to it shifting her weight from one foot to the other. "No." She swallowed, tried hard to catch her breath. "No, not at all. I just…I don't know what happened." Squinting in the light, she focused on Marti, saw the uncertainty and hurt on her face. "I'm sorry. I'm just not feeling well tonight."

"You seemed to be feeling fine a couple minutes ago." Marti didn't mutter it, but she came close.

Spencer took a breath to respond, then closed her mouth.

"Seriously, what is going on with you lately, Spence? You're distant. You're busy all the time. You still haven't brought a single box over." She ticked off the list on her fingers, her voice now matter-of-fact, an attorney listing evidence. "What's going on?"

"Nothing's going on," Spencer said, her voice a bit harsher than she intended, but she hated when Marti shifted into fact mode on her. Even if she was right. "I just don't feel well, okay? Am I not allowed to feel crappy once in a while?"

Marti blinked at her, obviously startled by her tone. "Of course you are." She swallowed audibly. "I'm just worried about you is all."

Spencer nodded, felt awful now. "I appreciate that. I do. I'm fine. Just…coming down with something, I guess. A summer cold, maybe." Lame, lame, so very lame, but she ran with it. She had no choice at this point.

Their gazes held for a moment before Marti asked, "You're sure that's all it is?"

"I'm sure." The lie slipped off Spencer's tongue so easily, it alarmed her. Was this who she was now? Taking a second to pull herself together, she put on her robe, moved toward the door, cleared her throat, and said, "Listen, I'm kind of wide awake, but it's late. I'm going to go out to the living room and watch TV. Okay?"

Marti studied her for so long, Spencer worried she would drag the conversation on even further. Finally, she lifted her chin, pressed her lips together in a line for a beat, then said, "Sure."

They stared at each other across the expanse of Marti's bedroom for what felt like hours but was surely only a few seconds. Then Spencer turned to go, the light clicking off before she'd even crossed the threshold of the doorway.

In the dark kitchen, Spencer pulled open the refrigerator and removed the open bottle of Pinot Grigio on the door. She poured herself a very generous glass and carried it to the dark living room where, rather than clicking on the TV, she steered herself to her little craft corner and took a seat, clicked on the small lamp.

Though the supplies here were still a mere fraction of all those she possessed, Spencer kept her workspace very organized. Every finding, every tool, every roll of wire had its own space, its own little square plastic container, its own peg to hang on (well, at her house the tools were hung on pegs). So unlike her thoughts lately, which were a mishmash. A jumble. A ball of her beading wire, hopelessly tangled and knotted.

Confidence had never really been a problem for Spencer. She

wasn't overly confident; she had normal worries and concerns like any other girl growing up in a male-dominated world. But overall, it wasn't really an issue for her. Not in school. Not at work.

Not until Chelsea.

"No," she whispered aloud, in the quiet of the house. "We're not going there." Instead, she picked up her flush cutter and a length of wire and snipped, envisioning a necklace for Lucy. Something fun and colorful, something that represented the joy and cheer her new friend gave her on a regular basis. She used the bead board (even though the table was too small) and measured out the necklace, estimated size and how many findings she'd need, then got to work.

Spencer's interest in jewelry-making had started with a class she'd attended with her mom. Jennifer had been the hostess (Jennifer hosted every kind of party imaginable, from jewelry making to wine tasting to sex toys) and the party had been at her house, complete with wine and munchies and an instructor to talk them, step by step, through making a bracelet. Spencer had found herself fascinated by all the tools, what each of them was for, how the design of each piece was totally up to the artist. Everybody's bracelet had been a bit different, and by the end of the party, Spencer's mind was racing with ideas. Designs for earrings, necklaces, and bracelets swirled in her brain until she couldn't *not* at least give it a try on her own. She'd started small, buying a very basic tool kit, 19-strand wire, and some findings and beads that appealed to her as she stood in the aisle at Michael's for what felt like hours and struggled to keep from being overwhelmed by the sheer volume of options.

She went home that night and made a necklace for Jennifer with alternating green and gold beads that Spencer knew would go beautifully with her favorite shirt. Jennifer loved it. Then she made a necklace for Travis, a hammered silver disk with the letter *T* on it, suspended on a brown leather thong. He never took it off, wore it until it nearly disintegrated. Spencer had replaced the leather three times so far.

Working on jewelry soothed her. Much like baking soothed some people. Or cleaning. Or reading. Somehow, she was able to set everything else in her life aside, any issues, any worries, anything causing her stress. It was simply pushed out of the way for a while, put in a box and put up on a shelf so she could focus her mind elsewhere, at least for a little while. Oh, it would all come crashing back in; that was inevitable. But for a short time, she could breathe.

Spencer alternated several different findings for Lucy's necklace. Bright pink and purple beads traded space with silver balls and transparent purple disks. All small and tasteful—she wanted Lucy to actually wear the thing—but a definite representation of Lucy's personality. She made it mid-length, to hang just below Lucy's collarbone, measuring it by making it a little shorter on herself due to Lucy's diminutive height. With her round nose pliers, Spencer made a loop in the wire, then switched to her crimp tool to fasten the wire to a clasp. When it was all finished and she was satisfied, Spencer held the necklace up, letting it dangle from her fingers.

It was perfect and so, so very Lucy.

With a grin, Spencer tucked it into a small black velvet pouch that cinched at the top with twine. She'd give it to Lucy on Monday at class.

Taking her wineglass to the kitchen, she set it on the counter next to the sink and took two steps toward the hall that led to the bedroom. Then stopped.

Doing her best not to spend too much time on why, she retraced her steps back into the living room, pulled the soft, fleecy blanket from the back of the couch, and covered herself as she lay down.

Each time she began to drift off to sleep, intense blue eyes filled her mind, staring at her, holding her captive, and Spencer did her best to shake herself free, to rid her brain of what had happened in bed with Marti.

She was mostly unsuccessful.

She remained mostly awake.

CHAPTER TEN

*S*he *never smells bad.*

It was a strange thought that jumped into Rebecca's head. Not for the first time. As a fitness instructor who worked in a gym, stinky, sweaty people were part of her everyday routine and, wow, some were so much worse than others. So much worse.

But not Spencer.

Like now. She was on the floor, up on her toes and forearms, struggling through a sixty-second plank that she wasn't going to make. Rebecca had put the bride class through the wringer today, and all five of them were flushed and drenched in sweat, including Spencer, who collapsed to the floor with twenty seconds to go, still smelling like sunshine and coconuts.

"No." Rebecca dropped down to her knees, her face very close to Spencer's. "You're almost there. Come on. Get up."

"Fudge nougat," was what Rebecca was pretty sure she heard Spencer whisper, and with a sound that was more a whimper than a groan, she pushed herself back up.

Before she knew what she was doing, Rebecca slid her palm underneath, set it up against Spencer's abs, which were quaking with exertion. "Tighten this. Right here. This is the sweet spot. This is your core. This is what you're making stronger." As if suddenly realizing she was touching Spencer, Rebecca blinked several times and snatched her hand away just as the timer went off.

All five women lay on the ground sucking in ragged breaths as if they'd just run a marathon.

"I know it may not feel like it, but I'm seeing some significant improvement. How do you guys feel?" Rebecca shifted her gaze from one to the next. Lucy stayed face-planted on the floor but lifted an arm and gave Rebecca a thumbs-up, which made her laugh. "You worked hard today. Good job. I'll see you Wednesday."

It was the fourth week of bride class, and September was closing in on them quickly. Rebecca had to admit to some pleasant surprise that all five women had stuck with the class and all five of them put in 100 percent. Some, a little more. And Rebecca hadn't been kidding. She was seeing results. Willow had gained some nice definition in her legs. Bella's endurance had greatly improved. Both Brittany and Lucy were lifting heavier dumbbells than when the class had started. And Spencer...

Rebecca shook her head as she left the gym floor and headed up to her desk. She was still way too aware of Spencer and didn't know how to shake it.

Off-limits.

It was the phrase she kept using, every time she found herself dwelling. She'd actually needed to scoot into the client locker room last week and had heard Lucy and Spencer talking about their upcoming weddings. Lucy was saying something about necklaces for her bridesmaids and Spencer had laughed that musical laugh of hers and Rebecca had smiled wistfully and pushed back out the door without them seeing her.

Off-limits.

Spencer had become a regular in Sherry's spin class, going at least once a week—if not twice—in addition to the bride class.

And it was showing.

"Nope. Nope. Not doing this," Rebecca muttered to herself, as she gathered her things. "I have a date. Let's put our focus there."

As if privy to Rebecca's train of thought, Sherry came up to her. "Good luck tonight." She gave Rebecca a one-armed hug. "Text me with a report."

"It's just coffee." Rebecca shrugged in a manner she hoped came across as nonchalant.

"Are you nervous?" Again, reading her thoughts.

Rebecca sighed. "A little. Yes. I mean, I'm hoping this one actually shows."

Sherry grinned. "What are the chances of two separate women from a dating site standing you up?"

Rebecca arched a brow. "We *are* talking about me here."

"Good point."

They both smiled and Rebecca slung her bag over her shoulder. "See you tomorrow."

An hour later, Rebecca had gone home, showered and changed, and was back near the gym, sitting at a small table in Grounded and nursing a mocha latte. It was a bit closer to her place of work than she'd like, but her date, Zoe, was a paramedic and only had a short time to sit with her. Grounded was the best location for her.

There was only one photo on Zoe's dating profile and it didn't really pull Rebecca in, but she liked her details. She liked that Zoe loved animals, hated politics, and was into biking, golf, and hikes. Everything had been in complete sentences (Rebecca surprised herself when she realized what a turn-off it was if a profile was in fragments and had misspellings). When Zoe had invited her to coffee, Rebecca figured, "why not?"

She walked into the coffee shop on a little wave of energy. Zoe was small, but large, if that made any sense. It was the only way Rebecca could describe her. Petite in stature, large in personality. It was obvious immediately. In the way she waved at the baristas. In the way she scanned the shop and seemed to make eye contact with everyone. In the way her gaze landed on Rebecca and stayed there.

She approached confidently, hand outstretched, friendly smile on her face. She was dressed in her uniform…black pants and shirt, several patches on it embroidered with various logos and phrases, and a gold name tag that said "Hernandez." Her dark hair was short, her eyes a deep brown and accented by thick lashes, and she was cute in a boyish sort of way. "Rebecca?"

"Guilty as charged." Rebecca stood, shook hands. Zoe's grip was unsurprisingly firm. As she sat, Rebecca asked, "Did you want to get some coffee?"

Zoe waved a dismissive hand. "I'll get one on my way out so

I can have it with me for a while." She leaned her forearms on the table. "Anybody ever call you Becky?"

"Nobody who's still living."

Zoe grinned. "Noted. So, Rebecca not Becky, you're a trainer?"

"I am. For about ten years now. And you're a paramedic."

"Yup. Same timeframe, roughly. Kinda cool."

"You enjoy it?" Rebecca sipped her coffee.

Zoe nodded. "Definitely. Never a dull moment."

Rebecca felt at ease with Zoe. Instantly, like they were simply old school friends who hadn't seen each other in a while. "What was your craziest call so far?"

"Oh, man, we get so many." Zoe sat back in her chair, crossed one leg up and rested her ankle on the opposite knee. "I can tell you that recently, we had a guy who was convinced he was a flamingo."

"Seriously?"

Zoe nodded with a grin. "Yup. Like, doing the weird walk, standing with one leg up, arms folded like wings."

"Please tell me he was on a bad trip."

"*Such* a bad trip. His roommate called us because he wouldn't come off the front lawn. Said he was going to stand there like flamingos were supposed to."

"Oh, so he thought he was a *plastic* flamingo."

Zoe's laugh was a startling yelp, which caused Rebecca to flinch as if she'd been poked. "Yes! A lawn ornament. It was nuts." When Zoe's laughter died down, she said, "What about you? Any crazies in your line of work? Any surprises?"

Rebecca sipped her latte again as she contemplated the question. "I wouldn't say I've ever had any crazies. I mean, it's a gym. But some of my clients can be more difficult than others. I get some that expect unrealistic results."

"Like, 'I've been here three times, how come I haven't lost forty pounds?' That kind of unrealistic?"

"Something like that, yeah. As for surprises...oh! I have one." She filled Zoe in on the Be Your Best Bride class. How it started, how Kara marketed it and how much Rebecca hated that, how she had to take over when Kara got sick. "I was honestly dreading the thing. I didn't go to school for this so I could listen to a bunch of bridezillas talk about how they need to fit into their size two wedding gown or they'll *just die*." She punctuated it with a roll of her eyes.

"I sense a 'but' coming."

"But..." Rebecca grinned at her while holding up a finger. "I'm finding it to be unexpectedly satisfying."

"Yeah? How so?"

"Well, the girls aren't bad. There are a couple that send me flashing back to the cheerleaders in my high school, but I'm getting to know them and they're okay. A bit too focused on what they look like rather than how they feel, but I can deal with that. There are two others that are much more...down to earth? I guess that's the best phrase. One just wants to be healthy. She's a tiny bit chunky, but I think that's more genetics than anything else, and she's working really hard. Plus, she's one of those women who's just...nice. You want to be around her."

"And the other?"

"She's working hard, too, which surprised me, given that her fiancée signed her up for the class without asking her first."

Zoe's eyes widened. "He did? What a prick."

"Not he. She."

"Her girlfriend signed her up?" Zoe's tone registered disbelief. "How do you know she didn't ask first?"

"My client said as much. She said her fiancée signed her up, so here she was."

"Man, I can't decide if I feel sorry for her or think she's an idiot."

"Me neither."

They shifted back and forth between Zoe's calls and Rebecca's clients, laughing the whole time. Rebecca found herself having a really good time, though...it didn't feel much like a date, and she wasn't sure why or what to do with that.

With a glance at her watch, Zoe said, "I need to get going."

"Don't forget your coffee," Rebecca reminded her.

Zoe stood and gave Rebecca a grateful smile. She took a step away from the table, stopped, then stepped back. Palms on the table, she leaned forward and said easily, "So, can we agree that there's, like, zero spark here?"

Rebecca blinked at her.

Zoe waited her out, her expression completely friendly and open. "I mean, right?"

A beat later, Rebecca inhaled slowly and let it out. "You're totally right. I've been sitting here trying to figure out why I'm having such a great time talking to you, but it feels like..."

"You're talking to your sister?"

"Yes!" Rebecca burst out laughing. "Oh, my God, that's exactly it."

Zoe's smile was wide, inviting. "I like you, Rebecca not Becky. I think we're gonna be friends for a long time." With a wink, she headed to the counter to get her coffee.

It was a weird, awesome feeling to know you'd made a new friend at thirty-five years old. So different from being a kid, being an age when you were actively looking for somebody to connect with, when you *needed* a friend. But in her thirties? Rebecca didn't need any more friends. She had plenty. That being said, she was keeping this one. She knew it immediately.

"Where's your phone?" Zoe was back, very large cup in hand. Rebecca pulled it out. Zoe rattled off her number. "There. Now you can text me any time. And then I'll have your number, too. Okay?" Zoe's brown eyes were soft.

"I think this may be the beginning of a beautiful friendship," Rebecca said, one corner of her mouth quirked up.

"Same." Zoe held up her cup in a makeshift salute. "Catch you later, Rebecca not Becky."

Rebecca watched her go as she sipped the last of her latte. Instead of being disappointed that yet another date hadn't worked out, Rebecca felt lighter somehow. Content.

"It was the weirdest thing," she said to Sherry later as she lay on her couch in her living room, phone pressed to her ear. "Like, we had this fantastic conversation. She's interesting, but she also listened. She was funny. And curious. She told great stories. But..."

"She didn't do it for you." Dishes clattered as Sherry must have been emptying the dishwasher.

"She didn't do it for me. And I didn't do it for her either, apparently." Rebecca had taken a bit to absorb that. "Isn't it funny, how we are? I mean, she didn't do it for me, but I didn't like hearing that I didn't do it for her. You know?"

Sherry chuckled. "Absolutely. Nobody wants to be unattractive to somebody else. To anybody else. I know I want everybody to think I'm hot. Always."

"Well, everybody *does* think you're hot, so you've got no worries there."

"Oh, thank God," Sherry said, and Rebecca could envision the playful smile on her face. "So, I think the takeaway here is, you *can* find a nice girl through internet dating. You did tonight."

"I found a friend, not a girlfriend. World of difference."

"But still. I think this should renew your faith, at least for a little bit longer."

"Maybe."

"God, you're stubborn."

"So I've heard."

They talked for a few more moments before hanging up. Rebecca clicked on the television, still feeling a bit wired. "This is why I shouldn't drink coffee after seven," she muttered to herself, flicking channels. A network that specialized in older movies was showing *Fly Away Home* and Rebecca stopped to watch for about the thirty-fifth time.

Her thoughts drifted back to her coffee date, to Zoe and how much fun she'd had. She picked her phone back up, scrolled to the number Zoe had punched in, and sent a text.

Had a great time tonight with a new friend. Let's do it again soon.

She added a smiley and sent it. A reply came almost immediately.

Same! I Facebook stalked you on my break. Accept my friend request, damn it. I'm getting a complex. The wink that followed took away any tinge of creepiness the text could have held. Rebecca chuckled to herself, then opened Facebook, found the friend request, and accepted it. Deciding to do a little stalking of her own, Rebecca scanned Zoe's timeline, noted her friends, and scrolled through a few photos, but before she even realized she was doing it, she'd typed the name Spencer Thompson into the search bar.

She popped up instantly, not hard to find at all, and Rebecca clicked. Her timeline was not private, which Rebecca knew wasn't smart and wanted to mention something next time she saw her, but how? How could she let Spencer know she should change her settings without admitting she'd been to her page? *Hey, Spencer, I was being a creeper and searched you out on Facebook and noticed your page isn't set to Private. Don't you know how many weirdos there are in the world that might photo stalk you?* Yeah, there was no way. Instead, she took advantage of the openness and wandered.

Spencer was fairly active. Not ridiculously so. Not like some people. Not like Sherry, who posted endless photos of her children and the details of every single thing they did on any given day, from winning a soccer game to eating a peanut butter and jelly sandwich, complete with commentary. It looked like Spencer posted every week or two, and most of her photos were of things, not people, though there were a few exceptions. Lots of photos of jewelry, it seemed. Rebecca wondered what that was about, remembered overhearing Spencer and Lucy talking about necklaces or something. There was what looked to be a family photo with Spencer, two people who were most likely her parents, given how much she looked like the older woman, a woman who must be a sister, and a young man of maybe twenty-five. A brother, must be. There was no caption. Lots of photos of dogs of varying sizes, colors, breeds, none of which seemed to be hers. And when Rebecca came across the photo of Spencer and another woman, it was as though her fingers suddenly had minds of their own and wouldn't let her scroll on past.

They stood in front of a pavilion. Maybe it was a picnic or an outdoor party? The taller woman had her arm wrapped possessively around Spencer's shoulders, the woman's smile wide.

Martina Daniels, the tag said.

This had to be the fiancée.

Rebecca zoomed. She had dark hair cut in a very professional-looking bob sort of style. Large brown eyes. She looked happy, standing there in black capris and a cream tank. She also looked... wealthy. Rebecca tilted her head, wondering why she thought that. Her clothes seemed fairly expensive. Her sandals definitely were. She glimmered with jewelry—a heavy gold watch, what looked to be diamond earrings, a gold chain with a charm on it that was slightly obscured by her collar and Rebecca couldn't quite make out. None of her jewelry looked like anything Spencer might have posted a photo of. That was something Rebecca noted right away. The other thing she noted was Spencer's smile. It was faint, more a ghost of a smile than anything else, an obligatory expression, something she maybe felt she was supposed to do.

"Oh, my God, McCall," Rebecca said, loudly, and quickly clicked off Facebook altogether. "What the hell are you doing? Stop it. Just. Stop."

She tossed the phone onto the coffee table and out of easy reach. Shaking her head in irritation at herself, she picked the remote back up. *Fly Away Home* had ended while she was stalking Spencer and about to stalk Spencer's fiancée, so she flicked quickly through channels until she found an episode of *Snapped*.

"Perfect. Let's watch overwhelmed women kill their spouses. That oughta cheer me right up."

I am officially ridiculous.

When *Snapped* failed to lasso all of her attention, she stretched for the phone and texted Zoe again, who texted back immediately.

I need a drink. Meet me?

"Yes," Rebecca said with relief.

Something else—some*one* else—to focus on was the perfect solution.

CHAPTER ELEVEN

"Hey, you," Spencer said as she swiped her membership card through the card reader at the front desk of BodyFit.

Lucy looked up and her perpetual grin grew wider. "Hi, Spence. How's life?"

Spencer parked a hand on her hip and slumped to one side. "Seriously, are you ever not crazy cheerful and happy?"

Lucy made a thinking face, then said, "Yeah, not really."

Spencer grinned at her. "The world needs more people like you. Hey, I have something to show you." She set down her bag, opened her purse, and took out a baggie filled with colorful beads. The bag flat on the counter, Spencer ran her hand over it so the beads were in a single layer. "I found some of these in packages I already had, and a few I bought because I thought they might work. See anything you like?"

Lucy ran her fingers over the beads, a soft "ooh" coming from her lips. "I like this one. And this one. This one here is very close to the color of the bridesmaids' gowns." She rested a fingertip on a rich mauve-colored bead.

"What are we looking at?"

Rebecca's voice was so close to Spencer, she gasped, then gave a soft chuckle. "You startled me," she said, glancing over her shoulder into those deep blue eyes.

"Sorry," Rebecca said and started to step away.

Spencer's guilt hit instantly, and she grasped Rebecca's wrist, tried not to notice the warmth, the softness. "No, no, it's okay. Stay."

Rebecca held her gaze for a delicious moment before moving her attention to the baggie. Spencer held on for a second or two longer than necessary, then let her grip slide away and felt unexpectedly sad about it.

"Spencer is making me necklaces," Lucy said, her voice bright, but her eyes focused on Spencer.

"Oh, yeah? You make jewelry?" Rebecca seemed honestly interested.

"I dabble," Spencer added with a shrug. Rebecca was still standing close. Spencer liked it, liked feeling her body heat, liked the sweet scent she gave off that Spencer couldn't pinpoint.

"Dabble?" Lucy looked at her like a third eye had appeared on Spencer's forehead. Turning to Rebecca, she went on. "She doesn't dabble. She creates. She's making me necklaces that reflect the colors of my wedding. I'm going to give them to my bridesmaids so they have something that nobody else has. Only the three of them."

Spencer felt her face flush. "I mean, they're not expensive. I just use glass and metal."

"Stop trying to make light of what you do. You make gorgeous stuff."

"Thanks, Luce." Spencer was keenly aware of Rebecca watching. Listening.

Rebecca reached for the baggie, sifted the beads through her long fingers. "Great colors in here," she said.

Lucy moved closer, stood on her toes, and pointed to the mauve bead. "This one."

"Oh, nice."

Spencer grinned at the two. Her friend and her...was Rebecca her friend? A strange question that came out of nowhere. And one Spencer didn't know how to answer, especially when Rebecca looked up from the baggie and snagged Spencer's gaze with her own. Held it.

Spencer felt her heart rate kick up a notch. Or seven.

God.

Then, suddenly, as if a spell had been broken, Rebecca blinked rapidly, seemed to make a concerted effort to tear her gaze away and force her eyes to the clock on the wall. "Yikes. Almost time for class. Better get ready." And then she very nearly race-walked away.

"She's growing on me," Lucy said, her eyes still on the baggie of beads.

Spencer nodded, her attention still pointed in the direction Rebecca had walked. "Mm-hmm."

"Come on. We'd better get changed."

Spencer followed Lucy to the locker room, where Lucy continued to talk about the necklaces. Spencer had to admit it was incredibly flattering to have somebody be so enamored of her work. It was one thing if it was her family. They sort of had to like her stuff. Or Marti, though she always seemed indifferent and had never asked Spencer to make her anything. It was quite another for it to be somebody as new to her as Lucy was. It was flattering, yes, but it also made her feel more pride than she had in a long time, and *that* was a nice feeling.

Once dressed and out in the gym area, they joined up with Willow and Bella. Before they finished their greetings, Rebecca joined them.

"Hello, ladies. No Brittany today, so it's just the four of us. I guess I'll have to divvy up her workout and give you each a little extra." She winked, and each of them let out a relieved sigh, then laughed when they heard each other. With an amused shake of her head, Rebecca said, "Let's stretch it out."

The foursome eased right into their usual stretching routines, and for the first time, Spencer realized she could do things more easily than when she'd first started the class. For example, the first step of the stretch was for her to bend at the waist, touch her hands to the ground, and walk them forward until she was very nearly in a push-up position. Next, she was to bring her left foot forward to meet her left hand, while the right foot stayed back. The first few times she'd done this move, she barely got her foot to her waist. She then had to scooch it in little skids to get it where it was supposed to be. Now? One step. Push-up position, left foot to left hand, done.

"Your flexibility has really improved," Rebecca said quietly, as if she was in Spencer's head and reading her thoughts like a magazine.

Spencer grinned at the praise, and as she turned to meet Rebecca's eyes, she felt a warm hand on the small of her back.

"Keep your back flat here. Don't arch."

Spencer nodded, did as she was instructed.

"Perfect."

Rebecca moved on down the line and Spencer again tried to ignore her disappointment when the hand slid away. *What is going on with me?* She furrowed her brow. *Better yet, what's going on with her?* Spencer was getting whiplash from the changes in demeanor. First, Rebecca hated her. Then she seemed to tolerate her. Then she hated her again and in addition, wouldn't touch her. Then she liked her once more and touched her a lot. Switching legs in her stretching, Spencer mentally shook her head. *I'm so confused.*

The rest of the class went along in similar fashion. Rebecca was friendly and pleasant, and if Spencer didn't know better, she'd think Rebecca was trying to touch her any time a chance popped up. Adjusting her stance in a stretch or tilting the angle of her elbow as she lifted weight or—Spencer's personal favorite, if she was telling the truth—shifting her hips during a move.

Standing at her locker now, Spencer recalled the feel of Rebecca's hands on her hips, moving them to the left, her voice very close to Spencer's ear. "Keep your hips straight. Don't twist."

Rebecca was causing her to gaze into space way too often.

Spencer shook herself, literally, and forced her brain back to the present. Lucy had left, Spencer moving way too slowly for her to stick around and wait. She'd given Spencer a funny look but then gathered her things and headed home, so Spencer didn't dwell much on it. Sucking in a large breath, she released her ponytail and brushed her hair, finished getting her things together, and finally—*finally*—closed her locker.

Her determination to stop daydreaming and concentrate on the other important things in her life was short-circuited by the sight of Rebecca sitting alone at her desk, staring off into space. Spencer had to walk right past her, and almost had when Rebecca shifted her focus and made eye contact.

Spencer lifted one hand in a casual wave.

"You've continued going to spin classes," Rebecca said, out of nowhere.

Spencer stopped and gave a nod. "I have."

"Good for you. Sherry's tough."

There were five spin instructors, and Spencer wondered if she should find it interesting that Rebecca knew which one she preferred. "She's *brutal*. Kicks my ass every time. Every. Time."

Rebecca laughed. "Well, it's doing you good. I can see it." A beat went by and Spencer watched, fascinated, as Rebecca's face slid from casually friendly to nearly mortified, seemingly by her own words. She held up a hand. "I'm sorry. That was…was that too personal?"

"Not to me," Spencer said. "A girl can never hear that enough, really." She punctuated that with a scoff. "It's not like anybody else tells me." And then it was Spencer's turn to grimace. "Now I'm getting too personal." They stayed like that for several seconds: Rebecca seated at her desk, Spencer standing, both of them looking slightly uncomfortable. So it was a bit surprising that Spencer couldn't seem to get her feet to move. "Do you not want to go home either?" The question was out of her mouth before she even knew she was going to ask it.

That seemed to give Rebecca a bit of a jolt, but a smile followed, and she held out an arm to indicate the chair next to her desk.

Spencer sat. "How did you become a fitness instructor? Did you always want to be one?"

Rebecca seemed to honestly contemplate the question. "No, I wanted to be a physical therapist."

Spencer tilted her head from side to side. "Similar field."

"Yes, but…" Rebecca gazed off into space as if searching for words. "I got in an accident when I was twenty. A bike accident."

"Oh, no."

"Yeah. I got hit by a car while I was riding. My own fault. I wasn't paying attention. I broke my femur and fractured my pelvis."

Spencer sucked in air through her teeth. "Ow."

"You have no idea. It was ironic that I needed physical therapy, given I was studying it. And let me tell you, that PT almost killed me."

"Painful?"

"Left me in tears almost every day. It was awful." Rebecca's features had softened, emotion clear on her face. Something Spencer hadn't seen often. She liked it. It made Rebecca seem more...human. "So I recovered and finished my studies and got a job in PT."

Spencer raised her eyebrows. "But?"

"But I hated causing that kind of pain to other people. I mean, I know it's part of their recovery, that they need to push through in order to get better. But I think having been the one on that table or balancing on those parallel bars, I had a better sense than my colleagues of just how much pain our patients might be in at any given time. And I just couldn't do it." Rebecca swallowed, then cleared her throat, her eyes bright.

Spencer sensed she hadn't quite finished and simply waited for her to continue.

"I had heard several doctors and fellow PTs say the same thing more than once, though: that if this person or that person had been in better shape—stronger, leaner, had more endurance, whatever— their recovery might be quicker or less painful or easier. And that stuck in my head for a good year or two before I decided *that* was what I wanted."

"To help people get stronger."

"And thereby healthier, yes."

"I like that." Aware that she was very close to seeing Rebecca in a new light somehow, Spencer smiled softly.

"My turn," Rebecca said, propping her chin in her hand and her elbow on the desk. Her blue eyes focused on Spencer, she asked, "Why don't you want to go home?"

"Oh, I want to go to my house, but I can't. Tonight I'm supposed to go to Marti's house, and...I just don't want to." Though startled that she'd answered so honestly, Spencer accepted it. Apparently, this was how she was with Rebecca now. Well, at least for tonight.

"And Marti is your…?"

"My fiancée."

"Right," Rebecca said with a nod. "The one who signed you up for this class."

"Yes."

"Without checking with you first."

"Right."

"Which was…okay with you? 'Cause I've got to tell you, that would have given me a bit of a complex."

Spencer swallowed. Rebecca's tone was gentle enough so that Spencer didn't feel accused or ridiculed, but they still weren't words she enjoyed hearing, and she was torn between defending Marti and being outraged by Marti. "Well, I could stand to lose a few pounds. I've always been a little chunky."

"Spencer." Was that the first time Rebecca had ever said her name to her? Spencer racked her brain and couldn't think of another instance. And she was pretty certain she'd remember because of how much she liked the way it sounded rolling off Rebecca's tongue. "So many things right now." She chuckled gently. "So many things. Okay, first of all, you are not chunky."

"I need some toning."

"As do most people. Fine. I'll let you have that, so long as we can agree you are not chunky."

Spencer nodded her consent.

"Two, while I am never going to downplay the importance of physical fitness—for everybody—I need you to help me understand how it's okay with you that Marti did what she did." Leaning in a bit closer, she added, "Marti *is* a she, right?"

Spencer grinned. "Yes. Marti is a she."

"Okay. Good."

"Good? Why is that good?" Spencer held Rebecca's gaze, her head cocked slightly, her tone definitely flirty, which she hadn't intended. Had she?

Rebecca poked the inside of her cheek with her tongue. "It's good because…" Then she seemed to think better of her answer and shook her head, waved her hands in surrender. "Nope. Not going there." But her face was open and her words came with a background of gentle laughter.

Spencer's turn to prop her chin in her hand, recalled the lunch date that hadn't showed for Rebecca. The *female* lunch date. "So, it seems that we play on the same team."

"Seems so."

"Interesting."

Spencer felt tethered to Rebecca in that moment. Tethered to her and safe with her, and she let herself simply sit with that. Rebecca seemed to as well, because they stayed that way for what felt like a long time…Rebecca sitting back in her chair and looking at Spencer, Spencer gazing back at her, chin in hand.

Something between them shifted right then. Spencer felt it as significantly as if some part of her world moved and clicked audibly, like a puzzle piece snapping into place.

Things will never be the same.

The thought ricocheted through Spencer's head, loudly and out of nowhere and so, so *weird*, startling her enough to make her flinch out of her reverie and sit up straight. What the hell was that? And what the hell was she doing? "I need to be going," she said suddenly, very aware of how weak her voice sounded.

Rebecca must have thought so, too, as her brow furrowed. "Oh. Okay."

Spencer stood so quickly, the chair toppled over behind her and she muttered, "Son of a biscuit."

"And yet another creative replacement for a curse word," Rebecca said, the amusement in her tone helping to alleviate a bit of what Spencer could only classify as the disappointment on her face.

"Yeah, I hardly ever swear."

"We'll see about that." Rebecca's half grin was almost too much for Spencer at this point. She had to get out of there, away from Rebecca, back to Marti where she was expected, where she was supposed to be.

"Okay, so, Friday then."

"Friday." Rebecca gave one nod, and that was the last of her Spencer saw because she needed to leave. *Needed* to.

She did her best not to actually flee Rebecca's presence, but she felt like she should be doing just that. The disillusionment and shame in herself, combined with the guilt—*God, so much guilt!*—flooded her system until she worried she might throw up right in the parking lot next to her car. She stood there, hand on the roof, braced for impending vomit, for several breaths before the feeling subsided. Without looking back at the building, she got in her car, started it, and pulled away. Too fast and too recklessly, but nobody else was around, thank goodness.

Marti's car was, surprisingly, in the driveway. Spencer parked next to it, gathered her things, and hurried in. Marti was in the kitchen, holding the refrigerator door open as she peered in. With a glance up at Spencer, she said, "Hey, babe."

Spencer dropped her stuff, walked up to Marti, and burrowed into her. Wrapped her arms around her, snuggled her head under Marti's chin, held tight.

"Wow," Marti said, her chuckle rumbling through her; Spencer could feel it. "This is a nice surprise. You okay?"

Spencer felt a tender kiss pressed to the top of her head, and even as her eyes welled up and she squeezed them closed, Spencer couldn't understand. This was her spot. This was where she was supposed to be. Safe and loved, enveloped in Marti's arms. Right? Wasn't it?

So how come the only thought in her head was that she wished it was Rebecca instead?

❖

Rebecca had been discreet about it, but she'd watched out a window as Spencer practically sprinted from the gym. Then she'd stood at her car, one hand on it, seeming to keep her upright as she swayed slightly. Rebecca was tempted to follow her out there, to make sure she was okay, but something kept her feet rooted to the floor where she stood.

"Nothing wrong with looking," Zoe had said the other night

as they'd shot some pool. "Nothing even wrong with touching if it's part of your job."

"You think?" Rebecca had been skeptical.

"Sure. I mean, you're not trying to seduce her, right? You said she's engaged. So, you do have boundaries." Zoe sank a solid orange ball, which was Rebecca's. "Damn it. As long as you keep them in your sights, I say take advantage. It's fun to be close to somebody you find attractive."

Rebecca lined up a shot. "Okay. That makes sense, I think."

"And for the love of all that's holy, stay off her girlfriend's Facebook page. That'll just make you crazy."

"That also makes sense," Rebecca had agreed, with a self-deprecating grimace.

She'd replayed that conversation a few times in her head, and when Spencer had arrived, standing at the front desk with Lucy, looking all fresh and pretty, Rebecca had decided to take Zoe's advice for a spin. Why not?

Rebecca was careful. She didn't go overboard. There'd been no unnecessary touching, only when Spencer needed help with her form. But Rebecca's fingers had tingled every single time, and now, after Spencer's hasty departure, she wasn't sure what to do with that. Instead of feeling satisfied, she was more confused than ever, and that made her a little bit…irritated. With Zoe. With Spencer. But mostly with herself.

Maybe Nick was rubbing off on her, making her think it was fine to touch a woman just because she found her sexy. In the next breath, she shook her head at her own gross overgeneralization about men. Nick would never do such a thing, and that made Rebecca feel even worse.

She watched out the window as Spencer stood up and dropped her head back as if looking to the sky for some kind of answer, her long, elegant throat a feast for Rebecca's eyes. Then she got in her car and drove away a bit faster than was safe, in Rebecca's opinion.

Rebecca stood there long after Spencer was out of sight, her thoughts racing through her head like cars around a Nascar track.

This had never happened to her before. Sure, she'd been attracted to lots of women in her life. She'd even been attracted to more than one client. But she'd never reached this level of…What was it? Frustrated desire? Unwelcome arousal? She'd had her reservations about Spencer from the beginning, and realized now that Spencer had never actually answered the question Rebecca had posed: why it was okay that Marti had signed her up, had basically told her she needed to get in better shape. Instead, she'd redirected the conversation and…

Rebecca's brain tossed her the image of Spencer's face, her chin in her hand, her cheeks still flushed from her workout, her eyes sparkling and giving Rebecca such intensely direct eye contact that she felt it in the pit of her stomach. And lower.

A breath of frustration pushed itself from her body, and Rebecca gave her head a hard shake. "All right," she said aloud. "Enough already. This has to stop. Enough."

She had all day tomorrow and most of Friday to get her shit together before she saw Spencer again. That should be more than enough time.

CHAPTER TWELVE

By Friday, Rebecca was back to being the standoffish, made-of-stone fitness instructor Spencer had met on the first day, and she was both disappointed and relieved by that. Their bride class workout was tough. Spencer had learned quickly that her least favorite line of Rebecca's was "We're gonna burn some calories today," as that meant it would be nearly an hour of cardio. Spencer's least favorite exercise. At least with spin class, she could picture being on a country road or pedaling up a gorgeous hillside. On the stupid elliptical and variations of it, she just felt annoyed.

After forty-five minutes of climbing to nowhere, raising and lowering resistance, sprinting and climbing steadily, Rebecca pulled them off and brought them downstairs to the floor area. Spencer knew what was coming.

"All right." Rebecca strolled in front of them, avoiding even the slightest glance at Spencer, which was how it had been the entire time.

We're back to this again.

"Plank positions. Sixty seconds. Some of you can do it and have, others are getting close but need to *work harder*."

Spencer wrinkled her nose at the stress on the last two words, as she knew they were directed at her. She and Lucy were the only two who hadn't made it the full sixty seconds yet, but Spencer could feel Rebecca's gaze. That's what she did: looked at Spencer when Spencer wasn't looking. And Spencer could feel it. Every time. It unnerved her.

And she was dreading this. Her emotions had been running very close to the surface for the past two days, her brain swirling with a confused jumble of thoughts, her body PMSing in a big way, the combination ready to make her scream in anger or burst into tears—or both—at any moment.

I could just leave. I mean, I pay for the class. It's not like I have to stay here.

But that would be...noticeable. She didn't want that. Rather, she wanted to sink down and blend right into the floor so nobody would see her. With a quiet sigh, she got into position.

"And go." Rebecca's voice was strong, and despite her cool demeanor, she looked absolutely edible to Spencer, who'd tried hard not to notice and who'd also failed spectacularly. Rebecca wore shorts today, mesh athletic shorts that Spencer immediately loved for no other reason than they left her legs bare. Spencer's eyes had roamed over them like fingers; God, they were beautiful. Shapely, lean but strong, astonishingly feminine. Spencer swallowed hard as her arms predictably began to tremble after a mere twenty seconds. Rebecca's dark hair seemed extra shiny today, and every time she tucked it behind her ears, Spencer's attention was pulled to her hands, her wrists, her bare arms.

Stop it!

Spencer swallowed down her exasperation with herself, tried to erase the image of Sexy Rebecca from her head.

Which Rebecca then made impossible when her black-and-pink Nikes stepped into Spencer's view and stayed there.

"You're halfway there," she announced to the group.

Next to Spencer, Lucy groaned.

Spencer squeezed her eyes shut, feeling her body weaken by the second. God, how she hated these planks.

Rebecca's feet didn't move. She was going to stand there until Spencer dropped. Spencer was sure of it.

"Twenty seconds to go," Rebecca said.

Spencer lasted another three before collapsing.

"No," Rebecca said, and suddenly, her face was next to Spencer's. "Get up. Get up. You have fifteen more seconds to go."

Her voice wasn't gentle. Or encouraging. It was almost angry, as if Spencer was purposely failing at this task.

Spencer turned to look at her and their eye contact was so intense, Spencer was sure she could reach out and touch it somehow, run her fingertip along the invisible line that connected them.

"Get up," Rebecca said again.

Spencer felt her own nostrils flare as aggravated resentment battled with sheer frustration, even as she pushed herself back up into position and held it for the remaining time.

The timer went off and all five women dropped to the floor with agonized groans and gentle laughter. Spencer stayed with her forehead pressed to the floor, mortified to feel tears well up in her eyes as Rebecca dismissed them and told them to have a nice weekend.

"You okay?" Lucy said, and Spencer could feel her getting to her feet.

Spencer nodded, but stayed face down.

"Want me to wait for you?"

Spencer knew she would, even though she also knew Lucy had friends to meet in twenty minutes. "No, no. I'm good. Thank you, though."

"You're sure?"

Spencer felt Lucy's hand on her head, a gesture of concerned friendship that only created more wetness in Spencer's eyes. "I'm sure," she said, not looking up. "Have fun tonight."

She lay there for another minute, then pushed herself to a sitting position and just…breathed. Her head was still a jumbled mess. Had been since Wednesday night and her ill-advised flirtation moment with Rebecca. God, she couldn't get it out of her mind…Rebecca's playful grin, the sparkle in those blue eyes that had looked so deeply disappointed in her tonight. She'd barely eaten. She'd hardly slept. Marti had gotten so annoyed with her tossing and turning last night, it was a relief to know she had a client dinner this evening and Spencer could go home to her own house—the only place she felt like herself anymore, not like she was pretending to be someone else.

A deep, loud rumble came from Spencer's stomach and she realized she'd eaten nothing since breakfast, so she slowly climbed to her feet and headed toward the smoothie bar.

A young man of college age was working that evening, his hair blond with fun streaks of electric blue. He greeted her with a smile and asked what he could do for her. She put in her order and he went to work. In a short time, she had a large cup of pale pink smoothie in her hand and took a sip through the thick, green straw. It was going to hit the spot.

"Thank God, something good out of this day," she muttered as she turned and headed for the locker room downstairs. At the bottom of the steps, she glanced to her left to pinpoint the strange noise she heard as somebody pushed a cart in the opposite direction. She swiveled her gaze forward just as she turned the corner.

And ran smack into Rebecca McCall.

Strawberry banana smoothie went all over the floor, all over the wall, and all over Spencer, its chilly temperature causing her to suck in her breath even as a loud "*Son of a bitch*" came from Rebecca.

"Oh, my God, I'm so sorry" burst out of Spencer, as she dropped her bag to the floor.

They stood for a moment, as if freeze-framed, staring at each other, smoothie all over Spencer's neck and chest and running down her right leg. She noticed immediately that Rebecca had one drop on her cheek and that was it.

Of course.

Before Spencer could say anything else, apologize again, or come up with a rarely used curse to toss back at her, Rebecca sighed loudly and grasped Spencer's wrist. "Come with me."

As she was tugged unceremoniously down the hall, Rebecca called in to the room on the left as they passed, "Bobby, can you clean up the smoothie spill in the hall?"

"You got it," came the reply, and Spencer saw him leap to his feet. "I'll do a great job."

Spencer allowed herself to be pulled along like a badly behaved toddler until they entered a locker room she'd never seen before.

Rebecca led her past the lockers and into a bathroom that was a bit nicer than the one the members used, less generic with more personal-looking décor. She was just reaching the conclusion that it was the staff locker room when Rebecca stopped them at a sink, turned Spencer so her back was against it, and grabbed a towel off the shelf.

Rebecca wet part of the towel and stepped close, into Spencer's personal space, and began wiping the smoothie off. Something in Spencer's head clicked and her anger began to simmer. She pushed at Rebecca's hands.

"Stop it."

Rebecca ignored her.

"I can do it myself," Spencer said, her ire growing. "I'm not a child."

Rebecca didn't look at her, just kept on with her attempts to wipe the remnants of smoothie away, moving the towel along Spencer's neck, her throat, switching from a gentle touch to a rougher one then back so quickly, Spencer had trouble figuring out which it was, and that made her a little crazy. When Rebecca moved the towel to Spencer's collarbone and dangerously close to her breasts, that was it.

Spencer snapped.

"What is wrong with you?" She slapped at Rebecca's hands, her voice filled with frustration. "Why are you all over the place with me? What have I ever done to you?" Again, her eyes welled up and again, she was supremely irritated by the fact.

Rebecca's hands stopped moving, but she didn't step back, and her gaze stayed just below Spencer's eyes, for a long stretch, and Spencer tried not to think about the fact that Rebecca was looking at her mouth. When she finally did look up, make eye contact, her expression caused Spencer to go completely still. Rebecca's eyes were filled with so much. So, so much. Confusion. Anger. Sadness.

Desire.

That last one was just registering in Spencer's mind. Her lips parted in realization and she inhaled a quick breath—which was all she had time to do before Rebecca moved. Not away, but closer and then she dropped the towel, grabbed Spencer's head with both hands, and crushed their mouths together.

Suddenly, they were kissing. No, they weren't kissing. They were full-on making out, and it wasn't gentle. There was nothing tentative about it. Rebecca pushed closer to Spencer with her entire body, pinning her against the counter. Spencer felt every single inch of them that touched. Breasts, hips, pelvises, thighs. She felt Rebecca's fingers slide into her hair, clutch the back of her head, felt Rebecca's tongue press into her mouth, and God help her, Spencer moaned and kissed her back. With abandon.

Reckless abandon.

The rest of the world fell away. There was no other sound but their kissing and the occasional soft hums or breaths. There were no other smells but Rebecca's usual scent of brown sugar and something uniquely her. Spencer felt nothing else but Rebecca's hands, in her hair, on her back, Rebecca's mouth taking her, owning her in the most delicious of ways, and Rebecca's body under her own hands. Her slim waist, her firm shoulders, muscles flexing, bunching.

Time didn't exist. Spencer had no idea how much had passed, nor did she care. She'd never been kissed like this before. Not with this much passion, this much heat. She'd never in her life felt this wanted. She didn't want it to end; it was like an instant addiction. It had never been this difficult for her to *not* begin undressing the person before her. As if they had minds of their own, Spencer's hands slipped under the back of Rebecca's shirt, and the smooth warmth of the skin there sent a surge of her own wetness to her center, her body already preparing for more.

A sudden, sharp knock on the door shocked them so thoroughly, the two of them literally jumped apart, like young teens caught by their parents.

"Rebecca?" It was Bobby, his cheerful voice seeming entirely out of place, given what they'd just done. "Hall's all clean and I left that blond lady's bag out here."

Rebecca tried to speak, croaked instead, and cleared her throat, her eyes never leaving Spencer's. "Thanks, Bob."

Spencer couldn't find her voice. She couldn't find words. She could barely find thoughts. She brought her fingertips to her swollen lips and felt her eyes widen with the realization of what she'd just done. They stood that way for what felt like hours, neither saying a word. She wondered what Rebecca was thinking, almost asked, but decided it was probably better if she didn't know. It took massive effort on her part, but Spencer finally managed to pull her gaze away from Rebecca's, to untangle herself from that eye contact she'd craved for so long and now wanted—needed—to be free of.

With a hard swallow, she turned the knob and opened the door. Bobby was gone, thank God, but her bag was right there on the floor, just as he'd said.

Without looking back, she scooped it up and left the room, bound for her car on unexpectedly wobbly legs, moving as quickly as she dared, the only thing on her mind being escape. Because if she stayed around Rebecca, she knew exactly what would happen.

CHAPTER THIRTEEN

Rebecca barely slept Friday night, and by five thirty Saturday morning, she was so aggravated by her own tossing and turning that she muttered a "screw it" and hauled herself out of bed.

In fact, everything was aggravating to her at the moment. Her coffee seemed bitter and a bit too strong. Of course, that might have something to do with the fact that she was on her fourth cup. The *Law & Order* reruns she'd been staring at from the couch for the past four hours were from the only season she didn't like. The brilliant September sunshine was far too cheerful and happy, and Rebecca wished she had a switch so she could dim it just a bit.

None of it really mattered, if she was being honest, because truthfully, that stuff was only taking up part of her thought process. The rest was taken up by one single subject.

Spencer Thompson.

Okay, maybe not one single subject because she was also thinking about Spencer's eyes. And Spencer's hips. And God, Spencer's mouth. That soft, warm mouth and—

"Oh, my God, stop it, McCall. You're going to drive yourself crazy." She said it aloud, and it seemed to ricochet around her empty living room before returning to settle right back on her chest.

Another half hour went by before she managed to drag her body into the shower, making the water as hot as she could stand it and letting it beat down on her shoulders. She stood there, eyes squeezed shut, trying to see anything but Spencer's eyes in her mind.

She was only mildly successful.

Maybe a walk would do her good. Early September was gorgeous, Rebecca's favorite time of year besides the Christmas season, and she put on a pair of yoga pants and a T-shirt. Deciding to let her hair air-dry, she was just reaching for her Nikes when her doorbell rang. She left them in the closet as she glanced at the clock, then padded barefoot to the door. At ten thirty on a Saturday morning, she expected to see Jehovah's Witnesses. Or possibly a politician stumping early for the upcoming campaign season.

What she didn't expect to see was Spencer.

They stood for a beat, just looking at each other, apparently neither one of them knowing what to say. Spencer looked unsurprisingly beautiful in denim capris and a white button-up camp shirt. Sandals were on her feet, and Rebecca noticed her purple toenails. Oddly, it occurred to her that she'd never seen Spencer's feet, that she was always in sneakers when they were together. Eyes roaming back up, Rebecca took in the golden waves of Spencer's hair, held back over her ears by the sunglasses perched atop her head.

"Spencer," Rebecca finally managed to say, her voice slightly hoarse. "Hi."

"Hey," Spencer said, her eyes darting from Rebecca's face to somewhere behind her to her feet and back again. "Listen, can I talk to you for a second? I promise it won't take long."

Rebecca cleared her throat and stepped back, held out an arm toward the interior of her house. "Sure. Come in."

Spencer stepped into the small foyer but didn't enter further. Rebecca shut the door and they stood there. Silent. Spencer's sandals must have had a slight heel, and with Rebecca barefoot, they were exactly the same height.

"Your hair's wet," Spencer said softly.

Rebecca blinked at her, then reached up, grasped some with her fingers. "Yeah. I just…got out of the shower."

Spencer nodded, stared for a moment before seeming to force her eyes away. She looked around the room, like she was taking it all in. After a beat, she cleared her throat. "Look. Rebecca. I just needed to address what happened last night."

Rebecca nodded. She'd hoped they could just go on about their lives and never have to discuss it, but Spencer apparently didn't agree. "Okay."

"It can't happen again."

A beat. "Okay."

"I mean it. I'm engaged. I have a...you shouldn't have...I mean, *I* shouldn't have..." Spencer inhaled sharply and glanced off to her right as if frustrated with her stuttering and looking for a way to collect herself.

When she returned her focus to Rebecca, her eyes had that same gleam from last night and Rebecca felt her entire body straighten to rigidity, brace itself, because somewhere, somehow, deep down, she knew what was coming.

With a soft whimper, Spencer repeated, "Your hair's wet." Her shoulders sagged with what seemed to be defeat. As the breath seeped out of her, she said very softly, "Goddamn it."

And the next thing Rebecca knew, Spencer was in her arms, grabbing her face, kissing her. Just like last night, there was nothing gentle. Spencer moaned loudly as Rebecca wrapped her arms around her tightly, pulled her close, kissed her back with all she had.

Rebecca backed Spencer up against the door, a soft "oof" pushing from her lungs. Rebecca pulled the sunglasses from Spencer's head and set them on a small table nearby, then dug the fingers of both hands into Spencer's glorious hair, the waves seeming to immediately wrap around them as if celebrating the lack of her usual ponytail. Spencer's hands trailed down Rebecca's back and she felt them cup her ass, squeeze it. Rebecca grinned against Spencer's mouth.

Seriously, had she ever kissed anybody like this before? Rebecca had wondered the same thing last night. What was it about Spencer? Why was kissing her so astonishingly arousing? Rebecca had kissed her share of women in her thirty-five years, but not one of them had made her feel like this. Desperate. Needy. Uncontrolled. Not one.

Freeing a hand from Spencer's tresses, Rebecca moved it down and slowly unbuttoned Spencer's shirt until it hung completely open, exposing bra-clad breasts and a bare stomach to her feasting eyes.

Rebecca moved her mouth from Spencer's and slid her tongue down the side of her neck to that sweet spot where it met her shoulder. She closed her mouth over the skin there, savored the softness, the sweet taste of it. Her other hand still in Spencer's hair, she tugged gently just like last night, forcing Spencer's head back, allowing Rebecca free access to the long column of her throat. With lips and tongue, Rebecca bathed it even as her free hand slipped slowly up Spencer's stomach and cupped one very full breast through her bra.

Spencer gasped and the sound yanked Rebecca back to her senses long enough for her to glance up and see the desire, the naked arousal on Spencer's face.

"Rebecca..." Spencer whispered, and it cut straight through Rebecca, down to her center, made her throb uncomfortably. "I can't..."

Rebecca dropped her head, took a small step back. "You came to me," she said quietly.

"I know." Spencer grasped the sides of her unbuttoned shirt as if to button it back up. "I know."

It started to simmer a bit, low in Rebecca's stomach, the confusion seasoned with a pinch of irritation. "What do you want, Spencer?" she asked, then wiped her fingers across her own swollen lips. "I can't figure you out."

"Join the club," Spencer muttered.

Her eyes welled up, and just like that, Rebecca's irritation vanished. She wanted to wrap Spencer up in her arms, protect her from the world. That was something she hadn't felt in a very long time, and she didn't know what to do with it.

They stood there, each seeming to absorb the presence of the other, when Spencer's expression changed. In an instant. It was like her resistance simply left her, and she gave in. Rebecca actually saw it happen, saw the moment it fell away. And then Spencer's hands were reaching for her.

Rebecca locked her eyes to Spencer's, searched them for

permission, found it. She moved in closer, returned her hand to where it had been, kneaded Spencer's breast through the bra, then dipped in and pulled it out, freed it for her eyes, her mouth to feast on.

Spencer's hand in her hair tightened, clenching, guiding, small whispers of "my God" and "yes, please" reaching Rebecca's ears as she ran her tongue over an erect nipple. She was lost in sensation, in the feel, the scents, the sounds of Spencer and her body, and she did her very best to ignore the tiny voice in the back of her head that kept promising her this was a terrible idea, that it would end badly.

I don't care.

It was the truth. She couldn't have stopped now if she wanted to…and she didn't want to. Rebecca had never wanted anything, anyone, so much in her life. And Spencer wanted it, too. That much was startlingly clear. Spencer's hesitation had completely vanished. Her hands were everywhere, tugging at Rebecca's clothes, as she kissed her with authority.

With *need.*

Wrenching their mouths apart, Rebecca said through heaving breaths, "We're not doing this here. Our first time isn't going to be in my living room." She grasped Spencer's hand and led her to the bedroom, barely recalling the trip, and they didn't miss a beat once they were there. Standing next to Rebecca's bed, they undressed each other in record time, as if they couldn't wait. And they couldn't. Rebecca looked into Spencer's eyes and saw her own want reflected back at her. It spurred her on, made her fumbling fingers move faster. Spencer was down to only her underwear—a simple white pair that matched her bra—in a matter of seconds, and Rebecca wasn't far behind. By unspoken agreement, they climbed onto the bed.

The eye contact was unexpected. Rebecca had to admit that. What they were doing, it wasn't a good thing. She had to concede that, but still. No, she didn't care in the moment. All she wanted was to feel Spencer underneath her, her warm skin, her wet heat. And if Spencer showed any hesitation, any signs of second-guessing this, Rebecca vowed to back off immediately. This bargaining had gone on in her head without her even realizing it, but when she met Spencer's gaze, saw the certainty there, the unwavering desire, and when Spencer reached for her, Rebecca threw caution to the wind. She had no choice.

The bed she'd made barely an hour ago was suddenly unmade. They slid between the sheets, mouths fused together, legs entwined, bare skin sliding deliciously against bare skin. Rebecca wasted no time running her hands over every inch of Spencer she could reach. Her shoulders with the light dusting of freckles, her arms that had become so much stronger, the stomach she was so self-conscious about, down the curve of her hip to the new solidity of muscle in her thighs.

"God, you're beautiful," Rebecca whispered as she pulled her mouth away from Spencer's. She saw the blush as it happened, starting at her throat and sliding its way up over her chin, her cheeks blooming splashes of pink. Rebecca ran her fingertips across Spencer's swollen lips. "I mean it."

"Thank you," Spencer said, just as quietly. "I love that you think so."

"Oh, I do."

"I feel the same way about you. I have since the first day I laid eyes on you."

That was news to Rebecca. News that made her feel warm from the inside. Warm and a little mushy. "Really?"

"Mm-hmm. Even though you didn't like me."

It was Rebecca's turn to blush. "I didn't. You're right. Which wasn't to say I didn't find you hot. 'Cause I totally did."

Spencer's chuckle rumbled up from her abdomen. Rebecca could feel it where their stomachs touched. Her eyes sparkled as she looked at Rebecca. "We're going to revisit the fact that you hated me on sight." Then those eyes darkened, went all sultry, and her voice got low. "But later. After."

Rebecca arched a brow playfully. "After what?"

"After I have my way with you."

And just like that, Rebecca found herself on her back, staring at her own ceiling while a gorgeous blond woman used her mouth to do erotic things to her breasts. Rebecca's breathing became ragged, her fingers closing and opening in Spencer's hair, trailing down her bare back. Sounds came from her own throat that she didn't recognize, as Spencer worked her way down, sliding Rebecca's underwear along her legs and off, baring her completely.

Never a fan of being exposed—to anybody—Rebecca was shocked by her own comfort. Spencer spread her legs wide, settled herself between them, and looked up Rebecca's naked body. Met her eyes. Held them. Rebecca had never felt such a connection. Ever in her life.

And then Spencer took her. Dove in with abandon. Lips, fingers, tongue. She *took* Rebecca. Owned her. Owned her in a way Rebecca had never experienced, had never known she wanted to experience, and frankly, had no idea Spencer was capable of. She tried to keep track of what was where, when it was a hand or a tongue or a finger, when it was touching her thigh, her folds, sliding in, but everything blended into one giant wave of sensation, until there was nothing but joyous pleasure. Rebecca let her head fall back onto the pillow, the sheet gripped in her fingers, and gave up trying to concentrate, allowed herself to simply feel.

And feel she did.

She didn't register right away that the soft pleas, the whispered exclamations of Spencer's name, actually came from her own lips until her orgasm dropped on her out of nowhere, tightening every muscle and ripping Spencer's name, loudly, from her throat. Her fingers clenched into fists—one in the sheets, one in Spencer's hair—and her hips lifted off the bed as the contractions pulsed through her body.

Spencer held on, kept her mouth pressed tightly to Rebecca's center, gripped her hips with strong fingers, until Rebecca began to come down. Ever so slowly, her body settled back down to the mattress as her lungs struggled for air and quiet "oh, my Gods" slipped from her mouth.

Rebecca felt rather than saw Spencer crawl up her body, kiss her forehead, settle next to her.

"Holy shit," Rebecca finally muttered, still trying to catch her breath.

"Yeah? I'll take that." Spencer's head was on her shoulder, and with her fingers, she drew lazy circles on Rebecca's stomach, and again, Rebecca was surprised by the comfort she felt. By how... *normal*...it all seemed. How *good*. She felt her brain drifting, trying to drag her back to the reality of their situation, but she put the brakes on, envisioned herself digging in her heels. Turning her head, she cupped Spencer's face and kissed her, and that was all it took. She rolled them both until she was on top, until her knee was between Spencer's. Until she groaned at the wetness that coated it. Until she pressed up and into Spencer's center, pulling a sexy whimper from her.

Rebecca wanted to take her time. She really did. She wanted to explore Spencer's body, to look at it as well as feel it and taste it. But her willpower had apparently been decimated by her orgasm, because she had none. The feel of Spencer's mouth under hers, of Spencer's hands on her back, of Spencer's hips pushing up and into her just a bit...all of it combined to send Rebecca into sensory overload, and she had no other option than to slide her hand down Spencer's stomach and into the hot, wet folds nestled between her legs. A sound escaped her the second her fingers reached their destination, a sound of disbelief mingled with joy mingled with sensuality. She plunged in, no preamble, no hesitation, and Spencer wrenched her mouth from Rebecca's so her cry had someplace to go.

And then they were moving. In rhythm. As one. Eyes locked. Bodies tethered. And when Spencer came, she came hard. Fast. Loud. Her nails dug into Rebecca's back and Rebecca basked in it, basked in the pain, basked in its source.

Rebecca collapsed, did her best to keep from laying her full weight on Spencer. They stayed there for a long while, all ragged breathing and pounding hearts, and in time, they calmed. Settled. Rebecca did her best to continue to keep the reality of what they'd done at bay, but she was weak. Spent. Had little strength left. And when she glanced up at Spencer, saw the faraway, contemplative look in her eye, what was left of that strength went away, too.

"Hey," she said finally. "It's okay."

Spencer turned to her then, met her gaze. "Is it?" Those blue eyes held a combination of such hope and such sadness, it made Rebecca's heart crack in her chest just a little.

Rebecca wanted to say yes, to insist. But she also knew this was something Spencer had to deal with on her own. Instead, she reached a hand up to Spencer's face, stroked her cheek, stayed quiet.

"We can't undo this," Spencer said, so softly that Rebecca wondered if she was talking to her or to herself.

"I don't want to undo it."

"We have to live with it now."

Rebecca nodded, unsure if a response was expected. Instead, she burrowed in a bit closer, and they stayed that way, quiet, for a long time.

"I need to go," Spencer finally said, and her tone was equal parts determination and regret.

"Okay." Rebecca moved to let her up, then watched as Spencer dressed, watched as Spencer didn't look at her. It wasn't unexpected, if Rebecca was being honest, but it still stung.

When she was finally dressed, Spencer did look. Her face said so many things to Rebecca in that moment: that she was sated, that she was sad, that she regretted what they'd done, that she didn't…

As Spencer turned for the door, Rebecca sat up and spoke. She felt like she had to. Had to say something. Anything. She could only come up with one word, though. "Spencer."

Spencer cleared her throat. "Yeah, we can't do this again."

Rebecca leaned her head to the right, smiled tenderly. "You said that about last time," she said, her voice soft.

Spencer's throat moved as she swallowed. "I know." The two words were whispered so quietly, Rebecca barely heard them. And then, without warning, Spencer crossed the room, was in Rebecca's arms, her face burrowed into Rebecca's neck, her grip tight, like she was afraid if she let go, she'd be swept away. Rebecca did what she'd thought about earlier: wrapped her arms around this beautiful, conflicted woman and held her tight, uncertain what else she could do.

And then, again without warning, Spencer let go, turned, and left. Rebecca heard the front door close and Spencer's car start up.

Rebecca sat, staring at the empty doorway of her bedroom, the alluring scent of sex still hanging in the air, and tried without success to figure out where to go next. And don't get her started on the wild emotions running through her head right then like a bunch of dogs let off their leashes.

It was fine.

She started there.

Everything was fine. They'd had a little fling, nothing more. No big deal. Happened all the time. It was fun (and could be much *more* fun), but Spencer was spoken for and Rebecca had to accept that. Consciously shutting down that part of her brain, closing it off from the rest, she did her best to shake it away.

It was a one-time—okay, *two-time*—thing and it was done now.

For sure.

No more.

CHAPTER FOURTEEN

By Monday morning, Spencer was very confused. By several things. Her head was a jumble of thoughts, emotions, and feelings, none of which seemed to want to be sorted. They just tumbled together in her head, like a load of wet towels in a dryer, mixing and mingling colors, until they were a blur of spin-art, swirling in her brain, making her slightly nauseous.

Since the moment she'd left Rebecca's house, Spencer had waited for the guilt, the horror of her actions, to come crashing down and bury her. *What have I done? What was I thinking? That was so unlike me!* That was the big one. What she'd done was completely out of character. She was a good girl. She did what she was told. Always had. What in the world had come over her?

She waited the rest of the day on Saturday, but aside from those three thoughts running on a loop through her head, that was it. She'd waited all day Sunday. She'd gone to Marti's house Sunday afternoon to watch football and braced herself. Marti had pecked her on the lips, popped open a beer, and sat down with a few work pals she'd invited over. Two guys and a girl, a bowl of salt and vinegar chips, some cheese and crackers, and her Jets on the television.

Spencer had stood in the kitchen and literally looked around, searching for a tumult of awfulness that never came.

Marti barely noticed when Spencer muttered something about some work stuff she'd forgotten and left to sleep at her own house. Spencer didn't want to be around strangers. She didn't want to be around Marti.

She was not at all happy about what she'd done. That was certainly not the case. She felt bad about it, guilty, and in fact, she was horrendously disappointed in herself. She'd gone over to Rebecca's to apologize for letting things progress on Friday, to tell her not to worry, it wouldn't happen again. And then she'd literally thrown herself at Rebecca. *She* had made the move! Spencer! The girl who didn't make the moves anymore. God, she was annoyed with herself. For not having better self-control. For giving in to temptation so quickly. For not feeling horrible, like she should.

Why don't I feel horrible?

That question had plagued her for the remainder of Sunday and was there waiting for her bright and early when she opened her eyes on Monday, as if it had camped out in a chair in the corner of the bedroom while she slept.

And now it was settling in, what had happened on Saturday. What she'd done. Probably because she would see Rebecca tonight.

God, Rebecca...

Her brain started to drift as she lay in bed, tossing her flashbacks and images of Saturday at Rebecca's house. In Rebecca's arms. Rebecca was an amazing kisser...Spencer had never been kissed like that. So thoroughly, so painstakingly, as if Rebecca's only care in the world was to make sure Spencer was enjoying the act of kissing. And oh, how she had enjoyed it. Before they'd even come close to traveling beyond the kissing, before any buttons had been unfastened, Spencer was already more turned on, more pleasured than she'd ever been with Marti. Or Chelsea, even. Anybody. She and Rebecca might have butted heads in many other aspects of life, it seemed, but when it came to sex, they excelled.

She let her hand drift up to her face, brushed her own lips with her fingertips, and closed her eyes with a soft exhalation.

Opened them. She was going to have to face this.

She took the pillow next to her, held it tightly over her face, and screamed as loudly as she could. Again and again until she was empty of the frustration, the anger, the worry, the guilt.

Then she called in sick.

And then she called her sister.

❖

The Hummingbird was a small café not far from the house where Spencer's parents lived. They met there often for coffee or lunch, and the staff—and many of the customers—knew them and greeted them whenever they arrived. Rather than a flood of working folk, the Hummingbird catered to an older, more laid-back crowd. No hustling, bustling yuppies or business people. The clientele was made up of mostly retired folk, all of whom knew one another and all of whom were there three to four times a week. Maybe more.

Mary Beth Thompson was the exception. She was not retired and, aside from Spencer, she was probably the youngest human in the place, but everybody still knew her, thanks to past introductions from her parents. Mary Beth was a financial advisor. Her clientele spanned all ages, but Spencer was pretty sure about 70 percent of her retired clients met her through her parents. Folks waved and called out greetings to her, and Mary Beth had to stop and chat three times before she was able to reach the table where Spencer sat, menu in hand, sipping a Diet Coke as she watched her big sister mingle. She looked professional and competent in her navy blue pantsuit, her modest heels clicking across the linoleum of the floor as she finally made her way to the table, her light brown hair pulled back in a twist.

"Hey," Mary Beth said in greeting, as she bent to kiss Spencer's cheek.

"Hey, M.B."

She took a seat across from Spencer, folded her hands on the table, and studied her. Part of the reason Mary Beth Thompson was so good at her job was her uncanny ability to read people. Spencer included. "You okay?" she asked.

Spencer reached into her bag and pulled out a little black velvet pouch, handed it to her.

Mary Beth loosened the drawstring and tipped a pair of earrings into the palm of her hand. They were gold and black, dangles, simple, but somehow a bit elegant. "These are beautiful," she said, then looked back up at Spencer. "And now I know you've got something on your mind."

"How?"

"You make jewelry when your head is messy. I've met you."

Spencer inhaled deeply, then let it out very slowly. With a nod of acknowledgment, she took a sip of her soda and looked around the café. She wanted to talk to Mary Beth about what was on her mind, but she didn't want to look at her while she did, didn't want to see the disappointment in her eyes. A hard swallow and a nibble on the inside of her cheek steadied her. "I did something."

"Okay."

They were interrupted by the waitress. Mary Beth hadn't even glanced at the menu but ordered anyway. A tuna melt with Swiss cheese and a Diet Coke. Spencer hadn't been hungry, but her sister's order suddenly sounded delicious, so she ordered the same.

"This thing you did," Mary Beth said once the waitress had left. "Is it bad?"

Spencer nodded.

"Are the police looking for you?"

The twinkle in her eye tugged one corner of Spencer's mouth up against her will. "No."

"All right, well, that's a relief."

Spencer nodded, slowly twirled her straw in the nubbly plastic red tumbler that all cafés and diners seemed to use.

"Are you going to tell me or should I just start guessing which figurine you broke?" Her tone was kind, gentle. She knew Spencer well, and this was how she'd always gotten her to talk. She'd coax her along, make tiny jokes to bring tiny smiles until Spencer felt comfortable enough to spill whatever secret she'd been holding. This had been Mary Beth's method since Spencer was five and broke one of her mother's favorite knickknacks, the pepper half of Winnie the Pooh and Piglet salt and pepper shakers. They'd gone to their mother, hand in hand, and told her what had happened. Well, Mary Beth had told her. Spencer had stood silently as fat, hot tears rolled down her cheeks. "It wasn't Mom's Elmer Fudd glass, was it? Please say no. I'm not sure I could protect you if it was."

Another small grin made its way onto Spencer's face. She couldn't help it.

"There's a smile." The waitress delivered Mary Beth's soda and she unwrapped the straw, took a sip. "It's okay, Spence. Tell me what happened."

Spencer swallowed again, knew there was no way her sister could guide her if she didn't tell her what she'd done. Staring into her soda, she said, very quietly, "I slept with someone."

"I'm assuming you're not talking about Marti," Mary Beth said, a meager attempt to make her smile that almost worked, but not quite.

"No."

"So, you cheated on your fiancée."

Spencer's eyes snapped to her and widened in slight horror.

"Spence, we've got to call it what it is here. Don't we?"

"Yeah. I guess we do." Spencer dropped her head down, shook it slowly. "I don't know what to do, Mare."

"All right. Let's look at it logically." This was exactly why Spencer had called her and not her mother. She needed logic over emotion right now, and she was pretty certain her mother would be mortified by Spencer's actions. Rightfully so.

The waitress arrived with their sandwiches and left them to it.

Mary Beth took a bite, chewed thoughtfully. "You need to answer some questions, I think. Things only you know the answers to."

"Like?"

She repeated the process of biting, chewing, thinking. "I don't want you to answer them right now. I want you to think about them for a bit."

Spencer nodded, chewing a bite of her own sandwich, savoring the blend of the creamy tuna and the sharp tang of the cheese.

"First question: What caused you to do it? Is there something missing in your relationship with Marti? If so, is it something that can be fixed?"

Spencer nodded again, happy not to speak as she absorbed the questions.

"Two: The person you slept with"—she held up a hand—"don't

tell me who it is. I don't want to know yet. But this person, do you have feelings for her?" She leaned forward a bit and said, with a comically arched brow, "I assume it's a her?"

Spencer allowed herself a slight chuckle. "Yes. Still gay."

"I figured." Mary Beth ate the rest of the first half of her sandwich. "Three: Are you still letting what happened with Chelsea dictate the decisions you make today? Because I think you have. For a long time now."

Feeling her eyes well up, Spencer shifted her gaze to the window and willed the impending tears away.

Her sister, maybe sensing that she needed her to keep talking, did. "And finally: How do you feel about all of it? What do you want to do? Do you want to double down on your future marriage and focus on that? Do you want to end things with Marti and pursue this other girl? Do you want to be on your own?" She studied her for so long that Spencer squirmed slightly in her seat. "I think that last batch…those are the big ones. And any of those choices are okay. You know? They're *all okay*." Her expression softened, and her eyes filled with love for Spencer. "You're a smart woman, Spencer, and I'm pretty sure you know that you wouldn't have strayed outside your relationship if something wasn't missing from it. I think you need to figure out what it is." Leaving half a sandwich, she slid the plate to the edge of the table, then folded her hands and looked Spencer square in the eye. "I'm not always the biggest Marti fan. You know this. But she deserves better than what you've done, so you need to figure it out. You're a better person than this."

She'd allowed a bit of her disappointment to seep in, and while Spencer knew she was right, she still felt ten years old again, like she'd touched Mary Beth's hairbrush or favorite CD without permission. She would much rather have her sister, her parents, her friends be angry with her than disappointed in her. But she had done this to herself. She could have stopped Rebecca that first time. She could have stopped herself the second time. Sure, Rebecca knew Spencer was taken, but Spencer had flung the door wide open and invited her in. Easy as it would be to push some of the blame onto Rebecca, she knew she couldn't.

No, Spencer had done this to herself. And now she had to either fix it or live with it.

She wasn't sure how to do either.

❖

Once Spencer had left her, satisfied but at the same time not, Rebecca had spent the rest of the weekend alone. At first, it was alone with her thoughts. But when that became too much to deal with, she went to a movie. Being able to focus on something else for two hours was awesome, but as soon as she left the theater, Spencer came screaming back into first place in her head. Visions of her sexy eyes, soft hair, gorgeously feminine curves pummeled Rebecca's mind until she wanted to shout for them to leave her alone—especially when the accusatory thoughts about how she'd overstepped her bounds as a trainer began to seep in. So the rest of the weekend was spent with Lysol. And Comet. And Tide. And Pledge. And Windex. Whenever Rebecca got stuck in a rut of endless thoughts, she cleaned.

By the time she got to work on Monday, she felt the slightest bit better and her house sparkled like the calm ocean in the sunshine.

She would talk to Spencer. That was the plan.

It made her nervous. With every hour the clock ticked away, the butterflies in her stomach kicked things up a notch. But she was sure it was the right thing to do.

"I don't want to." Mrs. Chase gave Rebecca a stubborn look as she sat on the upper body ergometer. It was basically an exercise bike that you pedaled with your hands instead of your feet, and Mrs. Chase's doctor had sent her for a bit of conditioning and rehab.

Rebecca sighed internally, as she went through this very same argument with the elderly woman every other time she came to the gym. "Mrs. Chase, you know this will help you get your strength back in your arms and upper body. You were in the hospital for a long time. You need to work back to your normal self again."

"I'll never be my normal self again." Her eyes welled up, not for the first time, and Rebecca put a hand on her shoulder.

"How about we do it in short spurts. Okay? Let's start with two minutes. You can do two minutes, can't you?"

"I don't want to," Mrs. Chase said again, but with less ire.

"I understand that. But...*can* you?"

The woman blew out an obviously annoyed breath. "Fine." She began pedaling with her hands and Rebecca quickly set the monitor for two minutes.

"Terrific. See how good you're doing already?"

To Rebecca, people like Mrs. Chase were perfect examples of why you should get yourself in shape and stay that way from a young age. A couple months ago, she'd taken a spill down the stairs in her house and, because of her sedentary lifestyle, had little muscle tone. Recovery was taking much longer than it should. If she'd been a bit stronger, she'd have cut weeks off her hospital stay.

Now it was up to Rebecca to help her understand that, even at seventy-six years old, exercise and health were paramount to living a long, productive, and independent life.

"I hope you have a wastebasket nearby in case I throw up," Mrs. Chase said, a little fire in her gaze.

"I'm not worried." Rebecca managed somehow to not roll her eyes at the drama queen that her client could be.

They finished up in twenty more minutes that felt like five hours to Rebecca. She helped Mrs. Chase to the women's locker room. "See you on Wednesday, Mrs. C."

"If I'm still around" was the response, as Mrs. Chase walked away from Rebecca and into the locker room.

This time, Rebecca just shook her head, a small grin on her face. When she turned around, she saw Spencer walking in her direction, scrolling on her phone. She looked up, saw Rebecca, and faltered, did a little stutter-step to a halt.

"Hey," she said, from about six feet away.

"Hi," Rebecca responded, even as she felt her palms start to sweat. "Um, listen, Spencer, can I talk to you for a second?"

Spencer looked hesitant, glanced around as if some other obligation would present itself.

"Just for a second. I promise." Rebecca held out an arm behind her. "There's an empty office over here." At the look Spencer gave her, Rebecca forced herself to smile and said, "We'll leave the door open."

Seeming to realize she was being a bit silly, Spencer grinned. "Sure." She followed Rebecca to the office, sparsely appointed with a simple metal desk and two chairs.

Neither of them sat, and Rebecca stared at the industrial gray carpet for a moment, scrambling for the words she'd rehearsed all day. "Listen, Spencer, about Saturday…" She looked up at the ceiling, hunting through her brain for the right way to say what she wanted to say. There was so much. So many things. Finally giving up, she blurted, "Can we be friends? Please?"

Spencer blinked at her, the surprise on her face clear. "Really?"

Rebecca's smile was genuine this time. "Yes, really. I like you. Physical attraction aside, I like you."

"Really?" Spencer asked again. "'Cause I was pretty sure you didn't. Physical attraction aside."

The chuckle came from deep in Rebecca's stomach; she felt it rumble up. "Yeah, I know. That was on me and I'm sorry. I was an asshole for…reasons that had nothing to do with you."

Spencer studied her with those gorgeous blue eyes the color of an early-April spring sky, as if trying to read her thoughts. Several seconds ticked by before she said quietly, "I like you, too."

"Good." Rebecca gave one nod and tried to tamp down her relief. "Friends it is, then."

Spencer tilted her head. "Will it be awkward?"

"Not if we don't let it."

"Is it that simple?" Spencer pushed a grimace to one side of her face.

"I say yes."

"Well, okay then. As long as you say yes." The laugh that bubbled out of Spencer was cute and inviting, deeper than Rebecca expected, but still very feminine.

"You'd better get yourself changed, young lady. You don't want to make your trainer mad because you're late for class."

Spencer groaned, dropped her head back toward her shoulder blades. "God, she's *such* a hardass."

"Hey!" Rebecca swiped playfully at her as Spencer dodged her, hurried out of the office and down to the locker room, where she disappeared inside. Rebecca breathed a sigh of relief.

Friends. This is good.

Things had changed during class. It was obvious. Spencer was more relaxed, even as she worked her ass off doing all the lunges and squats Rebecca demanded of her. Rebecca did her best to be encouraging and Spencer seemed to work extra hard. And there was joking. Fun teasing.

"You want to feel it deep in that ass," Rebecca said, of the squats the brides were doing.

"That's what she said," Spencer muttered, causing Lucy to bust out into a laugh that was quickly followed by the other three women. Soon, all five of them and Rebecca were doubled over in fits of laughter.

"You're all useless," Rebecca said, waving a dismissive hand at her class, her own laughter only just dying down. "Do some stretches, then get the hell out of my gym. See you Wednesday." She left them, shaking her head and smiling widely at the familiar joke, and headed to her desk, her day just about done.

It had been the first time that she actually enjoyed the bride class. They were fun. They worked hard. Rebecca was proud of them. Proud of Spencer. She wanted to tell her how well she was doing, that she could see changes in her, significant shifting of mass and building of muscle. But now she was a bit worried it could be taken the wrong way, so she'd stayed quiet, encouraging the class as a whole instead.

Now, her stuff gathered, she slung her bag over her shoulder and headed toward the front desk and door. A glance to her right told her Spencer was at the smoothie bar, and before she could think about it, her body turned and walked in that direction as if she wasn't in command of her feet.

Spencer saw her coming and held up her hands. "Back! Stay back, smoothie spiller!"

Rebecca barked a laugh. "That was so not my fault, little Miss Doesn't Watch Where She's Going."

"I'm on towels tonight, Rebecca," came Bobby Pine's voice, followed by the squeaking wheels of the cart he pushed. "I'm gonna wash 'em all up good."

"I know you will, Bob. Nobody's better at it than you."

He held out a fist as he approached and Rebecca bumped it with her own. "Was it a good day for you?"

Rebecca glanced at Spencer, then back toward him. "It was."

"I'm going to make my night good, too. I am determined!" He turned to Spencer. "Hello, blond lady."

"Hi," Spencer said with a grin. "I'm Spencer." Rebecca was pleasantly surprised to see that her face held no negative reactions to Bobby, unlike a large majority of people. No fear. No hesitation. Her smile was genuine and then she offered him her fist, which delighted him.

"Nice to meet you, Spencer. I'm Bobby."

"Nice to meet you, Bobby."

"Okay. I have to wash these towels now. And then fold them, which I don't like."

"I don't blame you," Spencer said. "Folding is my least favorite thing to do."

Bobby's face lit up at the discovery of common ground. He turned to Rebecca. "She's nice. I like her."

Rebecca grinned at him and waved him off in the direction of the laundry room. "See you tomorrow, Bob."

"Bye, Rebecca," he called as he pushed the cart away. "Bye, blond—er, Spencer."

They watched him go until he was out of sight. When Rebecca turned her gaze back toward the smoothie bar, Spencer was looking at her.

"You're good with him," she said.

"No reason not to be. He's a good guy. Works hard."

"Not everybody sees that first. They see that he's different and they judge. Immediately."

Rebecca cocked her head and raised her eyebrows.

"My brother is intellectually disabled."

"Ah," Rebecca said with a nod. That explained why Spencer had never been put off by Bobby. "I didn't know that."

"I have looked out for him all my life."

"That can be hard on a kid. He older or younger?"

"Younger."

"Well, he's lucky to have you for a big sister." She smiled as the girl behind the counter slid a smoothie in front of Spencer, noticed the color. "Blueberry this time?"

"If I had known you would be this close to me, I'd have ordered something with less staining power. Vanilla, probably."

"Oh, you're hilarious." But Rebecca couldn't keep the smile from her face. This was good. It felt...easier to be around Spencer since they talked. *Friends. Who knew?* "Okay, I've got to run." She reached out a hand, gave Spencer's shoulder a squeeze. "See you Wednesday."

"Have a good one."

Rebecca headed out the doors and to her car, the smile still there, her mind still a jumble of thoughts, but a different mix than the past couple of days. This was the right thing. Friends was the right thing. Much as she'd flashed back to their time in her house, as often as she thought about how amazing it was to kiss Spencer, to hold Spencer's warm, soft breast in her hand, she knew this was the right path. She'd let herself get sucked in, as had Spencer, and the best thing to do now was to step back. She had thoughts about the state of Spencer's relationship—so many thoughts!—but it wasn't her place to voice them. And really, what did she actually *know*? Like, for a fact? Only things she assumed, and assuming was never good.

She gave her head a literal shake as she slid into the driver's seat.

Forward. That was the only way to go.

Shifting into gear, Rebecca headed home.

CHAPTER FIFTEEN

The cool weather was probably the reason Turtle's was so busy that Sunday afternoon. The cool weather and football. While not a new bar by any stretch of the imagination, it was new to Lucy's fiancé, Ethan.

"He wants to check out the football-watching scene," Lucy had told Spencer on the phone that morning. "I need a friend to sit with because he's going to be glued to the TVs and I'll be bored inside of ten minutes."

Spencer laughed. "I don't know, Luce. My Sunday was going to be very exciting, what with the cleaning of the bathroom and the washing of my sheets. Not sure you can measure up."

"Ha ha. Very funny. Please. I'm begging you."

"I know better than to turn away a woman who's begging me, and I actually enjoy football. What time?"

It was after two by the time Spencer entered Turtle's, and she stopped inside to let her eyes adjust. It was sunny out, but also the end of September, so the temperatures were starting to cool down. When she could finally see, Lucy's hand was waving back and forth like she was at a concert. Spencer headed toward the small table.

"I'm so glad you're here," Lucy said as she stood and wrapped Spencer in a hug. "This is my fiancé, Ethan. Honey, this is Spencer."

"Ah, the infamous Spencer." Ethan was of average height and average appearance, but his dark eyes were inviting and friendly and his sandy hair made Spencer clench her fist to keep from ruffling it.

He just seemed…warm. She expected nothing less from the man who'd landed Lucy Schubert. "It's so nice to finally have a face to go with the name. Lucy talks about you all the time." He held out his hand, shook Spencer's with a firm grip, then indicated the empty chair. "Sit. Can I get you something?"

"The waitress is a bit overwhelmed," Lucy told her. "So we've been going to the bar to get drinks."

"I'd love a beer," Spencer said. "Anything light is fine."

"You got it." Ethan waved off Spencer's offer of money and sidled up to the bar.

"I'm so glad you're here," Lucy practically squealed again, closing her hand over Spencer's. "Thank you!"

"Hey, don't thank me until I'm sure this is more exciting than wiping out the inside of my microwave. Jury's still out."

"Where's Marti today?"

"She had some client brunch thing to go to."

Lucy nodded, and Spencer caught something flash across her face. Before she could ask about it, Ethan was back.

"One light beer and one Amaretto sour," he announced, delivering the women their drinks.

The next hour went by quickly; Spencer was surprised when she'd glanced at her watch. Turtle's only got busier, with more people arriving than leaving. Every barstool around the U-shaped bar was occupied, and the seven TVs showed several football games. Spencer was amused every time cheers went up in one part of the bar, but not the rest. Ethan was as absorbed in the games as Lucy predicted, so Spencer really didn't have much opportunity to talk to him, but it was fine. She liked him anyway, and chatting about mundane things with Lucy was always entertaining.

"My turn to buy a round," Spencer said as Lucy drained her glass. Empties in hand, she approached the bar, found a tiny sliver of space between a burly bearded man in his forties and a slim, college-age guy wearing a bit too much cologne, and slid into it sideways. "Sorry," she said when Beardy looked her way.

"Not a problem," he said, with a friendly smile and inched himself over to make more room.

In the several minutes it took for a bartender to even notice her, Spencer looked around. People watched. The crowd was overwhelmingly male, which was unsurprising, but there were a few jersey-clad women scattered among the guys. There were groups of friends, obviously there together, judging by their high fives and clinking of beer glasses. There were also a few that seemed solo, sitting quietly, sipping their cocktails, watching the various TVs. As Spencer scanned around the bar, her gaze stopped. Or rather was stopped. By a brunette directly across from where Spencer stood.

Rebecca.

She was full-on laughing about something (Spencer realized she'd never actually heard that laugh), head thrown back, teeth showing. Then she punched the large man next to her in the arm and pointed at the guy sitting on the other side of him.

"Miss?"

Spencer blinked and was pulled back to her own space at the bar by the bartender, who looked at her expectantly.

"Oh. Sorry." She placed her order, which came quickly, paid, and sent a last glance toward Rebecca before returning to Lucy and Ethan.

What are the chances?

Lucy thanked her. "We're probably heading out when this game is over."

And they did.

"I'm going to hang and watch some of the next game," Spencer said, as Lucy hugged her and thanked her again for "saving me from the dullsville of football."

Ethan also hugged her, saying, "Thanks for actually liking football."

Spencer smiled as she watched them go. Several people were leaving, as if it was a changing of the guards with the new games starting. A couple of stools opened up, and Spencer grabbed up her jacket, purse, and half-drunk beer, and snagged the one next to Beardy. Cologne Guy had apparently left.

As she settled in and got comfortable, she did her best not to look toward where she'd seen Rebecca. That wasn't why she'd stayed, right? She stayed to watch the next game get started and finish her beer.

Yeah. That's what she was doing.

She lasted about six minutes before her body betrayed her and her head turned away from the TV and in that general direction. Rebecca was looking right at her, what seemed to be a mix of surprise and happiness on her face. With a come-hither wave of her hand, she invited Spencer to sit with them, indicating what must have been an empty stool next to her.

Spencer thought about it. She did. Thought about politely shaking her head no. Thought about quietly slipping off her stool and leaving. And slip off her stool she did, once again gathering up her jacket, her purse, her beer. But then she was walking toward Rebecca, rounding the bar as she saw her lean toward the big man next to her and say something. Then both of them watched Spencer's approach.

"Hi," Rebecca said, when Spencer arrived. "What are you doing here?"

Spencer got up onto the stool and settled herself. "I met Lucy and her fiancé. We've been sitting at a table over there since two." She pointed with her chin.

"No way. I can't believe I didn't see you."

"It's busy here."

"True." Rebecca leaned slightly back in her stool so Spencer could see the big man next to her. "Spencer, this is my friend Nick." She pointed past him. "And that's Dwayne."

Nick held a meaty hand out to her. "It's great to meet you, Spencer. I've heard a lot about you." Spencer shook, not sure if she'd seen Rebecca kick him or if she'd just been shifting her feet.

"Nice to meet you both," Spencer said, shaking Dwayne's hand as well.

"You like football?" Nick asked.

Spencer tipped her head from one side to the other. "Yeah, I do. I'm not a rabid fan, but I like to have the game on on Sundays, even if I'm doing something else."

"Nick here is a TV sports whore," Rebecca said, sipping what looked like club soda with lime.

"I take offense to that," Nick said, and pressed a hand to his chest in obviously feigned shock. "Evidently, your friend here knows the pleasures of watching sports on TV." He shifted his gaze to Spencer. "Right? Do you watch baseball?"

"In the stadium, yes. On TV? Bores me to tears."

"Hockey?" he asked.

"If they're smashing each other against the Plexiglas."

"Golf?"

"God, no," Spencer said, enjoying the sparring and the way Rebecca was looking from Nick to her and back.

"Tennis."

"Often."

"Nascar."

"Nascar is cars driving in a circle, Nick. Zzzzz."

Rebecca's laugh burst out of her and Spencer noted it was the second time that day she'd heard it. And loved it. "She's got a point, Nicky."

Nick merely shook his head as he narrowed his eyes at Spencer. "I'm undecided about you."

"I completely understand." Spencer held her beer glass toward him, and he touched his to it with a chuckle.

"So," Rebecca said as the guys turned back to the game. "Come here often?"

Spencer grinned. "Original."

"I try."

"Actually, I've never been in here before." Spencer took a swig of her beer. "I've seen it. Driven past many times. But this is my first time inside."

"And your verdict?"

"It's…a bar."

Rebecca nodded. "That it is."

"What about you? Regular hangout for you? You don't seem like a sports bar kind of girl."

Rebecca feigned a gasp. "Why would you say such a thing?"

"Mostly because of the club soda," Spencer said, pointing at the glass with her eyes.

"Damn it. That gets me every time." They shared a grin and Rebecca went on. "I wouldn't say this is a regular hangout for me, but it is for Nick, and if I want to spend time with him, I generally have to come here. So by extension, yeah. I guess I am sort of a regular."

"And how do you two know each other?" Spencer asked.

Rebecca opened her mouth to answer, but Nick spoke first. "We were in high school together and Becks here fell madly in love with me. Sadly, the line of hot chicks ahead of her was very long and she got tired of waiting. Decided she'd have better luck with the ladies."

Rebecca punched him playfully. "A small part of that story is true."

"The better luck with the ladies part?" Spencer asked. Rebecca touched a finger to the tip of her nose and Spencer laughed. "Also... Becks?"

"Don't do it," Dwayne warned her. "I tried once."

"What happened?"

"She threw a glass at me!" Dwayne's eyes were wide in mock horror.

"Plastic cup," Rebecca muttered to Spencer.

"I almost lost an eye!"

"It bounced off his head," Rebecca clarified. "He hardly felt it."

"She's crazy," Dwayne went on. "Don't cross her."

"Word," said Nick with a sage nod, and sipped his beer.

"I hate both of these men," Rebecca said to Spencer. "I really do. No idea how I ended up sitting with them."

"Because you can't resist our charms," Nick said.

"Word," Dwayne said, stealing Nick's comment.

"I like them," Spencer said and meant it. "They're funny."

Nick turned to look at Rebecca. "Why don't you switch stools with her? She's a lot nicer than you."

Rebecca nodded enthusiastically. "First true thing you've said in hours. I completely agree."

Spencer watched this banter for the better part of an hour, sometimes included, sometimes just listening and then laughing out loud. It might have been longer than an hour. She hadn't checked her watch once since sitting down next to Rebecca. They were so much fun, these three. It was obvious how much they cared about each other. Even more interesting was how much more relaxed Rebecca was around them. Not that Spencer had ever thought of her as tense or uptight…it was simply a level of comfort that was very apparent. And it looked good on her.

When halftime arrived, Spencer reluctantly began gathering her things.

"You leaving?" Rebecca asked, her tone tinted with an obvious touch of disappointment.

"Yeah, I really need to. I have to swing by my parents' house, and I've got some work stuff to catch up on before tomorrow."

"Real estate stuff," Rebecca said.

Spencer was pleased she remembered. "Yes. Real estate stuff."

"Well, it's not like I won't see you again tomorrow."

"Very true."

"I'm glad you came and sat with me." Rebecca's smile was different this time. It felt like it was just for Spencer.

"Me, too." Spencer slid off her stool, then touched Nick's back. "It was great to meet you guys," she said when Nick and Dwayne both turned to her.

"Same here," Nick said. "We're here every Sunday."

"And sometimes Mondays," Dwayne offered.

"Occasionally Thursdays," Nick said.

Spencer laughed. "Got it. You live here. I'll come visit." Turning her gaze back to Rebecca, she reached out, touched her upper arm. A beat passed as their eye contact held. Finally, Spencer squeezed, let go. "I'll see you tomorrow."

A weird duo of feelings tangoed in her head as Spencer headed out to her car, a mix of a necessity to leave and a desire to run back inside and stay until…whenever. She forced her feet to keep moving, got in her car, and drove out of the parking lot faster than she should have.

❖

"Wow," Nick said, not looking at Rebecca.

"What? What does that mean?" She squinted at him.

Nick casually took a swig of his beer and dug into the massive plate of nachos he'd ordered to share with them (though both Rebecca and Dwayne knew he'd eat most of them). "Nothing. Just wow."

"Wow, this game sucks? Wow, these nachos are awesome?"

"Wow, you really like her, and she likes you." Nick crunched a chip, his eyes on the TV.

"I told you. We're friends. We talked about it."

"Friends who've fucked."

"God, you're so eloquent." Rebecca reached for a chip, took one with a jalapeño on it.

"I'm just stating the facts."

Rebecca slumped a bit on her stool, not happy with what Nick was saying but knowing it had a bit of truth to it. She *did* like Spencer. She was growing to like her more and more with each chance they spent time together. For the first time, part of her began to second-guess the "friends" part of their equation. "Doesn't matter. She's engaged. She's taken."

"Yeah? Where was her fiancée?"

"I have no idea."

"Nope. And you didn't ask."

"No."

Should she feel bad about that? Rebecca knew that Nick was making a point, but she didn't think it was her responsibility to inquire after Spencer's significant other. If Spencer wanted to talk about her, Spencer could bring her up. That made sense, right?

She reached for another chip, crunched it, and was content to let the conversation be over.

Nick had other plans.

"So," he said, actually turning to her as there was a commercial on. "How do you think this friendship is going to work?"

"What do you mean?"

"I mean, have you ever seen me stay friends with a girl I banged?"

"Again with the eloquence. And I've told you a million times, Nicky, it's—"

"Different for lesbians than for straight couples. I know you say that, but I don't buy it."

Dwayne apparently decided to join in, but surprisingly, took Rebecca's side. "I don't know, dude. It makes sense. Girls do friendship differently than guys."

"Thank you, Dwayne."

Nick simply shook his head and continued to eat. "I just want you to pay attention, Becks. You're walking through a minefield, my friend."

Accepting that there wasn't going to be a resolution to this discussion, Rebecca shrugged and said, "I will. I promise."

"That's all I ask."

The game was back on and the trio focused their attention on it, but Nick's words stuck with Rebecca for the rest of their time together and well into the evening. Home alone, folding laundry, his minefield comment reverberated through her brain.

Was that what she was doing by trying to be friends with Spencer? Walking through a minefield, the possibility of getting blown to bits right there all the time?

Rebecca wasn't sure she agreed with that.

She understood the limits. She understood the lines. Yes, they'd both crossed them, Spencer with regard to her engagement, Rebecca with regard to her job. They'd both made the same mistake. But they'd talked about it. Sort of. They'd agreed that they'd like to be friends. And while Rebecca couldn't speak for Spencer, she did know that she enjoyed Spencer's company more and more, and she didn't think she should feel bad about that, as Nick seemed to think.

Laundry folded and put away, Rebecca pulled out her laptop and sat down on the couch, determined to catch up on some of the fitness reading she did every Sunday evening. Notebook by her side, she'd jot down interesting things she learned and how they could benefit which clients.

At the very least, it would take her mind off her conversation with Nick. Off Spencer.

Until tomorrow, anyway.

CHAPTER SIXTEEN

H ave a good day." Marti kissed the top of Spencer's head as she walked past her in the kitchen.

"You, too. See you tonight." Spencer sat parked along the breakfast bar, working on her laptop and sipping her coffee. She watched as Marti left, looking ridiculously entrepreneurial in her new charcoal gray suit. Spencer would be spending the evening with Marti at a nice restaurant with some of her work friends, as Marti had new clients to wine and dine. Her role of partner was demanding, but she seemed to be loving it. It was something she'd worked hard for; Spencer knew that, and she was proud of Marti.

Only one more class to get through this week. She'd managed both Monday and Wednesday without too much personal contact with Rebecca. Which wasn't easy. Sunday had been a bit of a wake-up call for Spencer. When the reality of how much she'd enjoyed spending time with Rebecca, of how much she'd have rather stayed on the barstool next to her than do just about any other thing in the world, hit her, it hit her hard. Friends was one thing. Being friends with Rebecca was fine. Perfectly acceptable. But being really close friends could be dangerous.

"Careful there…"

Mary Beth's warning on Sunday night echoed through her head. After she'd stopped at her parents and spent a little time with them, she'd called Mary Beth from the car on her way home, told her where she'd been that day.

"Careful there..."

It was all she'd said about it, but those two words weighed a *ton* as they settled on Spencer's shoulders. They'd stayed with her the rest of Sunday and into the week. She'd gone to class. She'd enjoyed it, but every time she and Rebecca made eye contact, every time Rebecca smiled at her, Spencer heard it.

"Careful there..."

She'd avoided spending any alone time with Rebecca all week and instead, had focused on paying more attention to Marti, who barely seemed to notice.

Spencer was starting to feel adrift. Nothing to hold on to. No idea which direction would lead her where. Alone and lonely.

That was it, and the realization was like a slap.

She was lonely.

In her relationship. In her life. She was lonely. And she recognized now that she'd felt that way for a very long time, but hadn't even been able to put a name to it, to verbalize it.

She took a sip of coffee, but it burned like acid as it flowed down her throat, so she tossed the rest of it into the sink, gathered her things, and headed for work. She needed other things to take her focus because this kind of thinking wasn't helping her at all.

It wasn't unusual for Spencer to be the first one in the office, and today was no exception. Realtors worked crazy hours, worse than retail, and had to be at the beck and call of their clients. That meant their evenings and weekends were often marred by work. That also meant that very few of them were in by nine in the morning.

Spencer was okay with that. She enjoyed having the place to herself. It wasn't a big office, but she sort of felt like it was her domain. The Realtors worked outside, at houses and condos, but the office? The office belonged to Spencer. She took her time getting her things organized, checking the general email box, jotting down or forwarding any messages for the requested agents. She opened the miniblinds and watered the plants she'd added here and there to give the place a warm and inviting feel. Most importantly, she replenished the supplies around the Keurig. Her agents drank *a lot* of coffee.

She'd just doctored up her own cup when Jennifer arrived, consistently the first one there after Spencer.

"Good morning, Ms. Thompson," Jennifer said, with a big smile.

"Hey," Spencer said as they passed. She took a seat back at her desk.

Jennifer put her purse into her bottom desk drawer, then went to the coffee station and popped a pod into it. As she waited, she stared at Spencer, who could feel it.

With an audible sigh, she looked up from her computer. "What?" she said, staring back at Jennifer. "Why are you looking at me?"

The Keurig beeped and Jennifer poured powdered creamer into her cup, stirred it as she approached Spencer's desk. She pulled up a chair and sat at the end so she could cross her legs and stare some more. "You going to tell me what's been bothering you?"

Goddamn it. She could never keep anything from Jennifer. Still, she tried. "What do you mean?"

"Seriously?" Jennifer simply cocked her head and said, "Why do you even try?"

"I don't know," Spencer said, and dropped her head in defeat. Jennifer was a wizard at reading her and her moods. "Why aren't you a psychologist or something?"

"I'm not smooth enough." Jennifer sipped her coffee. "I have no time to waste on leading somebody to their problem."

Spencer gave a snort. "Yeah, good point. Probably better you're not."

"Just tell me what it is, damn it. Consider me your psychologist and tell me why your moods have been all over the place all week. I'm having trouble keeping up. You need a weekly wall chart or a daily sign on your desk so I know what I'm going to get each morning." When Spencer didn't laugh, Jennifer grew serious and sat up. "Okay. Talk to me. What's up?"

There was little internal debate. Spencer spilled. She told Jennifer everything, reiterating the beginnings of the bride class—which Jennifer already knew—to how she'd quit, to Rebecca's up and down and back and forth, to the spilled smoothie and the surprise kiss that had come of it, to Spencer going to Rebecca's house and practically throwing herself at her, and Rebecca's request to be friends, and up to now. She was slightly winded when she finished, and she absently wondered if she'd taken a breath at all anywhere during the telling.

Jennifer's eyes had widened several times, but she didn't say a word. And now she sat quietly, staring at Spencer, her mouth opening, then closing, then opening again.

Spencer waited, wondering if she'd just ended a friendship because she couldn't control herself and Jennifer disapproved.

"Well," Jennifer said finally, and sipped her coffee. "That is…a lot to process."

"Tell me about it."

"What have you decided to do?"

"What do you mean?" Spencer furrowed her brow.

"I mean, you cheated on your fiancée, Spence."

"Yeah, I'm aware."

"Are you going to tell Marti? Leave her? Do you want to be with the fitness instructor? What are you going to do?"

Spencer turned her gaze toward the window. The little bit of morning sun had vanished behind clouds that were blowing in fast. It was going to storm, and Spencer willed it to come. It would match her mood. "I have no idea," she said quietly, surprised but not at how much Jennifer sounded like Mary Beth. "I really, really don't."

❖

Class went along smoothly, and despite Rebecca wearing some tight-fitting pants and doing a lot of smiling, Spencer was able to focus on the moves, on the workout, and really put herself into it. Truth be told, she was starting to see results herself, not just hear about how they'd be noticeable eventually, and it was invigorating. Made her want to work harder and more often. In fact, there was a spin class tomorrow she might hit and a yoga class on Sunday afternoon she was interested in.

The divide in the class had decreased as well, which Spencer credited Rebecca for. She talked to them all about health and wellness, about how their diets were just as important as their workouts, how their weight was simply a number and didn't matter at all if they felt good, if they felt strong and healthy. Even Brittany seemed on her way to believing she didn't need to be a size 2 to look and feel great at her wedding.

They finished up class, and Rebecca bid them all a good weekend, then went off to do whatever it was she did after class. Spencer watched her go. She tried not to, but those pants...

"What exciting things are on your Friday night schedule?" Lucy asked her, yanking her back to reality.

"Oh," Spencer said, shifting her attention. Together, they fell into step and walked to the locker room. "My car's in the shop, so Marti is picking me up and we're going to meet some of her work friends for dinner and drinks."

"That sounds fun." Lucy spun the dial on her lock, popped it open.

Spencer shrugged. "It'll be fine. I don't know these people very well and they always end up talking business, even when they promise they won't. So we significant others will have to start up our own conversations or sit there and twiddle our thumbs."

"Well, if it wouldn't seem weird for your fiancée to bring *two* people with her, one of whom is a total stranger, I'd totally go with you and chat with you while they talk shop. I owe you for last weekend." Lucy's smile was bright, as always, and again, Spencer wondered what it must be like to be that happy all the time.

"You're a swell friend."

"That I am." Lucy slammed her locker shut and shouldered her bag. "Catch you Monday."

Spencer took her time changing out of her workout attire and back into her work clothes. Eyeing herself in the mirror, her gaze was critical. As usual. Marti's work friends made her uncomfortable, and Spencer didn't blame them. It wasn't their issue. They never *tried* to make her uncomfortable. It was all Spencer. She never felt on the same level as them, with their designer clothes and seventeen different college degrees. She always felt a bit "lesser than" around them.

Staring at her reflection in the mirror and scrutinizing her black slacks, white button-up top, and black pumps took much longer than it should have. When Spencer glanced at the clock on the locker room wall, she gasped and muttered, "Son of a nutcracker." Marti would be getting impatient. When her things were stuffed haphazardly into her gym bag, she fished out her phone and turned the sound back on. Three texts from Marti.

Coming out soon?

Where are you?

We're going to be late!

That last one was crucial because Marti hated to be late. It completely stressed her out, therefore, it completely stressed Spencer out. She slammed her locker and headed for the exit as quickly as she could without actually running.

The sight that greeted her in the parking lot nearly made her stop dead in her tracks. It was only by sheer force of self-preservation that her feet kept moving, because Marti was out of the car, standing at the open car door, her forearms braced across the top of it. She was grinning as she talked to none other than Rebecca McCall.

"There she is," Marti said as she saw Spencer. "About time."

"Sorry," Spencer said, as Rebecca turned and their eyes locked. "I got distracted."

"What else is new?" Marti asked, her tone light. But Spencer knew she was irritated. "I was just about to come in and get you when Rebecca here came out. I asked her if she knew you. She said she did, very well."

Spencer didn't dare look at Rebecca.

"She's my star pupil," Rebecca said, surprising Spencer.

"Yeah? Well, that's quite a surprise," Marti said.

Spencer opened the back door to the car and tossed her things inside, slammed the door and stood beside Marti.

Every single thing about this situation felt weird to her. Every. Single. Thing.

"Why a surprise?" Rebecca asked, and Spencer did look at her then. Her gaze was riveted on Marti, and Spencer was pretty sure she saw the quick flash of an angry nostril flare.

"Spencer isn't exactly the most athletic of women," Marti said with a chuckle, and there was something about the way she said it, as if it was the most obvious fact in the world, that set Spencer's teeth on edge.

"I guess you've never seen her in the gym," Rebecca said, her voice very, very low.

Marti's grin didn't reach her eyes, and that did nothing to help Spencer's discomfort. "I haven't. You're right. But she's always been a little...soft." Marti put her arm around Spencer's shoulder and squeezed her closer. "Don't get me wrong. I like her that way."

Rebecca's eyes never left Marti, and Spencer could all but see the storm brewing in them. "She's anything but soft. She works really hard in class and she's getting results. Visible results."

The way Rebecca emphasized the word "visible" sent a flood of warmth rushing through Spencer. The how, the why, the what-the-hell-is-going-on, all of it shot through her like fast-moving water, and she had such a barrage of mixed feelings hit that she worried for a split second she might faint.

"If you say so," Marti said, that same chilly smile on her face as she shrugged.

"We should get going," Spencer finally managed to make herself say, and ducked out from under Marti's arm. Her eyes met Rebecca's as she passed, the storm clouds still gathering in them, and she gave Rebecca's arm a quick squeeze as she continued by and around the car. "Have a great weekend, Rebecca. See you Monday." A little wave later, she got into the passenger seat and emptied her lungs in a whoosh.

Marti slammed her door shut and keyed the ignition. "Jesus, she's uptight, huh?" She shook her head as she shifted the car and drove them out of the parking lot.

So many things flew through Spencer's mind at the moment. So many possible replies, most of which were not gentle or kind or happy. But they were on their way to meet people, and the last thing

Spencer wanted to do was walk into the restaurant in a fight with Marti. Nothing would make the evening drag on more.

She kept quiet.

In her sideview mirror, she could still see Rebecca. Standing tall like a sentry. Standing up for Spencer.

A small smile crept its way onto Spencer's face.

❖

"Ugh. She was just...smarmy. You know what I mean?" Rebecca shook her head in disgust and sipped her club soda. "So fucking smarmy."

"I like that word." Zoe swigged her beer as she leaned an elbow on the bar and regarded Rebecca. "Smarmy. It's a good word."

"I mean, Spencer was standing *right there*. Right next to her. Who does that? Who calls their partner soft and unathletic in front of somebody they just met?" Rebecca had hoped the boiling of her blood would ease a bit once she got to the bar and met Zoe, once she had some nice, icy cold club soda in her system, but no such luck. She was just as annoyed as she had been an hour ago as she'd watched Spencer sit silently next to her fiancée and drive away. "For Christ's sake," she muttered, turning to face the bar and bracing her forearms on it like a regular. She glanced up at Zoe, who was looking at her with what Rebecca could only label amusement, but she couldn't seem to stop. "I mean, she obviously hasn't looked at Spencer at all lately. Like, *at all*."

"No? What makes you say that?"

"Because she's got muscles!" Rebecca's voice was louder than she'd intended, and she sank her head down into her shoulders a bit and lowered the volume. "Because she's been working hard and she's getting results, and how does the person who loves her not even notice that?"

"Yeah." It was all Zoe said and when Rebecca glanced her way, she was shaking her head, eyebrows raised as she took a swig of her beer.

"What?"

Zoe continued to shake her head slowly, but added a shrug for good measure. "Man."

"What?" Rebecca asked again.

"You got it bad for this one."

Rebecca opened her mouth to protest. Her brain scrambled for arguments, sifting through a variety of options. Instead, she inhaled a big breath and let it out slowly. "Goddamn it." It was true. She did have it bad for Spencer. And she'd been fine until the sex. She hung her head and let out a tiny cry of despair. "Why did I have to sleep with her? Why did I let that happen?"

"Because we are weak, silly creatures, my friend."

Rebecca groaned, then downed her club soda like it was a shot of whiskey and slid the glass across the bar for a refill. When a new glass was in her hand, she turned to Zoe and said simply, "I want to protect her. I want to stand up for her. Is that weird?"

"Absolutely not," Zoe said and signaled the bartender for another bottle. "It says a lot about the kind of person you are."

"Stupid and self-deprecating?"

"Exactly." Zoe let out a chuckle and touched her beer bottle to Rebecca's glass. "Nah," she amended, after they'd sipped. "You're okay."

"I need to get her out of my head, Zo. I've got no business messing in there. I need to step off."

"You do." Zoe's eyes tracked a young, pretty blonde across the bar. "Too bad the heart wants what the heart wants, huh?"

Rebecca scoffed.

"Right now, mine wants that." She pointed at the retreating figure. "Be right back. Maybe." And Zoe was off, sauntering across the bar toward the pool table where the blonde had stopped to watch the game.

Rebecca spun on her stool and sat with her back against the bar. She'd been excited to get the invitation from Zoe to join her out for a drink after work. Rebecca's first client that morning had come in at 5:30 a.m. and she'd gone nonstop ever since. A relaxing drink after a busy day sounded great. And despite how often they texted, she hadn't seen Zoe face-to-face in quite a while.

And then she'd walked into the parking lot and been a nice person and veered toward what was obviously a businesswoman who had gotten out of her car and was waving Rebecca over, poised to ask a question.

Marti Daniels. That was her name. That was how she introduced herself when she shook Rebecca's hand, but the name hadn't clicked. She wasn't unattractive. A little plain, maybe, but neat, well-dressed, great smile. Her dark hair was sleek and expensively styled. Her suit was designer. Her car was a Lexus. Then she asked if Rebecca knew Spencer Thompson.

Pieces started to snap into place.

"She's my girlfriend and she was supposed to meet me out here"—a glance at her gold watch—"fifteen minutes ago."

"Oh, you're the fiancée," Rebecca had said, before she could stop herself.

"I am. You know Spencer?"

"I'm the instructor of the bride class. Rebecca McCall."

"Ah, the infamous Rebecca."

Rebecca wasn't sure what that meant, but chose to let it slide by. "You signed Spencer up for the class." Again, not what she'd thought about saying, but it popped out and, in that moment, Rebecca was very curious to hear some details.

And then Spencer had appeared, and there went Rebecca's chance.

Zoe swaggered back to the bar a few minutes later and sat on her stool.

"Shot down?" Rebecca asked.

"Like an intrusive drone," Zoe answered, with a disappointed shake of her head. She turned to Rebecca. "How're you doing, my friend? Rehashing the parking lot scene?"

"Every last word."

"Women, man."

They sipped in tandem.

"Women." Rebecca exhaled slowly. "What am I going to do, Zoe?"

CHAPTER SEVENTEEN

"All right. What is it? What did I do?" Marti stood next to their bed in her LSU T-shirt and underwear as she watched Spencer pull throw pillows from it and toss them onto the floor.

"Nothing."

With a much put-upon sigh, Marti flopped onto the bed. "You've been quiet all night, and you've barely looked at me."

Spencer stopped what she was doing and did look at her then. *Really* looked at her. Marti didn't appear all that worried. She didn't seem terribly concerned. In fact, she looked slightly bored, like this was something she dealt with all the time and it tired her. That only fanned the flames inside Spencer's gut.

"I am not soft, Marti."

Marti's eyes widened for a moment. That was followed by the furrowing of her brow and some rapid blinking. "What?"

Spencer threw down the last pillow and yanked the covers down. "I. Am not. Soft."

It still took a beat or two before Marti caught up. "Oh. Oh! The trainer at the gym." She laughed and slid under the covers, reached for a book on the nightstand.

"'Oh, the trainer at the gym?' That's all you're going to say?" Spencer stood next to the bed, covers gripped in one hand, and stared at this woman she was beginning to wonder if she even knew at all.

"I don't know what you *want* me to say, Spencer." Marti was clearly frustrated, dropping her book down into her lap so she could meet Spencer's angry gaze.

And that was the problem, wasn't it? Marti never knew what to say to her because she needed to make sure it was what Spencer *wanted* her to say.

"You know what? Never mind. It's fine. It's whatever." Spencer slid under the covers and turned onto her side so her back was to Marti. She was being alarmingly passive-aggressive and she knew it, but it was as if all the energy left her like she was a deflated balloon, and she simply no longer had it in her. It was there, the fight, the spark, and then it was gone. Just like that. Suddenly, she was so tired she could barely think.

"You sure?" Marti asked, and the warmth of her hand landed on Spencer's shoulder.

It took everything Spencer had to keep from shrugging it off. "I'm sure. Good night."

"'Night, babe."

It wasn't the first time Spencer had silently cried in bed while Marti lay next to her, often awake.

I'm a mess.

That sentence played over and over again, ran through her head like a train on a circular track. Round and round, never changing, never altering its course.

Chelsea had done this to her.

No.

She had *let* Chelsea do this to her. Big difference. Chelsea had mowed her down like a combine over a field of wheat, and Spencer hadn't been able to get up again. She sometimes felt like she was still lying there, flattened, worthless, completely unable to read any sort of feeling or sign or emotion from another, a failure of epic proportions. Other times, it was as though she'd managed to get to her hands and knees. Or even to a squat. But it had been a disturbingly long time since she'd felt like she was actually standing tall, to her full height. She always felt a little bit hunched. A little bit bent, like she was hiding, flying under the radar so she wouldn't get called on. Called on to what, she wasn't sure. To speak? To be seen? To live? Who knew?

Rebecca saw her.

Those three simple words bolstered her somehow. In a world where she'd become the background, where she'd begun to feel like nothing more than window dressing, Rebecca saw her.

And then the bolstering faltered. Because *did* Rebecca see her? How could Spencer be sure? She'd thought Chelsea saw her as well, but that ended up an enormous disaster because Spencer had wildly miscalculated. Maybe that was exactly what was happening now.

It wasn't like she didn't have options. She did. One choice was to run. She could throw everything away, be honest with Marti, move the very small amount of her belongings she'd brought over back to her house, and be done. She could do that, even though it made her a little ill to think about it. Or she could double down on this relationship, on her upcoming marriage. Stop worrying so much, stop analyzing every aspect of it and just focus. Pour all her energy into being the best wife she could be to Marti. She did care about her. That wasn't in question. She had been in love with her once, hadn't she? She could be again, right? She just had to work on that...

Enough!

Spencer mentally shook herself. Going around and around about all of this crap was a surefire way to drive herself completely off the deep end, and she'd come close more than once. This wasn't the first time she'd listed out her options.

It was just the first time that somebody else had forced her to do so.

❖

Six a.m. on a Saturday was early, but if you'd been awake for most of the night, as Spencer had, it was actually late. By four, she'd given up trying to get anything more than quick dozes in and had hauled herself out of bed. When she glanced back at Marti's deeply sleeping—and still snoring—form, she briefly toyed with poking her awake. Her snuffling and snorting sounds hadn't helped Spencer to drift off. But the idea of having to maintain morning conversation with her was more than Spencer could bear, so she snuck into the bathroom and put on her workout clothes.

She had decided early on that those tight-fitting workout pants were made to shame people like her. Women who weren't model-thin, who weren't lean and muscular and curved in all the right places. That's why she'd started out in loose-fitting sweats. But as she'd attended more classes and had started to feel herself getting stronger, Spencer didn't mind those pants so much. They still showed many more of her imperfections than she'd like, but they also showed her progress. So she fought her way into them, donned a sports bra and her racer-back lime green tank, and headed for the gym.

She was going to make this spin class her bitch.

The Saturday morning crowd at BodyFit was a different mix than during the week. When Spencer came to the bride class on weeknights, the crowd seemed mostly made up of men and women coming right from work. The locker rooms were bustling and the hum of conversation was steady. On the weekends, though, the vibe was different. Mostly women, mostly without their kids (the on-site day care room was nearly empty), mostly quiet. Friendly smiles and gentle hellos drifted around the locker room, but there was little conversation and the volume was kept at a minimum.

Spin class was almost full. By the time Spencer picked her bike, adjusted the seat and the handlebars to fit her, clipped her feet onto the pedals, and began her warm-up, there were only four bikes left without riders. A quick glance around the room told her the class was mostly women and that a lot of them knew each other. Sherry wasn't the instructor on Saturdays. This was Amanda. She was tall, lean, annoyingly cheerful, and Spencer was pretty sure she would kick their collective ass.

Good.

She needed an ass kicking.

One of the best things about spin class, she'd decided as Amanda turned up the pumping music and got them moving, was that she needed to focus. She couldn't let her mind wander because

Amanda had her concentrating not only on not falling off the bike, but on shifting gears. Up and down, up and down, standing, sitting, standing, sitting. Spencer had no choice but to pay attention, follow directions, and—her favorite—track the counter that told her how many calories she'd burned.

There was no time for dwelling on anything else.

Forty-five minutes later, Spencer was pretty sure she was dying. Which was par for the course and meant spin class was going exactly as planned. She stood and pumped her legs as Amanda shouted for her not to drop her ass, not to give up on this hill, to keep pushing, pushing, pushing! Sweat rolled down the center of Spencer's back, dripped from her temples, covered her chest. Her lungs heaved, her quads burned, and still she pushed, pedaled, sprinted, doing her best to outrun those damn demons that refused to leave her alone.

When she finally hit the cool-down phase, Spencer sat back on the bike, hands on her hips, and pedaled easily, the sense of accomplishment washing over her. This. This was why she continued to go to class. This feeling right here? This pride? This feeling of triumph? It's what kept her going. Not to mention that her legs and heart felt stronger.

Back in the locker room, Spencer felt infinitely better. Things still weighed on her, of course, but that rush of endorphins definitely did what it was supposed to, and she felt at least a tiny bit lighter. What made her feel even lighter still was the text on her phone from Lucy.

Future mom-in-law driving me nuts. Time for coffee? Lunch? Anything? Please? Save me.

With a grin, Spencer texted her back, and half an hour later, they sat at a little café halfway between the gym and Lucy's place. Spencer dug into her plate of scrambled eggs, suddenly famished.

"You didn't kill her, did you?" she asked Lucy.

"Who? Ethan's mom? No." Lucy grinned. "She's really very nice. She's just…a bit on the exuberant side when it comes to the wedding. I think she's bummed she's the mother of the groom and not of the bride because she really wants to be a part of all of it, and I can almost see her forcing herself not to be."

"Aww, that's kind of sweet."

"It is. But also, exhausting." Lucy sipped her coffee and eyed Spencer's breakfast.

"Help yourself," Spencer told her, pointing to the plate with her fork. "I won't eat it all. But spin class makes me so hungry."

"I'm so impressed with your drive." Lucy's face lit up, her pride in Spencer evident.

Spencer gave a half shrug. "Thanks."

"You really enjoy it, huh?"

"What? God, no. I hate it. Every second of it. It's awful. But I like the way I feel when it's over."

"Fair enough." Lucy snagged a slice of Spencer's toast. "Was Rebecca there?"

Spencer shook her head, an odd mix of relief and disappointment around her answer swirling through her. "No, I didn't see her. I'm not sure she works on the weekends."

"She was in the parking lot yesterday when I left talking to some woman with a Lexus."

"Yeah, that was Marti."

"Your Marti?"

"Yep. I was running late, and she was picking me up." Spencer thought back on the conversation. "You know what? Rebecca stuck up for me."

Lucy's brow furrowed. "What? What does that mean? I'm going to need details, please. She stuck up for you how? Against who?"

"Whom."

"What the fuck ever, just tell me the story," Lucy demanded, with a laugh.

"Against Marti."

Lucy's eyes went wide. Then she made a rolling gesture with her hand, urging Spencer to continue.

"It was no big deal. Just...Marti jokingly said I was not athletic and that I'd always been kind of...soft." She didn't like saying it. True or not, it still stung. Spencer pursed her lips and pushed them sideways, making a face.

"Wait." Lucy held up a hand. "Your *fiancée* told your trainer you were soft? Like, squishy? That kind of soft? Not, like, softhearted or a pushover or something? But literally soft of muscle? Like, flabby?"

"Exactly like flabby."

"Wow." It was as if Lucy needed a moment. She sipped her coffee, took another bite of toast, chewed. Finally, she asked, "What did Rebecca say?"

Spencer scooped up the last of her eggs, held the fork aloft as she squinted, pretending to search for words that she knew by heart. "She said I was anything but soft. That I work really hard and that I'm getting results. Visible results." She didn't add the low timbre of Rebecca's voice, how it had felt a bit threatening, like Rebecca was protecting Spencer. She didn't mention how much she'd liked that.

"And Marti's response was…?"

"'If you say so.'" Spencer made air quotes around the other sentence she wouldn't forget.

"Wow." Lucy blinked at her, seemingly stunned into silence. "Just…wow."

"Yeah." Spencer picked up her mug as the waitress stopped at their table and warmed up Lucy's. They sipped quietly for several moments.

"Hey, Spencer, can I ask you something?"

Spencer nodded. "Sure."

"I might be overstepping," Lucy warned, her face hesitant.

Spencer reached across the table and closed a hand over Lucy's. "You can ask me anything. Despite only knowing you a short time, I trust you. It's weird."

Lucy smiled. "I feel the same way."

"Good. Shoot."

Lucy looked down, studied her coffee in the mug. When she looked back up, her eyes were soft. Tender. "Are you happy?"

Three little words. That's all they were. Three little words. Four syllables. Eleven letters. But they settled down onto Spencer's shoulders with the weight of the lead vest the dentist used when taking x-rays, heavy and constricting, making it hard to take a full breath. She let the question roll around inside her, twist and turn, spin one way, then the other, until finally, she knew she had to answer. She owed Lucy an answer. An honest one.

"About four years ago, I was head over heels in love."

Lucy seemed to settle back into her seat, as if she knew some major information was coming her way.

"Her name was Chelsea and she was an anesthesiologist. Beautiful. Tall, long dark hair, huge brown eyes. I had never fallen so hard, so fast as I did with her. We dated for over a year, but I knew from the first month that I wanted to marry her." Spencer knew her voice had gone a little dreamy, but she couldn't seem to help it. That was how she'd felt in those first few blissful months with Chelsea: like she was in a perpetual dream state. "We didn't talk about it, of course. No better way to scare somebody away than tell them you want to marry them after five dates." She laughed, but there was an edge. "But I planned it in my head. I could see it. We'd have beautiful lacy white dresses and our fathers would walk us down the aisle and it would be magical. When I came out, I assumed that kind of a wedding was no longer an option, but with Chelsea, it felt like I got it back, like the possibility had returned."

Spencer glanced at Lucy, whose face was a mix of enthralled anticipation and dread. It was obvious she knew the story didn't have a happy ending.

"It was our fourteen-month anniversary—I was silly like that back then, celebrated monthly anniversaries like a child—and I decided this was it. I was going to pop the question. I planned it so meticulously. Made reservations at our favorite restaurant. For both of us as well as several of our friends and my parents. I had them all set to come in after us and sit behind Chelsea so she didn't see them. The waiter was to drop the ring in her glass of champagne and we'd toast and I'd get down on one knee and ask her. And then we'd have a big celebration."

Spencer didn't go back there often, didn't allow herself to. But it had been a while, and she was surprised to find that it hurt the smallest bit less than last time as she envisioned that gorgeous restaurant, the white linen tablecloths, Chelsea's little black dress and upswept hair.

"What happened?" Lucy asked, her voice so quiet, Spencer wondered if she was afraid of breaking something with it.

"She said no."

"Oh, Spencer."

"Not only did she say no. She laughed at me and then got angry. Asked me how I could be so stupid as to think she'd want to get married, that she was *never* going to get married and how could I not know that about her. She didn't realize we had guests there, so all our friends and my parents heard all of it. When she saw that, she got even angrier, said I'd humiliated her and stormed out of the restaurant."

"Oh, no." Lucy brought a hand to her mouth. "Spencer."

"I spent the next year wondering how I could have possibly misread the signs so badly. Any confidence I had, Chelsea took with her when she left the restaurant. I tried to crawl back up from that but found myself second-guessing everything I did, every decision I made."

"And when did you meet Marti?"

Spencer inhaled slowly, let it out, feeling a sense of relief at having told the story to Lucy. "About a year later. We were at a party together and she came up to me, said hi, brought me a drink. She did most of the talking but was charming and sweet, and I liked her right away."

"You started dating?"

Spencer nodded, thinking back to that time when things were new and fresh. Though, if she was going to be honest, she had to admit that one thing that kept her in it. "Marti's very assertive. She's decisive."

"So you could just follow along." Lucy said it with no accusation, but Spencer heard it and, for the first time, actually absorbed it. Felt embarrassed. Felt shame. Felt weak. "And she said, 'let's get married,' and you said, 'okay.'"

Spencer grimaced. "Not quite. I tend to just…go along when

it comes to Marti. It wasn't an actual proposal. More of a 'hey, we should do this at some point' kind of thing."

Lucy shook her head. "Oh, Spencer."

"I know. I know." Spencer hung her head. "I'm a mess."

"You are, but I don't understand why. You're wonderful. You're smart and beautiful and funny and I adore you. Why don't you?" When Spencer didn't answer, she asked, "When's the last time you were happy? Be honest."

Spencer didn't need to think about it at all. "Last Sunday in the bar with you guys and then with Rebecca and her friends."

Lucy smiled. "Why?"

"Because I felt like I could be myself."

Lucy sat back with a smile and folded her arms across her chest as if she'd accomplished something. "There you go." She said it like she'd just solved the problem, like the solution was crystal clear and sitting in the middle of the table.

Was it?

CHAPTER EIGHTEEN

Turtle's was a mob scene on Sunday. The weather had turned and it actually felt like football season. Toss in the drizzle that fell from the sky, and apparently everybody had decided to watch the games from this particular bar.

Nick had gotten there first, as always, and saved their usual barstools. Rebecca sat next to him on one side, Dwayne on the other, and Kevin had been able to join them as well. The Giants scored on the TV across the room, and that half of the bar erupted in shouts of happiness and applause.

"How's Michelle feeling?" Rebecca asked, as she leaned in and snagged a stalk of celery off Nick's enormous plate of wings. Only three remained.

"Morning sickness," he replied, his eyes not leaving the screen above them as he put an entire wing into his mouth and pulled out a bone like a cartoon character would. It never ceased to amaze Rebecca. Nick flexed his left hand, then grabbed another wing.

"Ugh. That's got to suck," she said, turning back to the game.

"Oh, come on, ref!" Dwayne said, from Nick's other side. "Put your glasses on, goddamn it."

"She seems to be doing okay with it," Nick said.

"And are you being helpful?" Rebecca asked him, her voice gently scolding as she bumped him with her shoulder.

Nick held up a hand like a Boy Scout. "I swear, I am. I even offered to hold her hair back this morning, but she shut the bathroom door in my face."

"Maybe I'll go see her tomorrow, see what she needs." Again, the other side of the bar erupted in cheers. "Man, the Giants are killing it today." Something hit her thigh, and when she looked down, there was a large spot of wing sauce on her jeans. "Aw, Nick, come on, man, stop dropping food on me." She looked up to see Nick's eyes widen in confusion and his face drain of color. "Nick. Nick!" Rebecca slid off her stool and reached for him. "What's wrong?"

"I don't...know..." He grabbed his left biceps with his right hand. "I feel...weird..." Then he moved his hand to his chest. "Trouble...breathing..."

Dwayne picked up on the situation, jumped off his stool, and put a hand on Nick's shoulder. "Dude. What's going on?" He looked at Rebecca, panicked. "Jesus, is he having a heart attack?"

"I don't—" Before she could finish her sentence, Nick dropped to the floor like his legs had been yanked out from under him, and somebody was screaming to call 911 in a horrified shriek. Rebecca didn't realize right away that the shrieking was coming from her.

❖

"I hate hospitals," Kevin said, as he paced back and forth in front of the row of chairs. "The sounds. The smell. God, the smell." He made a face and ran his hand through his hair for what must have been the fiftieth time, judging by how it stood straight up on its own now.

Rebecca sat in one of the very uncomfortable chairs. They were deceiving, really, those chairs. All nicely upholstered, pleasing color schemes of turquoise and terracotta, very Southwestern, which was maybe meant to relax visitors. But they were hard as slate. Rebecca's ass protested. It felt like she was sitting on plywood. Just one more thing to add to her already skyrocketing stress levels.

"God, when will they tell us what's going on?" Dwayne's voice was a near whine, and as he lifted his hands out from his side, Dave came skidding into the room as if he was wearing only socks on his feet.

"What the hell happened?" he asked, breathless. They'd called him out of the theatre where he was on a date, and he hadn't hesitated. "Is he okay?"

"Michelle's in with the doctor now," Rebecca told him. "We're waiting."

"Jesus Christ, he had a heart attack, didn't he?" Dave dropped into a chair next to Rebecca. "I knew this would happen. I knew it. I kept telling him it was only a matter of time. The way that guy eats."

"Shut the fuck up," Dwayne said quietly.

"Dude, you know I'm right."

"Yes, I know you're right. I just don't want to hear about it right now. Okay?" Dwayne glared at him and Dave held up his hands in surrender.

"Yeah, okay. Okay. Sorry, man."

Quiet settled over them again, no sound in the waiting room except for the soft hum of the wall-mounted television in the corner broadcasting the local news.

Rebecca was worried. She couldn't remember the last time she'd been this worried. Nick's face, the gray pallor of his skin, the terror in his eyes as he fell. He didn't know what was happening to him, to his body. She'd held his hand the entire time he lay on the floor, waiting for the ambulance. The bar had gone eerily silent, people standing around him, trying not to stare and failing. The ambulance had arrived in record time, thank God, and they'd loaded him in and promised Rebecca they would take good care of him as she reluctantly let go of his hand and watched them zip away with her best friend in the back.

Dave was so right about Nick's eating habits. His exercise habits—or lack thereof. Honest to God, if he pulled through this, Rebecca was going to beat him into shape with a club if she had to. Damn him. Why didn't he listen to her? Why didn't he listen to anybody?

If he dies on me…I swear to God, if he dies on me…

She didn't have time to finish the thought because Michelle appeared in the doorway. Everybody looked up at her, and it was as if every movement in the world stopped. Just froze. Breath held. Nobody blinked. Michelle's expression was still worried, but Rebecca could sense a slight relief.

"He's going to be okay," she said, and the entire room let out one huge breath.

"Thank fucking Christ," Dwayne muttered.

"What did they say?" Rebecca asked.

"An acute case of angina, which can mimic the symptoms of a heart attack." Michelle shook her head. "He's had this pain before, just not as bad. I keep telling him he has to take better care of himself..." Her eyes welled up and Rebecca crossed the room, wrapped her arms around her best friend's wife.

"He's a stubborn bastard," she said. "It's going to take more than some heartburn on steroids to keep him down."

They all laughed softly as they gathered around. Michelle looked at them. "They're going to keep him overnight for observation, but he said to send you guys home." She reached out and laid her hand on Dwayne's cheek. "Come by the house tomorrow night and visit him."

"You're sure?" Dwayne asked.

Michelle nodded as he leaned in and kissed her temple. "I'm sure." As Rebecca turned to gather her things, Michelle held fast. "Not you. He wants to talk to you."

❖

Spencer sat back in her chair and squeezed her eyes shut for a minute. They burned a little bit, given how long she'd been focusing through the freestanding magnifying glass. The day had been fairly gray, but now she realized it was evening. Her living room was dark, except for the light from her craft desk, and for a moment, she had a vision of those old black-and-white films where the bad guy was being interrogated and the entire room was void of anything but a simple table, a chair, and one swinging lightbulb.

In one hand, she held an almost-finished earring, a simple green stone accented with gold. In the other, her crimping tool. Another pair of earrings for Mary Beth, this time for Christmas, and Spencer would add them to the pile of things she'd made since yesterday. It was slightly alarming, that pile, as she had been creating nonstop since her talk with Lucy, a pretty accurate sign that she was stressing out.

The internal conversation started up again.

When had she become so incredibly passive? When? On what day, in what moment, had she decided it was totally fine to let life just go on along without her participation? When had she made that decision? To be a follower? To let somebody else choose her path and then follow along blindly?

She could blame Chelsea. She *did* blame Chelsea, at least partly. Chelsea had shattered something inside her, something important, something independent. She used to be strong and feisty, but now? Now she just…wasn't. She could blame Marti, too. Sure. But that was the thing: it wasn't Marti's fault. Marti was just being Marti. In all their time together, she had never acted any way other than who she was. Spencer had to admire that. Was actually envious. Marti knew who she was. She knew what she wanted. Reached for it. Grabbed on.

Not Spencer, though. Spencer had apparently forgotten how to reach for things. How to grab on. Now she just kind of floated. Drifted.

Spencer had become a flounderer.

Emotions bubbled up in her again. They'd started yesterday, after her talk with Lucy, after her forced look in the mirror. Things had begun to simmer, with an occasional bubble here and there, like a thick sauce in a pot, left on low on the stove, a bubble here, a bubble there. It was a mix of disappointment, shame, and anger, combining into a sour stew in her stomach. That last one had been most prominent, much to Spencer's surprise: the anger. It was a weird realization, to understand you're angry at yourself. But she was. She had anger. Lots of it. Brewing up from deep within her, bubbling like lava, threatening to eventually spill over and out. Spencer wasn't an angry person. She rarely yelled. She never swore. But right now? She was dangerously close to her breaking point. She didn't understand it, but she could feel it.

Thus: jewelry.

She finished the earrings, put them in their own little velvet pouch, and reached for her bead board. On to the next project. She'd go all night if she had to.

Creativity and her focus on it—they were the only things keeping her sane right now. Keeping her from examining what a disaster she'd made of her life. Of what she was doing to Marti's life. They were going to have to have a talk. Soon. She owed Marti that. She had no idea what she was going to say. Or how. She hadn't thought it through yet. After spending time with Lucy, Spencer felt an odd combination of relieved and lost, like she had finally solved a difficult riddle but had nobody she could explain it to.

A roll of black leather had been on sale a couple months back and Spencer had snagged it from the craft store with no idea what she'd do with it. Travis's necklace was brown leather and thicker, so she couldn't use this one next time he needed a repair. Her brother thrived on routine, and a change as simple as his necklace going from one color to another could send him into a tailspin. So the new leather roll sat in the stack of other spools of various wire and elastic. Now it caught her eye. She picked it up, looked at it as she turned it in her hand, and an idea formed in her head.

She needed to stay busy. To not think. To not analyze. To not dwell.

Just focus on the leather, the silver, the tools. Feel them in your hands. See the piece in your mind.

Spencer reached for more findings and kept working.

❖

In all the years Rebecca had known Nick Scarfano—and she'd known him longer than she *hadn't* known him—she had never seen him look quite this bad. Not after the hit he took in college that had broken his collarbone. Not the day he was going to propose to Michelle. Not the morning after his bachelor party. No, this was far, far worse. He lay in the bed with his eyes closed, his skin a sickening gray, his hair stringy. Somehow, his enormous frame seemed small in the white sterile room. Nick had always been a huge presence. Strong and loud and big, the guy who sucked all the air out of the room, the guy you couldn't help but notice. This quiet, subdued, *small* man was the complete opposite of what Rebecca was used to seeing, and it made her stutter-step in the doorway, have to brace herself against the frame and take a second to just breathe.

Nick opened his eyes then and focused on her. Without hesitation, she launched right in, because the best way to deal with this was head-on.

"Jesus, you look like shit," she told him as she crossed the room and waved a finger up and down his body. "This gray and sallow thing you've got going on? Definitely not a good look for you."

Nick's body moved as he gave a silent chuckle; Rebecca saw his shoulders move. "You don't like it?" His voice was more of a croak than anything else, and he cleared his throat.

"Absolutely not. I recommend going back to that healthy flesh-tone color you wore earlier."

"I'll take that under advisement."

Rebecca pulled a chair close to his bed and sat. She closed her hand over his forearm and they stayed that way for several moments. Finally, Rebecca spoke. "My God, your arms are hairy."

Nick's laugh bubbled up from deep within him and rumbled out of his mouth. Then he groaned. "Ugh. Don't make me laugh, Becks. Come on."

"Seriously. It's like a little bear cub lying here on the sheet."

"Stop," he pleaded, as he laughed harder. "Ow."

"You big baby," Rebecca said, but her tone was gentle. Once his laughter subsided, her eyes welled as she whispered, "You scared me."

"Get in line."

"I'm glad it wasn't more serious."

Nick studied her for a beat before he spoke again. "You know what went through my mind? In the midst?" Rebecca shook her head and Nick shifted his gaze to the acoustic tile on the ceiling. "I'm having this pain in my arm and I can't take a breath, like there's a fucking hippo sitting on my chest. I'm sure I'm having a heart attack. The first thing—the *only* thing I could think was that I'd never see my baby." His dark eyes filled with tears, and as Rebecca watched, one spilled out the corner, left a wet path across his skin.

Rebecca tightened her grip on his arm, uncertain of what to say. His tears were a foreign sight to her and they took her by surprise, so she stayed silent and present.

Another beat went by before Nick cleared his throat and took a swipe at his eyes. "So," he said, his voice firmer than it had been since Rebecca came into the room, "I need your help."

She gave him a nod. "Anything."

"If there's one thing an almost heart attack will teach you, it's that life is too fucking short. You can be gone in the blink of an eye." He finally shifted his focus from the ceiling to Rebecca, snagged and held her gaze with his. "Life is too. Fucking. Short."

She nodded, captured by the intensity of his stare, feeling like it was boring into her, burrowing deep, planting a seed.

"So. I need you to help me get into shape."

Rebecca blinked, felt released, and gave him another nod. "Absolutely." Then she absorbed the words, replayed them in her head, and a smiled widely. "You know I've been waiting to hear those exact words from you for, like, our entire friendship, right?"

"I know," Nick said, with a sigh. "I know. And I don't want any I told you sos. Got it? Just…help me."

"Got it. I will not say I told you so. I promise." And then she was on her feet, pacing, ideas and meals and an exercise regimen already forming in her brain. Then she stopped, pivoted to face him. "There will be ground rules, you know."

"Terrific." He arched an eyebrow and looked decidedly unamused.

"If I'm going to be your trainer, you're going to have to listen to me. No complaining."

"No complaining? Seriously, Becks, do you even know me at all?"

"Fine. A *minimum* of complaining."

"Done."

Rebecca started ticking things off on her fingers. "We'll get you into the gym at least three times a week. More if we can manage. I've got some great books for you to look at about how to eat better, but still have what you like…"

"Becks."

Rebecca stopped and looked at Nick, saw the softness in his eyes, the friendship, the love.

"Thank you."

She took a moment, smiled tenderly at him before saying, "Are you kidding me? Whipping your ass into shape? This is a dream come true for me."

Nick shook his head. But he was still smiling.

CHAPTER NINETEEN

The only good thing that had come out of Nick's ordeal, at least for Rebecca, had been that it had shifted her focus away from Spencer Thompson. Since Sunday, all her attention had been on Nick. Getting him home from the hospital, convincing him to take the week off and just rest, talking to him about the changes in his diet and in his overall lifestyle they were looking to make. All of it had taken the majority of Rebecca's concentration, and that was a good thing.

She'd canceled the bride class on Monday, taking the day to get Nick home and settled into his easy chair, make sure Michelle didn't need anything, running to pick up prescriptions. The poker gang had all been in and out, but Rebecca's presence was near constant, until Michelle finally told her, gently and kindly, to go home. Rebecca obeyed, and once there, had dug out her books and checked her bookmarked websites to help her work up a new regimen for her best friend. He was going to live a long and healthy life if it killed her.

Tuesday, she'd gotten back to the grind, and it was a full day of clients. She was helping Phil on the dip machine that evening when she happened to glance up at the windowed wall of the spin room and saw Spencer pedaling away in all her sweaty blond glory. The sight did things to Rebecca. Many things. It made her smile, filled her with trepidation, tickled her with longing. Phil had to say her name twice before she forced her eyes away and back down to him. When she looked up again, class was over and Spencer was gone.

Rebecca was both relieved and disappointed.

After work, she'd called Nick to see if he needed anything from the store, since she was going anyway. Then she picked up two bags of vegetables and other produce and a six-pack of non-alcoholic beer and took it over to the Scarfano house to help Michelle make him a healthy, filling dinner. To Nick's credit, he only whined once.

By the time Rebecca got home, fed a very irritated Veruca Salt, and dropped into bed, she felt like a discarded dishrag: soggy, flimsy, and useless. Veruca rolled in a ball on Rebecca's stomach and began to purr, and that's all it took. Sleep claimed her instantly.

Rebecca knew it was a dream.

It had that strange, foggy, soft-lit quality to it, like she was watching through cheesecloth or gauze. The lighting was too perfect and there was background music. Large, ornate double doors opened in front of her, and she was faced with the interior of a church full of people as she stood at the end of the center aisle. No sound other than the music, which was something pretty but unrecognizable to her. Strings and a piano, maybe? Coming from above. Unaware that she made the decision, she began walking down the aisle, the strangers that filled the pews on both sides watching her, but saying nothing. When Rebecca looked up, to the end of the aisle, two women stood there.

Spencer was stunning. Ethereal in a white flowing dress that was made just for her. It was strapless, leaving her shoulders and the top of her chest exposed, an inviting expanse of creamy skin. The top edge of the dress was scalloped, the lacy pattern encompassing Spencer's full breasts. Not caring that she was in a church and shouldn't be gawking, Rebecca let her eyes follow the bare shoulders down Spencer's arms to the small, tasteful bouquet of white daisies she held with both hands, and when Rebecca got closer, looked up and into those beautiful blue eyes, they were filled with confusion, with hurt, and with something else...hope? Spencer didn't speak. Every emotion she conveyed, she did with her eyes.

Rebecca turned to the other woman. Marti. Of course. Her dress was almost as gorgeous as Spencer's, but not quite. She didn't have the same curves, the same inviting aura that Spencer did. Marti was attractive, but not warm, as though she wore an invisible force field to keep people at arm's length. Rebecca met her brown eyes, but her emotions were much clearer than Spencer's. And there was only one: anger. Rebecca did a double take when she saw Marti's mouth moving, but no sound came out. Was Rebecca the only one who couldn't hear her? Marti pointed back down the aisle, obviously telling Rebecca to get lost, but when Rebecca tried to reply, she found she had no voice of her own, couldn't speak even when she felt as though she was making a massive effort to do so. The only sound continued to be the soothing notes from the music, a confusing and bizarre soundtrack to the otherwise silent film playing out before her.

Rebecca looked to Spencer again. Their gazes held and something passed between them. Rebecca felt it like warmth, like a gentle summer breeze off the ocean. Again, she tried to speak to Spencer but made no sound. Spencer looked down as if studying the flowers in her hands as Marti continued to flail and point, and it was the only moment Rebecca was glad for the lack of speech. She didn't need to hear what Marti was saying to understand it. What she didn't understand was why Spencer made no effort to talk. She said nothing. Her mouth never opened. She simply looked on, watched what was happening around her as if she had no other choice.

Rebecca had never felt the need to rescue somebody so deeply before in her entire life. Dream or no dream. She wanted to wake Spencer up, so she tried. She reached out, grabbed her by those sensual bare shoulders and gave her a shake. She screamed at her without sound, told her to look around, to understand her own worth, to participate in her own life, for God's sake, that she deserved so much better than she was settling for, that *life was too fucking short*. Spencer simply looked at her with a small, sad smile.

Rebecca woke up.

She lay there in her bed, eyes adjusting to the pre-dawn light in her room, and stared at the ceiling. Rebecca wasn't one of those people who remembered her dreams in vivid detail. Most of the time, she barely remembered bits and pieces. But this dream…

With a slow inhale, she rehashed every single element of it. She could still see the church, could almost smell it. She remembered the anger on Marti's face, the rage as she flailed her arms. Rebecca found it interesting in that moment that, while she'd been able to reach out and touch Spencer (she could still feel the warmth of her bare shoulders under her palms), Marti had made no attempts to physically remove Rebecca from the scene.

I certainly would have if the roles were reversed. I'd have shoved her out of that church so fast...

Mostly, though, she focused her memory on Spencer. On the beauty of her dress. On the corkscrew curls that dangled near her ears and all around her upswept hair. On the sadness in her eyes.

A glance at the bedside clock told Rebecca it was four a.m. She had a five-thirty client and would normally sleep for another forty-five minutes, but she was wide awake and she knew it. With an irritated groan, she threw off the covers and headed for the shower.

Unlike normal dreams that tended to fade away as the day progressed in wakefulness, this one stayed with Rebecca. Any time she wasn't focused on a client or an email or a fellow employee, her mind drifted back there. Back to Spencer's lack of words, to her resigned smile, to her sad, sad eyes.

Was this simply Rebecca's mind messing with her? Punishing her for what she'd done? Or was it something more? Something bigger? A sign of some sort? Sherry was big on that kind of thing. After all, yoga was all about the mind-body-spirit connection. During her training, she'd immersed herself into a lot of that type of thing, and she was always pointing out "signs." Rebecca made the air quotes in her head because that was how she normally thought of such things. But this...this had thrown her for a loop because it seemed to come out of nowhere. Not the sexual desire, but the emotions. She could still feel them from the dream, as strongly as if they had happened in a real-life situation. Her frustration, her worry, the urgent need to rescue Spencer from something bad.

That last one got her. Rescue. Rebecca shook her head as she sat at her desk and pretended to be reading email. Spencer was a big girl. She didn't need rescuing. If she was going to leave Marti, if she needed to leave Marti, that wasn't for Rebecca to say. In fact, it had nothing at all to do with Rebecca, and she'd do well to keep reminding herself of that.

Right?

With another hard shake of her head, Rebecca blew out a breath and squinted at her computer just as Sherry dropped into the chair nearby.

"Hey."

"Hey," Rebecca said in reply. "Housewife yoga over?" That's what they called the two o'clock yoga class, as it seemed to be filled with women who dropped their kids off in the child care room on their way in.

"Yep. Nearly fifteen today."

Rebecca raised her eyebrows and nodded. "Impressive."

"Yep." Sherry managed to stay quiet for a good ten seconds before asking, "So, what's up with you? You're all over the place. Is it Nick still?"

"Yeah. I mean, he's going to be fine and he's been great about listening to me when I talk about exercise and eating better."

"So it's not Nick, then."

Rebecca could feel Sherry's eyes on her, feel her stare, and hated it. Sherry could see right into her like she could read her thoughts. Even Nick wasn't that good.

Sherry sat back in her chair with a grunt of affirmation, like she'd solved a puzzle.

Rebecca stared at her computer screen until she couldn't take it anymore and shifted her gaze to Sherry. She tilted her head and waited.

"It's your little cupcake," Sherry announced with certainty.

"I wish you wouldn't call her that."

"I know. You're right. It's condescending. And honestly, the way she's been kicking ass in my spin class, I don't think she's as weak and squishy as I may have thought. I'll have to come up with another nickname. Something harder. Something tough." It was an attempt at lightheartedness, but it fell flat and Sherry seemed to know it. "Seriously, Beck, what's the deal?"

"I slept with her." Rebecca's voice was barely a whisper, but she said it. She said the words, then squeezed her eyes shut and flinched as Sherry unloaded on her. As expected.

"You did *what*? Jesus Christ, Rebecca, what were you thinking? You know how inappropriate that is! You could lose your job." Sherry kept her voice down as well, looking around as she hissed at Rebecca, making sure nobody could hear them. "You know better."

"I know. I know."

"And isn't she engaged?"

Rebecca nodded.

Sherry was perched on the very edge of her chair, and when Rebecca finally ventured a glance, she wished she hadn't. A mix of frustration, disgust, and immense disappointment was splashed all over Sherry's face.

"Jesus Christ, Rebecca."

"I know."

"When did this happen? And, is it a regular thing now?"

"A couple of weeks ago. And no. Just the one time. We talked about it and agreed it couldn't happen again and we'd be friends."

Sherry nodded, gazing off into space as if she couldn't bear to look at Rebecca. Rebecca slumped a bit in her chair. "Well. That's good, I suppose." They sat quietly for what felt like a long time before Sherry seemed to collect herself, sat up a bit as if she'd been bolstered by something. "Look, I'm sorry. I shouldn't have yelled at you."

Rebecca shook her head. "It's fine. I deserved it."

"No. No, you didn't, because something else is going on here. Talk to me." Sherry's voice had softened. Rebecca knew her friend well. She led with emotion, and then logic and practicality followed quickly after. "Are you in love with her?" she asked quietly.

"No, I...I don't think so," Rebecca said. "I mean, I don't know her well enough to be. Right? But..." She searched for the right words. "I can't seem to get her out of my head. I had this crazy dream last night that I can't stop replaying." She told Sherry about the entire dream, still surprised that she remembered every detail. When she finished, Sherry sat with wide eyes. "I know, right?"

"Wow."

"I just...I worry that I'm giving way too much of my energy to something I need to just let go of. You know?" She turned to Sherry, looked intently at her. "But being her friend has become difficult because...I like her. I like her a lot. She's witty and smart and charming—"

"And taken."

Rebecca closed her eyes. "Yeah. That, too."

"Yeah, you did things so backward, girlfriend. You're supposed to get to know her first, *then* decide you like her, *then* sleep with her." Another attempt at humor that didn't go very far. More gently, Sherry asked, "What are you going to do?"

Rebecca sat back in her chair and let out a long, slow breath, like a bike tire losing air. "I know what I should do. And I know what I want to do. And they are very different things."

Sherry leaned forward, laid a hand on Rebecca's shoulder. "I find that when you're not sure what to do, the best thing to do is nothing."

❖

Spencer had made a decision. It had taken several days and an overwhelming amount of back and forth, of tears, of frustration, but she'd settled on a course of action.

"You're sure this is what you want to do?" Mary Beth had asked her on the phone the night before. To her credit, she did a commendable job keeping her own opinion out of her voice, even though Spencer suspected she didn't agree.

"Yes. I screwed up in a big way and I need to make up for that. I need to stop being so wishy-washy and focus on the life ahead. Marti deserves my full attention, not my confusion. Not my uncertainty. She's been nothing but patient with me, and I messed up. I have to fix that."

"I'm hearing a lot of 'I did this' and 'She deserves that,' but I haven't heard you say anything about what *you* want."

Spencer knew one thing she wanted: she wanted not to have to explain any more to her sister, because if anybody could make her waver, make her swerve back to being unsure, it was Mary Beth, Queen of Logic and Pragmatism. "Can you just support me here? Please?" She said it gently, but there was a pleading tone in there that made Spencer wrinkle her nose with distaste.

Mary Beth had been quiet for a few beats before saying, "Of course. You're right. It's your life, and only you can make these decisions. I'm behind you, no matter what."

Spencer's sigh of relief escaped from her lungs in a whoosh much louder than she'd intended. "Thanks, M.B. That means a lot to me."

"You're my little sister, Spencer. I love you. I just want you to be happy."

"I know. I love you, too."

She had her big sister's support.

So why did she still feel so alone?

Work had been very busy, and for that, Spencer was grateful. She didn't want to dwell. She'd done enough of that. Not to mention, she had bride class tonight. Rebecca had canceled Monday's class but hadn't said why, and Spencer had toyed with contacting her to make sure she was okay. Reason had won out, though, and she'd managed not to. Thank God there were only a few classes left in the program because being around Rebecca after making the decision to focus on her life with Marti was not something she looked forward to.

"Hey, don't you need to get going?" Jennifer's voice yanked Spencer out of the staring off into space she'd done several times that day. She tapped her watch. "It's five twenty."

"Oh. Right. Thanks." Spencer logged off her computer, then pushed herself back from her desk and bent to retrieve her purse from underneath.

"You okay?" When Spencer sat back up, Jennifer was looking at her with gentle concern. "You've been kind of quiet today."

"I'm good. I'm fine. Just tired. I didn't sleep well last night." Not the whole truth, but not a lie. She'd seen 1:37, 2:45, and 3:50 on the clock the night before.

Jennifer's face said she was skeptical, but luckily, she didn't press. "All right. Just checking on you."

"I appreciate it." Spencer forced a smile, then escaped the office as quickly as she could before Jennifer changed her mind and decided to probe further.

The locker room at BodyFit was full and buzzing. A shiny red lock hung from Spencer's usual locker and she wrinkled her nose as she glared at it. No sign of Lucy. Spencer figured she must be out there already. Choosing the next locker over, she opened it, put her purse inside, and set down her bag to get changed as she eavesdropped on conversations around her. The two women directly behind her were discussing some sort of recipe...chicken? No, turkey—one swearing that the slow cooker was the only way to go. They headed out and Spencer could then hear voices she recognized as Brittany and Bella, their tones joyful and excited, as they chatted from the next aisle over.

"It's red velvet with a buttercream frosting that's just ridiculous," Brittany was saying.

"Oh, red velvet..."

Bella must've made some kind of dreamy face because Brittany added with a laugh, "Yes! That's exactly how I looked."

"We decided on cupcakes, but the flavors are kind of exotic," Bella said then. "Key lime. Egyptian spice. Chocolate cayenne."

"Cupcakes are a fantastic idea! I almost went there, but I wanted a tiered cake."

"Totally understandable. Did you have fun?"

"I did. I think choosing the cake was the least stressful thing about the planning...though I haven't really minded any of it." Brittany sounded so happy, so incredibly joyous, and Spencer was surprised by the wave of envy that rushed through her. Their voices faded as they left the locker room, and Spencer gave herself a full minute before following.

After a ten-minute warm-up on cardio equipment, the five brides met Rebecca at their usual corner of the gym to find out what they'd be working on today. Spencer allowed herself ten seconds to soak up the tight-fitting black workout pants and red racer-back tank Rebecca wore before forcing her eyes down toward the floor and keeping them there.

"Hello there, my hardworking brides-to-be. We've only got four classes left. Can you believe that?"

"No way," Lucy said, then covered her mouth in an adorable display of *I didn't mean to say that out loud*.

"It's true, I'm afraid." Rebecca grinned at Lucy. "That just means I've got four more days to work in all the remaining torture I can think of." She winked and then her expression softened; Spencer allowed herself a quick glance. "You guys have made some amazing progress. I'm really proud of you and want you to know that. Also, I'm sorry about Monday. Rough day."

"Everything okay?" Lucy asked. Because of course, Lucy would ask. She was sweet like that.

Rebecca took a deep breath. "It is now. My best friend since high school had what we thought was a heart attack on Sunday, so I spent Monday helping his wife get him home from the hospital and settled."

Spencer let out a small gasp, and before she could catch herself, she asked, "Nick?"

Rebecca met her eyes, held them, nodded. "It was just a case of acute angina, and he's fine." She seemed to have to make a concerted effort to pull her gaze from Spencer, but once she had, she clapped her hands together once and smiled widely. "The good news is he's now going to actually listen to me about diet and exercise, so... silver lining?"

Chuckles went through the other four, but Spencer didn't join them. She could see the veiled worry on Rebecca's face, the slight shadows under her eyes that said she probably wasn't sleeping well, and all she wanted to do was wrap Rebecca in her arms. The sudden image of the two of them on a couch, Rebecca's head in her lap while Spencer played with her hair, was so strong, so solid, it made Spencer's breath catch in her throat.

"Okay, let's get to work."

Rebecca hadn't been kidding; she worked them hard, didn't

take it easy on them just because the classes were drawing to a close. Spencer concentrated, did her best to focus, to not look at Rebecca. Which was fine because Rebecca didn't seem to want to look at her either. The entire time Spencer exercised, with each new move or circuit Rebecca instructed her to do, she could feel her emotions inside going from a simmer to a slow bubble to a low boil, their intensity increasing as she pushed her body. She didn't understand it. She'd made a decision. She knew what she needed to do, so what on earth was the problem? Why couldn't her brain settle?

It was core work today, Spencer's least favorite, so that certainly wasn't helping her mood. They finished up the last set of crunches, all five women flat on their backs, groaning and panting, but when Spencer turned to look down the line, all seemed to be smiling. Happy.

Envy washed through her.

"Okay," Rebecca said, her sneakered feet moving past Spencer's head. "On your stomachs. You know the drill." She had her phone out, and presumably, the timer all set for planks. "Some of you got this and some of you are so close. Sixty seconds. Ready?"

Spencer didn't look at her—par for the course today—and got into position, her feelings roiling inside her like a cauldron full of something sour.

"Go."

All five women braced on forearms and toes and held it.

Spencer's brain was like a KitchenAid mixer, systematically blending every thought she had, yanking it into the beaters and combining it with every other. Her job and her living situation and Marti and Nick and Lucy and Ethan and Rebecca and spin class and her body and her jewelry and all of it. *All of it.* It blended together into a thick, ugly mess of feelings until Spencer couldn't take it anymore. Until she wanted to scream. She could feel her face heating up as the blood rose and her body quaked with exertion and when Rebecca's timer finally sounded, Spencer dropped to the ground and uttered a word she'd never said before in all her life with enough intensity to alarm herself:

"Mother*fucker.*"

A beat of silence passed before the rest of the girls burst out laughing.

"Oh, my God, *finally*." Lucy was on her stomach next to Spencer, and she laid a warm hand on Spencer's back.

Brittany and Bella broke into applause while Willow's laugh kept on.

Spencer ventured a glance at Rebecca, who was grinning widely. "I think you've arrived," she said to Spencer, with a wink.

It probably should have been a fun moment, something to laugh about, an amusing memory to have. But it wasn't. Instead, it made Spencer even more sad and confused and she simply stayed there, like a fish that had washed up on shore.

"You okay?" Lucy asked as she got to her feet and held out a hand.

Spencer waved it off. "I'm good. Just gonna stay here for a minute."

She could feel Lucy's eyes on her, but she kept her own gaze on the peeling rubber on the foot of the leg press several yards away.

"I'm worried about you, Spence." Lucy squatted, and her voice was soft, filled with concern. "You're not yourself lately."

Spencer managed to turn her grimace into a small smile and reached to grab Lucy's foot. "I'm okay. Promise."

Lucy looked unconvinced, but went with it. "I'm here. Okay? Just remember that. I'm here if you need me."

"I know. Thank you."

Another moment went by before Lucy sighed quietly and headed for the locker room. The truth was, Spencer didn't want to chat. She didn't want to deal with conversation right now. With anybody. And she was worried about Rebecca being worried about Nick. She wanted to talk to her, to ask her how she was, could Spencer help. Which was not her place. *So* not her place. But that didn't make the desire go away.

Spencer sat up but stayed on the carpeted floor for another ten minutes, just watching the bustle of BodyFit. The Crasher was in the corner with the free weights, dropping large plates with a loud groan after every set. Spencer could feel the reverberation in her ass as it shook the floor each time. The Redhead with Shoulders to Die For was on the pull-down machine, her earbuds in as she worked her triceps. Spencer wondered if she was even the tiniest bit aware of the glances she got as people walked past her. In the corner, two twentysomething guys were bench pressing and spotting each other, encouraging one another. Everybody was busy. Everybody oblivious to the darkness of Spencer's mood.

She pushed out a loud breath and got to her feet, grabbed up her water bottle and towel, and headed to the locker room. She'd timed it well, as the other four brides were gone, so she took her time opening her locker—after staring at the unfamiliar red lock in confusion for longer than she cared to admit before remembering somebody else had snagged her usual locker first. She found her own, twisted the dial, and got the combination wrong. The lock held fast. With a thud, Spencer dropped her forehead against the cool metal of the locker and just stood there, doing her best to take air in, let air out.

"Just breathe. Just be. You're fine." She whispered the mantra several times before trying the lock again, this time with success. Not wanting to dwell on the relief that coursed through her, she pulled her duffel out and unzipped it, tossed her water bottle in.

The little black velvet bag looked at her from inside.

Spencer reached in, retrieved it, pulled open the drawstrings. Her mind immediately flooded with Rebecca's face, with the worry she must have felt after getting the call about Nick. The panic that must have seized her. Spencer had seen the two of them interact. She knew firsthand how much they meant to each other.

Maybe it'll cheer her up.

That was the thought that spurred Spencer into action. She tightened the drawstring back up, pocketed the pouch, gathered her things, and went in search of her fitness instructor one last time.

❖

Rebecca was exhausted.

She'd spent most of her free time for the past three days either helping Nick and Michelle or doing research for them. She was pretty sure she'd visited every fitness and good health site she knew of a dozen times each and that she'd read about a million articles, blogs, and chat rooms. She was determined to find the very best regimen for Nick that she could, and she wouldn't stop until she had.

All the while, his words echoed through her head.

Life is too. Fucking. Short.

It was a simple statement, really. Not hugely original. People said it all the time. Every day. It was a common thing for one person to remind another. Rebecca knew all of this. So why had it stuck with her so completely? Like gum on the bottom of her shoe, it was always there and she kept noticing it because it would stop her progress for a second or two. Not only that, it took her focus. She found herself staring off into space on a regular basis over the past three days—like now—and it weirded her out. She was getting so little accomplished at work, but she felt like she'd developed instant attention deficit disorder and couldn't concentrate on one thing for longer than a couple minutes before she ended up staring off, once again, distracted by blond hair, blue eyes.

"Hey." Spencer's voice startled Rebecca enough to make her flinch in surprise. Spencer wrinkled her nose and put a hand on Rebecca's shoulder. "I'm sorry. I didn't mean to scare you." Then, as if noticing she was touching Rebecca, she snatched her hand back.

"Oh, no. No problem. That's what I get for daydreaming." Rebecca forced a smile onto her face. This was a situation where she couldn't not look at Spencer. She didn't want to, mostly because looking at Spencer did things to her. Sexual things. Things low in her body. Things she didn't want to think about. At least in class, there were four other women she could rest her eyes on and it wasn't obvious that she wasn't looking at Spencer. But now? It would be rude to avoid any and all eye contact when it was just the two of them. Mentally bracing, she looked up from her seat, into soft blue eyes that seemed…uncertain. "What's up?"

It was a little unnerving, the way Spencer studied her, tipped her head to one side, those eyes not allowing her to look away. With a glance behind her, Spencer grabbed a chair, pulled it toward her, and sat. "Are you okay?" she asked finally.

"Me? Sure. Of course. Why do you ask?" Rebecca knew her eyes darted a bit, tried to prevent that, but was unsuccessful.

Again with the head tilt. "I know how close you are with Nick. You must have been terrified for him."

"I was." Rebecca nodded, cleared her throat. She looked down at her hands, scraped at her thumbnail. "But he's doing pretty well."

There was a beat. Another. Finally, Spencer gave a nod, though her expression showed skepticism. "Okay. Good." Then it was her turn to clear her throat as she reached into her jacket pocket and pulled out a small black pouch. "Listen, um, I was just goofing around with my stuff the other night and I made this for you." She held it toward Rebecca.

It was like Rebecca's arm moved in slow motion and she couldn't speed it up. Very, very slowly, she reached out and finally felt her fingers brush Spencer's. A huge lump of…something…had developed in her throat and she worked to swallow it, to clear her airway. "For me?"

Spencer nodded, waved a dismissive hand. "It's nothing much. Just…an idea that came to me." She shrugged.

Rebecca tugged the drawstrings open, turned the pouch over, and dumped the contents into her hand. She blinked at it.

It was made of a black leather strap, not thin, but not wide. Small, so a bracelet rather than a necklace. Spaced out evenly were three small silver squares, each with a simple line drawing. One was a person on a bike, one was a person in the yoga pose of downward dog, the third was a person balancing a barbell above their head. It was simple, classy, and absolutely perfect. If Rebecca had seen it in a store, she'd have purchased it for herself. The lump got bigger and she stared for several beats more before raising her eyes to Spencer.

"This…" Rebecca cleared her throat for the tenth time in five minutes. "This is amazing."

"Well." Again, Spencer shrugged it off as less than significant, looked away.

"Seriously. Spencer." Rebecca waited until those blue eyes turned back to her. "Would you put it on me?" she asked quietly.

Spencer's nod was almost imperceptible as she reached for the bracelet.

Rebecca watched her hands—God, her hands were beautiful—as she opened the clasp and fastened it around Rebecca's wrist. The fit could not have been more perfect. Not too tight, not too loose. She stared at it, noticed Spencer's warm hands touching her skin longer than they needed to. Longer than they should have. And suddenly, Nick's voice was echoing through her head again.

Life is too. Fucking. Short.

"Don't marry her." The words were barely a whisper and were out and floating in the air between them before Rebecca even realized she'd spoken them out loud. But they gave her strength and she pulled her gaze from the bracelet that she already loved and looked at Spencer. Her blue eyes were wide, and Rebecca grasped her hands before she could pull them away. She kept her voice soft as she said, "Please, Spencer. Don't marry her. Not for me. For you. You are an amazing, vibrant, stunningly beautiful woman and you deserve so much better."

Spencer blinked at her. Blinked again. Too many emotions zipped across her face for Rebecca to identify them all. "How?" she whispered, and it almost seemed like she wasn't even asking Rebecca, just the world in general. "How could you say that to me now? How?"

In that moment, Rebecca would have happily explained it, would have been glad to have a discussion about why she thought this, why she believed Spencer deserved so much more. But she never got the chance. Spencer stood quickly, as if ejected from her chair, and her eyes darted around the gym as if she'd suddenly forgotten the way out. Then she moved her gaze to Rebecca, directly to Rebecca, held hers, cradled it for a moment as her eyes welled. Rebecca reached for her hand, but Spencer turned and fled before any contact was made.

I had to tell her.

That thought played over and over. She'd had to. Right? It was the right thing to do. It wasn't Rebecca being selfish, was it? She'd simply needed Spencer to know, needed her to understand what others thought of her. No, that wasn't it. She'd needed Spencer to know what she thought of her.

Right?

Her gaze stayed glued to the front door, and while a part of her wished for Spencer to come back through, to sit back down and talk to her, she knew that wasn't happening. With a long sigh, she scanned the front desk area and stopped at Sherry. Standing behind the desk, looking right at her, disappointment clearly etched across her face.

"Shit," Rebecca muttered.

CHAPTER TWENTY

Spencer was pretty sure she was being punished for her indiscretions. It was the only explanation for why this was all so hard. She'd made a decision. It was the one she was supposed to make. She was certain of it. She had to set her feelings for Rebecca aside...

Wait. Feelings?

She gave her head a hard shake. No. Nope. Not going there. She did *not* have feelings for Rebecca. She refused to. She was engaged to marry Marti. She'd made a commitment and she needed to honor that. She was a good person.

She was a good person.

She was a good person.

She was a good person.

Wasn't she?

In the driveway of Marti's house, Spencer dropped her head forward and rested it on the steering wheel. She felt like she was going crazy, like she was barely holding on to herself, and if one more thing hit her, she was going to spin off into oblivion. Alone. Forever.

Marti was home. Her car was in the driveway, the lights were on in the house, and Spencer realized that her entire very-planned-out schedule for talking to her fiancée had just been stepped up. She'd been waiting for the weekend to have this discussion, but in that moment, Spencer was ready.

"Okay," she said, to the empty interior of her car. "We're going to do this now." With a nod of determination, she pulled on the door handle and got out of her car. She shouldered her gym bag and her purse, looked up at the house, took in a deep, fortifying breath, and headed inside.

Marti was on the couch, her feet on the coffee table and crossed at the ankles. Spencer was surprised she wasn't on her laptop, since she was almost always on her laptop. The television showed somebody ripping a wall out of a bathroom, and Marti seemed engrossed.

"Hey," Spencer said, setting her duffel on the floor and her purse on the kitchen counter.

"Hey," Marti said, not turning around. She held a glass of wine in one hand and Spencer immediately decided she was going to need that. She helped herself to a glass and the open bottle on the counter.

Wine in hand, she went around the couch and sat on it, next to Marti. "Can we talk?" she asked after a large gulp of wine and a moment of steeling herself.

Marti turned to look at her and there was something different in her eyes. Something new. Something that gave Spencer pause. They were a little bloodshot and nearly devoid of mascara. "I think we need to," she said, her voice quiet, her face shuttered.

Spencer furrowed her brow. "Okay." She'd had a whole speech, a whole rehearsed monologue that she'd been rolling around. And suddenly, it was gone from her head. Just...gone. The expression on Marti's face—tired, determined, maybe a tiny bit sad—was not what Spencer had been expecting, and she felt like her world tilted just enough to make her plans slide off the edge.

Marti took in a deep breath, let it out slowly, then sipped her wine. She looked very much like she was gearing up, very much like she did before she practiced her opening argument for a trial. Silent. Pensive. Preparing.

Spencer waited with a growing sense of dread.

"I love you, Spencer," Marti said, still not looking at her. "I love you very much."

"I love you, too," Spencer said, automatically.

Marti did turn to her then, and Spencer was surprised to see her brown eyes filled with tears. "No. You don't." Spencer opened her mouth to protest, but Marti held up a hand, stopping any sound. "It's okay. Spence. It's okay. I get it."

Spencer blinked at her.

"We're not working. We haven't been for a long time. I know it and I'm sure you know it." Marti swallowed and her eyes cleared. Spencer knew she was now in the meat of her speech and all emotion had been removed. It was how she operated. "I was hoping we wouldn't go down this path, but"—she shrugged—"I shouldn't be surprised, really. There have been many signs along the way, especially recently. You can't seem to bring yourself to move a single box here from your place. You have yet to put your house on the market. Our intimacy is…sorely lacking, and has been for a while now."

Spencer's nostrils flared, but before she could protest that their lack of intimacy certainly wasn't all on her, Marti went on.

"We're not working." Her voice went soft, and she uncharacteristically let a sliver of emotion seep in. "I don't think…I don't think you know for sure what you want. And I think you need to figure it out." With a clearing of her throat, Marti took another sip of her wine.

Spencer sat. She blinked some more. She felt weird. This was so not how she saw this conversation going. She'd been prepared to apologize to Marti, to let her know that she'd been absent, but she was back. That she was ready to commit fully to their partnership. Marti had turned it all on its head.

So many emotions washed through Spencer. She chewed on the inside of her cheek as she sat there, vision blurred from unshed tears, and tried to name them. Sadness. Shame. Guilt. Embarrassment. Relief.

Wait.

Relief?

I don't think you know for sure what you want. And I think you need to figure it out.

Those were probably the truest, wisest words anybody had ever said to her.

"Marti." Spencer swallowed the lump in her throat.

Marti turned to her, her expression open for the moment.

"I'm sorry," Spencer whispered.

"I just wanted you to be happy," Marti said quietly, and if she had any hopes of them working things out, she didn't show them. At all. "I'm not perfect. I know that. But I really do care about you."

We've gone from "love" to "care about" in a matter of five minutes, Spencer thought. Which meant Marti was disengaging. Already.

God, it was happening so fast. Spencer couldn't help but feel a little blindsided. And then she did that thing that most people do when they see their relationship about to end, when they see their entire life about to change: she panicked and scrambled. "I can be better. I can. I promise I can. I've just been...distracted lately. But I'm better now. I really am. I can fix it. I can work on it."

Marti slowly shook her head as Spencer babbled. "I don't want my girlfriend to have to 'work on it' to be with me." She made air quotes as she spoke.

Spencer opened her mouth to protest more, but something stopped her. A thought. A realization. Divine intervention. She wasn't sure, but it was something, some feeling. She stayed quiet as unexpected tears suddenly formed and spilled over, coursed down her cheeks. Whether they were from sadness or relief, she wasn't sure. Maybe a little of both?

Marti sat up, scooted to the edge of the couch, and turned to face her. Her voice was gentle, which surprised Spencer. "You don't want to be here. If you did, you'd have moved boxes in weeks ago." She took Spencer's hand in hers, turned it, studied it. "You're an amazing woman, Spencer, and I'm really sorry I didn't make you feel like you are. That's on me."

Spencer cleared her throat and stared at their hands for a moment before meeting Marti's eyes. "You're right," she said softly, not wanting to cause more pain, but knowing she needed to say it out loud. "I'm not happy."

"No. And you haven't been for a very, very long time. I'm not even sure you *know* what makes you happy."

The tears were flowing freely now. "Me neither." But she had an idea...

Marti squeezed Spencer's hands, and in that moment, Spencer felt closer to her than she had in months. "Don't you think you owe it to yourself to find out?"

Spencer let the question hang in the air, but her brain was screaming an answer. *God, yes.*

❖

An hour and a half later, Spencer sat in her car in her own driveway, her back seat empty but her trunk almost full. It had been painfully obvious as she gathered her things from Marti's house just how right Marti had been. It had taken less than an hour to pack up the things of hers that she kept at Marti's. Her jewelry-making stuff, some toiletries, one drawer of clothes, two pairs of shoes, a jacket, a cookbook, and a coffee mug with Wonder Woman on it.

She'd cried. Marti had left, thank God, because Spencer was feeling a mix of stupid, humiliated, and devastated. She didn't want Marti to see that. More accurately, she was pretty sure Marti didn't want to see it. They'd hugged. It had been awkward. Then she left to meet her work friends for a drink. Maybe to mourn the loss of her relationship. Maybe to celebrate her freedom.

It didn't take more than three trips from the car to her foyer, and Spencer left all her crap in a pile on the floor, too depressed to deal with it any further.

What the hell had happened?

This was not at all how she'd expected the evening to go. Not at all. As she contemplated this, a little bubble of anger began to well up.

"Seriously?" she said, as she crossed the empty living room and headed toward the kitchen. "This is what you get for doing the right thing?" There was a half-full bottle of Chardonnay in the fridge, and she poured herself a glass, carried it back into the living room, and flopped onto the couch.

Spencer was at a loss.

What did she do now? What was the next logical step? Was there even a next step?

She sipped her wine and felt her tears well up.

No, this was not what she'd expected. Her whole life, her entire existence had just been altered. In a matter of a half hour, everything had changed. The year was almost over, and the view she'd had of the upcoming year had just been drastically transformed until she didn't even recognize it. By next spring, she was supposed to be married, living in one house instead of two, and feeling happy (which, she knew, would not have been the case). Instead she would be single, living alone, and feeling...what?

That was the weirdest part of it all: Spencer wasn't quite sure how to feel, and that scared her more than anything else. If she was good at only one thing, it was knowing what was expected of her. But right now? How was she supposed to feel?

She'd never felt so adrift in her life and it terrified her.

What was she supposed to do now?

❖

"Jesus, Mary, and Joseph, woman. What the hell is wrong with you?" Zoe was half joking, a grin on her face and a teasing eye roll to accompany it, but Rebecca also knew she was partly serious. Mostly because she'd asked herself the very same question multiple times.

"I don't know! Can't you help me? Please? I'm a danger to myself and others." Rebecca sipped her latte and looked around.

Grounded seemed unusually busy for a Wednesday night. Rebecca had been at Nick's place for a short time, but he was exhausted and Rebecca could tell that Michelle was, too. So even though she had a few things she wanted to go over with Nick, she left them to get some sleep without her hanging around, staring at them.

Thank God there had been a text from Zoe because Rebecca couldn't face going home and being alone with her thoughts. Even Veruca Salt had begun to look at her with pity in her green cat eyes.

Stopping for caffeine. Time to meet up?

Rebecca had arrived first. Zoe had shown up five minutes later on her break.

Now they sat at a table near the window and watched the headlights zip by. Something hip and folksy was playing over the speakers, and the hum of conversation was steady.

"You just blurted it out? Please don't marry her? Just like that?" Zoe's expression still registered disbelief; it hadn't changed at all since Rebecca had told her.

With a defeated sigh, Rebecca hung her head. "I did."

Zoe seemed to get that Rebecca wasn't happy about it either. She closed a hand over Rebecca's wrist. "What happened?" she asked softly.

Rebecca shook her head, tried to take herself back to the headspace she'd ended up in when Spencer had given her the bracelet. She wore it now on her left wrist, fingered it with the other hand. "Ever since Nick gave me his 'life is too fucking short' speech, I can't get it out of my head. It's so weird." She took a sip from her cup. Zoe was watching her carefully, intently. "It made me look at my own life. Am I happy? Am I doing what I want to? If I get hit by a bus tomorrow, what regrets will I have?"

"I get that," Zoe said, with a nod. She removed her hand, picked up her espresso, and sipped. "I've seen people die on my watch. I've also seen them come back from the brink, and that's the overwhelming lesson those who return have learned: life is too fucking short." She paused. "So, where does Spencer fit in?"

"That's just it," Rebecca said. "Everywhere. How is that possible?"

Zoe's brow furrowed and she shook her head.

"When I asked myself those questions, my brain asked them about Spencer, too. Is she happy? Is she doing what she wants to? What regrets would she have? I have no idea why. And then she showed up and gave me this bracelet, and all I could think was that she's so incredibly kind and sweet, and I'm worried that she's settling for less than she deserves."

"You know she's a big girl, right?"

"Yes," Rebecca said, on a sigh.

"And you know it isn't up to you to decide if she's making the right decisions for her life, right?"

"Yes." Grudging.

"Rebecca." Zoe waited until Rebecca met her eyes. "You've gotta let this go."

Rebecca's voice was a whisper. "I know."

"It's driving you crazy, and ultimately, she is not your responsibility." Zoe's words were gentle—and true—but still hard to hear.

Rebecca swallowed hard, looked out the window.

"Want my advice?"

Forcing a small smile onto her face, Rebecca nodded. "Please."

"I say focus on you. Get back on the dating site. Find things to keep yourself occupied. The bride class is just about over, right? So you won't have to see her as often, and she'll gradually fade away. Just take care of this girl." She tapped her forefinger on the back of Rebecca's hand. "I happen to like this girl. She's going to make some woman ridiculously happy. Soon. I know it."

It didn't help a ton, but it did help a little. "Thanks, Zoe."

"Absolutely." Zoe sat back in her chair, sipped, then a big grin split her face. "Now, do you want to hear about my worst call so far today?"

"Yes, please." The change of subject was good. Not 100 percent effective, but it was good. Zoe was an animated storyteller, hands waving all over the place, her brown eyes widening, and Rebecca couldn't help but laugh. Which was also good. It kept her mind off tomorrow. Because tomorrow was the day she needed to start really letting go of the woman she cared too much about…the woman she couldn't have.

How the hell was she going to do that?

CHAPTER TWENTY-ONE

February was easily Rebecca's least favorite month of the year. The holidays were long over, spring was still three months off, and she wasn't a skier or ice skater. In her opinion, there was nothing to look forward to that might ease the harsh cold of a northeast winter any time soon. Yeah, she intensely disliked February.

This lunch had been nice, though. Not stellar. Not life-altering. But nice. Rebecca watched as Stacy, her latest internet date, headed for the ladies' room. She was thirty-six, a broker, and seemed like a normal, intelligent woman. She was attractive and amusing, and lunch with her had been enjoyable.

The past couple of months had taught her not to expect anything more. If she had a nice time, some nice conversation with a woman who held her attention, she'd been given strict instructions from Zoe not to write that off. In fact, she was supposed to set up a second date, right then and there, if possible.

Rebecca had done that twice so far. This was her second date with Stacy, and Rebecca thought it might be time to move from coffee and lunch dates to dinner, which was more intimate. She pulled her phone out to check her calendar for the weekend and wished she was a bit more excited, instead of feeling like she was following a schedule of events somebody else set up for her.

"Rebecca?"

"Hm?" Rebecca looked up and into blue eyes. Not just any blue eyes, though. Blue eyes she knew well. Blue eyes she'd memorized. Blue eyes she'd missed. "Spencer. Hi." She sat up straighter, and the smile broke across her face with no permission from her. All on its own, just parted her lips, showed Spencer her teeth, made it alarmingly obvious how happy she was to see her.

Spencer gestured to Stacy's empty chair. "I don't want to interrupt. I just..." She jerked a thumb over her shoulder. "I was sitting over there and saw you, and..." Her voice trailed off for a beat, and she cleared her throat. "I wanted to say hi."

"I'm glad you did. I haven't seen you in a long time." The truth was, she hadn't seen Spencer since that day in the gym. The day she'd told her not to get married. Spencer hadn't come back to finish the bride class. Any time Rebecca asked Sherry if she'd seen Spencer in spin class—and she didn't ask often because she didn't want Sherry's judgey looks—she was told no.

"Yeah, I know." Spencer looked down at her feet, then up and out the window past Rebecca. "I'm sorry about that. I meant to text you. I needed...do you...I just..." A beat went by before she wet her lips, then returned her gaze to Rebecca's, snagged her eyes and held them. "Can we get together some time? I..." She looked down again, then back up, but didn't say any more.

There was something different about her. Rebecca couldn't put a finger on it, but it was there. A new shine. A polish. A surety. Before she knew what she was doing, Rebecca said, "I'd like that. Very much."

"I'm sorry, am I interrupting?" Stacy's voice startled Rebecca. And Spencer, too, if the slight flinch she made was any indication. She pointed to the chair where Spencer stood.

"Oh. No. Sorry." Spencer stepped to the side to allow Stacy access to her chair. "I was just saying hello to my..." Her smile was genuine and it made Rebecca feel warm. "Trainer."

Stacy studied Spencer as Rebecca watched with interest. They looked at one another, the smile on Stacy's face slightly forced. Spencer's smile was unassuming, but there was a flicker of something in her eyes that Rebecca couldn't quite place.

"Spencer Thompson," Spencer said, holding her hand out to Stacy.

That yanked Rebecca out of her analysis, and she winced. "I'm so sorry. Stacy, Spencer took a class of mine at the gym last year. Spencer, this is Stacy, my—"

"Date," Stacy supplied, before Rebecca could finish her sentence.

Spencer nodded, seemed to not miss a beat, and they shook hands. "It's nice to meet you." There was a quick moment of slightly awkward silence before she continued. "Well. I've got to run. It was good seeing you, Rebecca. And nice to meet you, Stacy." She turned and left, her heels clicking on the tile floor as Rebecca followed the exit with her eyes.

"Looks like I nipped that in the bud," Stacy said, her expression satisfied.

"I'm sorry?"

"I saw how she looked at you." Stacy smiled, gave a shrug. "I needed to mark my territory."

Rebecca blinked at her, brow furrowed, mind boggled.

❖

"I don't think she was *trying* to turn me off," Rebecca said to Nick later, as he sweated profusely on the stair climber and she stood next to it poking buttons and changing the resistance.

"Cut it out, goddamn it," he said, through heaving breaths. His gray tank top was drenched, as was his face, which he mopped with a white gym towel. "Nah, she probably wasn't."

"But that's what happened," she said. "She called me her territory. I felt like a tree she was about to pee on."

Nick chuckled. Or tried anyway, given how out of breath he was. He climbed in silence for another three minutes before he reached the twenty-minute mark and Rebecca told him to ease off. He stepped down, wiped his face again, then turned to her. "And what about the other one?"

"The other one what?" Rebecca asked, feigning confusion. She knew exactly what other one he was talking about.

"Spencer."

"What about her?"

They were headed toward the free weights, but Nick stopped and gave her a look. "Really? We're gonna play this game?"

Rebecca sighed. "I don't know about her. That's the truth." And it was. Coffee had been several hours ago and she'd taught a Power Fit class and met with four different clients, but the entire time, Spencer had been on her mind. Again. Just like that. Sometimes, in the forefront, super-prominent, with her beautiful smile and those ridiculous eyes. Other times, she hung out in the background and gave Rebecca a little wave if her thoughts drifted close.

"You wanna meet up with her?" Nick asked, as he situated himself in front of a mirror, a dumbbell in each hand.

"I don't know." Again, the truth. "I mean, nothing's changed, right?"

Nick shrugged, then began curling the weights. "Maybe. Maybe not."

"What does that mean?"

"It means you don't actually know."

"You know, call me crazy, but it's sounding to me like you actually want me to contact her."

"Do you want to?"

"God, I don't know, Nick." Rebecca could feel her frustration mounting. She'd felt it all day, which she didn't understand.

"You want to know my thoughts?" Nick said, and then grunted, the weights becoming harder to lift.

Rebecca sat down on a nearby bench, mentally counting his reps. "Do I have a choice?"

"Nope."

"That's what I thought. Two more, by the way."

Nick finished his reps, dropped the weights, and grabbed his water bottle. "I've known you for how long?" He took a swig of water and Rebecca did the math in her head.

"Twenty-two years? Twenty-three?"

"Right. And I've seen you through a lot of ups and downs with chicks."

Rebecca nodded and didn't bother to correct his descriptor. This time.

"And in all those years, I never saw you as..." He squinted as he looked off into the middle distance as if searching for the right word. "Affected. As you were by this girl. I don't know if that's a good thing or a bad thing. I honestly don't. Me and Michelle have had many conversations about it." He looked at Rebecca then, and she could feel the love he had for her. "I know I pushed you the other way before, but...I'm not sure you should let her pass you by without being completely sure. You know?" His voice went soft. "I don't want to see you miss out on somebody that might be your Michelle."

To say Rebecca was surprised would be an understatement. Nick was not an emotional guy. He didn't share feelings. In fact, he liked to pretend he didn't have any. But the softness in his brown eyes in that moment touched Rebecca deeply. So deeply that her vision blurred.

"No. Cut that out," he said, pointing, and swung his towel playfully at her.

Rebecca laughed and caught the one tear that had spilled over with a thumb. "Sorry. Crisis averted."

"Thank fucking Christ," he said. "There's no crying in the gym."

"Oh, trust me," Rebecca said, standing and pulling herself together. "There's plenty of crying in the gym. Plenty. Come with me and I'll show you."

There was no more talk of Spencer for the rest of Nick's workout. In fact, they joked a bit more than usual; Rebecca was sure Nick was trying to lighten the mood just a bit. It worked. By the time he high-fived her and headed to the locker room, she felt a lot better. And even more confident as she scrolled through her contacts to find Spencer's name right where she'd left it three months earlier, and stared.

What the hell should she do?

❖

Travis's birthday was February fourteenth. Spencer's parents always said he was their Valentine baby, and every year, they threw him a combination birthday/Valentine's Day party to celebrate. He requested the same thing each time: cheeseburgers, fries, and half-moon cookies frosted with hearts instead of the traditional half-vanilla, half-chocolate.

They'd finished dinner and the Thompson family was now sitting around the dining room table having cookies before Travis opened his gifts.

"Did your girlfriend at the bakery make these for you, T?" Mary Beth asked him, as she bit into the cookie he'd given her.

Travis's blush crept slowly up his neck until his face was a deep red. "She's not my girlfriend," he said unconvincingly, giving his shoulders a shrug and ducking his head a bit.

"I don't know. I don't think she makes birthday heart cookies for just anybody."

His blush deepened, which made his sister grin.

"Mary Elizabeth, stop teasing your brother." Their mother said it like she was talking to two elementary-aged children, must have realized it, and shook her head, an expression of quiet happiness on her face.

"No, it's okay, Ma. I can take it." Travis took a huge bite of his cookie.

Mary Beth threw Spencer a look and whispered, "He loves it."

"He does," Spencer agreed. Being teased about his bakery crush was one of Travis's favorite things.

"This one came in the mail today from Uncle Andy and Aunt Jeannie," Margie said as she slid a gift toward Travis. Her sister and brother-in-law lived in Phoenix, but always sent birthday and Christmas gifts for Travis and his sisters. Travis shoved the rest of the cookie into his mouth and reached for the brightly wrapped package. "Chew that," Margie ordered, holding tight to the box.

"How're you doing, kiddo?" Mary Beth took advantage of the distraction to focus on Spencer, who didn't really want to talk about it.

"Fine." Shrug. She watched Travis but could feel Mary Beth's eyes on her. They stayed long enough to make Spencer squirm, and she looked at her in defeat. "What?"

"You don't seem fine." There was nothing but love and concern on her sister's face. "You seem sad. And a little lost." Under the table, she grasped Spencer's knee, squeezed. "Talk to me."

Travis's whoop of joy over the video games he'd opened gave her cover.

"I ran into Rebecca the other day."

"Really? Where?"

"Coffee shop. I think she was on a date." Spencer worked hard to say it nonchalantly and was pretty sure she failed.

"Was that the first time you've seen her since…" Mary Beth let her voice trail off, leaving the sentence for Spencer to fill in however made her feel the least terrible.

"Since I've been single? Yeah."

"Did you talk to her?"

"I did. I asked if we could get together some time."

Mary Beth gaped at her; Spencer could see it without even looking, and it caused one corner of her mouth to tug up in a half smile of self-satisfaction. "Wow," her sister said. "I did not see that coming."

"I know, right? Neither did I. It just kind of…slipped out."

Mary Beth squeezed Spencer's knee again. "What did she say?"

"She said she'd like to, and then the date came back from the ladies' room, and it got all kinds of awkward. I ran out of there like I was being chased by zombies."

"I can shoot zombies now," Travis said, holding his game up for Spencer to see.

"Good. You can protect me."

"You got it." He held up a hand and she slapped it.

"Have you talked to her since?" Mary Beth asked, as Travis ripped open another gift.

Spencer shook her head. "Chickened out."

"You want to know what I think?" Mary Beth asked.

"Does it matter? You're going to tell me anyway." Spencer wrinkled her nose in fun.

Mary Beth glanced at the table where Travis had finished with his gifts and was talking animatedly to their father. She pushed her chair back and said quietly to Spencer, "Come with me." Spencer followed her, brow furrowed, until they were in the kitchen, just the two of them. Mary Beth turned to face her, put both hands on Spencer's shoulders, and told her, "I think you're ready."

That surprised Spencer. She wasn't sure she agreed. She didn't feel ready. At all. "You do?"

"I do. Because I've observed something." When Spencer didn't comment, Mary Beth seemed to take a different tack. She dropped her hands from Spencer's shoulders and instead twirled a hank of her sister's hair around a finger. "How long were you with Marti?"

"About two years."

Mary Beth nodded, still twirling, seemed to watch her own hand as she searched for the right words. "In those two years? I never once saw you as relaxed and just...*you* as you are now. Not once."

Spencer's eyes widened in yet more surprise. "What the hell are you talking about? Relaxed? I'm not relaxed. I'm a mess. I'm sad. I feel...lost. I..." She shook her head, not wanting to list more. When she turned her gaze back to Mary Beth, her sister was smiling, and she lifted her hand, rested her palm against Spencer's cheek.

"Yes. You're all of those things. But you're also *you*. You're back to being the Spencer who calls me a couple times a week and comes to family dinner and *stays*. I know you're sad, honey, but that'll pass. And to me, it's worth it just to have my little sister back. I missed her."

Spencer's eyes welled.

"Therefore..."

"There's more?" Spencer said, in a feigned horrified protest.

Mary Beth laughed. "Therefore, I think you should find out where Rebecca is."

Spencer grimaced.

"Can't hurt, can it? I mean, if she's not interested or she's got somebody now, you're no worse for wear. Right?"

That was true. It was a reasonable idea. A super-intimidating and terrifying idea, but a reasonable one.

"Spencer, you didn't finish your cookie." Travis bounced into the kitchen like he bounced everywhere, a grown man who walked like a happy toddler. He held out the remaining half of Spencer's cookie, but stopped when he saw her face. "Why are you crying?" he asked, his voice going soft, concern evident on his face.

"I'm not," Spencer said, wiping her cheek and sniffing. "I'm okay."

"You promise?" he asked, his innocent eyes wide. "I don't want you to be sad anymore. It makes me sad when you're sad."

"It does?"

He nodded, his expression serious, and Spencer held her arms open to him.

As he stepped in and let her hug him, she said, "I promise to stop being sad very soon. Okay?" She felt him nod against her shoulder. Then he pulled back.

"Here." He held the cookie out again. "Mom says you have to finish what you started."

Spencer looked at the offering, reached her hand out to take the cookie as the words resonated.

You have to finish what you started...

CHAPTER TWENTY-TWO

B y the beginning of March, the snow was still piled higher than most people liked. Spencer, however, didn't mind. She enjoyed winter. She liked curling up in a big, bulky sweatshirt and reading a good book on the couch. She had also begun to really enjoy snowshoeing this year, something new that Lucy had gotten her into. No, Spencer didn't hate winter. What she did hate about March, though, was the brown. Everything went from sparkling clean and white to brown and dirty and just kind of gross. The roads were wet. The cars in front of you spat dirty road spray onto your windshield. The banks of snow left looked like they'd been draped with a light brown veil of sorts. Any spots that were free of snow were simply muddy.

March was dirty, and therefore, Spencer's least favorite month of the year.

Except for this year.

This year, the beginning of March marked a change for Spencer. A lot of changes, actually. It marked the start of her new life. That was how she liked to look at it. She'd needed time, and she'd taken it. After she and Marti had split last November, Spencer had been reeling, that was true. Reeling for what felt like a lot longer than it was. But Mary Beth had been right. She was ready.

Spring meant new beginnings, and this was definitely a new beginning for her. She pulled the door to BodyFit open and walked in for the first time in more than three months.

The young man behind the counter was new to Spencer, his

sandy hair shaved on the sides and styled into a fun swoop at the top, as perfectly placed as the hair on a cartoon character. Absently, she wondered how much product he had to use to keep it from moving. Below the swoop, he had a silver hoop piercing his eyebrow, and his smile was friendly and welcoming.

"Hi there. What can I do for you?"

"I have my first appointment with my trainer." She gave him the name and he punched some keys on the computer.

"Terrific. Why don't you go get changed and I'll have her meet you in the cardio area?"

With a nod of thanks, Spencer headed to the locker room. She set her bag in a locker and pulled out her phone to silence it just as it pinged at her. A text message from Lucy.

You doing okay?

A small smile tugged at the corners of Spencer's mouth as she typed back. *So far.*

Seen her yet?

Spencer shook her head as she typed. *No. Avoided looking.*

Lucy sent a smile, then: *Text me when you're done.*

Spencer silenced the phone and slid it back into her bag, then changed into her black workout tights and a red tank. She hadn't been to the gym in three months, but she'd been snowshoeing with Lucy and Ethan and she'd dusted off the stationary bike in her basement, had begun riding it a few times a week. She actually felt almost good about her body. But she knew she could do better, that she just needed a little guidance. A little help. And she didn't intend to let her not-inexpensive gym membership go to waste, even if Marti had paid for it.

So. Here she was.

Spencer stood in front of the full-length mirror as she pulled her hair into a ponytail, then blew out a breath. "Here we go," she whispered.

Near the treadmills stood a cheerful African American woman dressed in calf-length workout pants and a white T-shirt with the BodyFit logo on it. Her dark hair was in a messy twist at the back of her head and her smile was open as she turned.

"Hey there. Spencer?" At Spencer's nod, she held out a hand and her smile grew. "I'm Aisha. It's really great to meet you."

Aisha knew her stuff. That became clear immediately. She was encouraging but firm, asking Spencer about any issues she might have with her back, knees, or any other body part that could give her trouble during certain exercises. She asked questions, made observations, and even cracked jokes. Spencer liked her right off the bat.

It was when they were wrapping up a circuit and Spencer was doing the dreaded plank ("Man, I thought I'd at least escape this on my first day with you," she'd whined at Aisha good-naturedly) when she saw a pair of bright pink Nikes walk nearby and stop near her face.

"You know," said a familiar voice, "if you make her do this long enough, you might get an *MF* out of her."

"Oh, yeah?" Aisha asked. "I'll keep that in mind."

"It's totally worth it."

The pink shoes moved away, and Spencer dropped to the ground with a groan, turned her head just in time to catch Rebecca disappear around a corner.

"Good day today," Aisha was saying, and Spencer mentally shook herself back to the subject at hand. "I can see some things that we need to focus on. I'll take the list of things you want to work on and incorporate what I saw today, and we'll come up with a great regimen for you, okay? We'll work together."

Spencer liked Aisha. They were a good fit. That's what she'd hoped for.

She'd also come for something else.

"Great. I'll see you on Thursday." She smiled as Aisha nodded and high-fived her. Instead of heading for the locker room, though, Spencer headed upstairs toward the offices.

"Hey, pretty blond lady." Bobby Pine caught Spencer off guard halfway up the staircase, and she blinked at him, at his unassuming smile for a moment before realizing his fist was hanging in the air, waiting. She bumped it.

"Hi, Bobby. How's life?"

"Life is awesome now that you're back," he said, with his usual exuberance. "Have a great day!"

Spencer smiled as she followed his descent with her eyes and wondered if he really had noticed she'd been gone. At the top of the staircase, she looked toward the offices and saw Rebecca looking right at her. She yanked her gaze away quickly when Spencer made eye contact with her and seemed to pretend to focus on her computer screen.

"It's now or never," Spencer whispered to herself. Then she took a deep breath, swallowed hard, and headed in Rebecca's direction.

She looked amazing. Again. As always. It never *didn't* surprise Spencer how incredibly attractive she found Rebecca. A tingling in her abdomen was near constant when she was around her, and that hadn't changed, apparently. Hand on her stomach, Spencer willed the feeling to ease up so she could think. Rebecca wore her usual workout pants, these in slate gray, and a muted green V-neck topped with a black zip-up hoodie with the BodyFit logo embroidered in red on one side. Her dark hair had gotten a bit longer and now skimmed her shoulders. Spencer liked it. Rebecca glanced up, saw her, and tucked some hair behind her ear, a gesture that seemed like a nervous one. Spencer found it endearing. And that's when she noticed that Rebecca wore the bracelet Spencer had made her, the black leather worn to softness and looking like it belonged wrapped snugly around her slim wrist. A pang hit Spencer low in her body and made her falter slightly before she pulled herself back together.

"Hi." She helped herself to the chair next to Rebecca's desk without waiting for an invitation.

Rebecca wet her lips. "Hey."

"How have you been?"

Rebecca nodded. "Fine. Fine. You?"

"I'm great."

Rebecca's eyebrows rose and dropped quickly, like she hadn't meant to move them and hoped Spencer hadn't seen. "Yeah? How was the wedding?" A surreptitious glance at Spencer's left hand did not go unnoticed either.

"There wasn't one."

This time, the dark brows stayed raised. "You mean yet?"

"No, I mean there wasn't one, and there won't be one."

It seemed that Rebecca had to take a moment with that. Then another. Her brow furrowed. "What does that mean?"

"It means Marti and I split up. I'm back in my own house, and…" She swallowed hard, then snagged Rebecca's gaze with her own and held it tightly. "I needed some time. I had a lot to sort through."

Rebecca nodded, studied her own hands. "What happened?" She looked up quickly then. "If it's okay to ask."

"It's okay to ask." Spencer took in a deep breath, gathered her thoughts. "I'm a little bit ashamed to say that it wasn't my doing." Rebecca made a face of such surprise that it made Spencer laugh. "I know, right? Turns out, I'm even slower than Marti."

Rebecca seemed to think it was okay to join in the laughter then, and it was a beautiful sight to Spencer, a beautiful sound.

"And it was the best thing she could have done for me because I was ready to commit totally. I mean, like, totally."

"But you weren't happy."

"I know. But I'd lost confidence completely. In everything. In my ability to read people. In knowing what's best for me. Marti cared about me, I knew that, and I thought that was enough." She paused and focused intently on Rebecca. "I was wrong."

"When did this happen?" Rebecca asked softly.

"The night you asked me not to marry her." A mask of guilt settled over Rebecca's face then, and Spencer nipped at it. "No. No, this was not your fault, Rebecca. Don't you see? You were right. You were so exactly right. You told me I deserved better."

"You do."

Spencer smiled. "I know that now. It took a while. It took a lot of tears and a lot of energy and a lot of soul searching. And I'm finally doing so much better." They were quiet for a beat. Then Spencer asked, "So, how's Stacy?"

Rebecca wrinkled her nose. "No idea."

Spencer took that in. "I see."

"You're back at the gym."

"I'm back at the gym."

"Aisha's good." Rebecca tried to hide what she was really thinking, but Spencer saw it. Spencer saw it and her heart warmed and her eyes welled up.

She reached across the desk and closed her hand over Rebecca's forearm. Just that simple touch sent a jolt through her system. "I hired somebody else because I didn't want you to get into trouble."

The furrowed brow again. "For what?"

"For dating your client." Spencer waited until Rebecca caught up. "I mean, that's frowned upon, right?"

Spencer sucked her bottom lip into her mouth. This was it. This was the moment she'd been rehearsing for. Weeks had gone by and she'd talked it through with Lucy, with Mary Beth. She'd played this scene in her head, tried to anticipate every outcome. Rebecca could laugh at her. She could get angry, kick her out. She could be hurt, upset. She could say some pretty rotten things, and they'd probably be true. Or…

Rebecca could do what she actually did.

She smiled. It was slow in coming, as if it was sneaking onto her face, quietly and unobtrusively, tiptoeing until it finally sat there comfortably.

"I mean, it *is* considered inappropriate," she said, drawing out the words.

"Yeah, that's what I thought. Thus, Aisha."

"You want to date me, huh?"

Spencer gave a tiny snort of a laugh and kept her voice low. "I want to do more than date you, Rebecca. But dating is a good place to start, I think. If you'll have me."

Rebecca shook her head. "God, we did everything so backward, didn't we?"

Spencer nodded in agreement. "We totally did."

Rebecca looked at her, held Spencer's gaze with those blue eyes of hers, and Spencer was reminded how much she'd missed this. The fun and easy banter, the zap of electricity between them. Not for the first time, she wondered how she could've been so blind, so naïve as to think this kind of a connection came along on a regular basis.

"I have one more client tonight," Rebecca said finally. She sat forward, leaned closer to Spencer. "Meet me in the parking lot and take me to coffee?"

Relief washed through Spencer like a wave over the sand, and she had no control over the enormous smile that erupted across her face. "I'd love nothing more."

Rebecca stood then, reached out a hand and brushed Spencer's hair off her face. "See you in an hour."

❖

Spencer sat in her car in the parking lot with ten minutes to spare. She was pretty sure time had slowed down to the speed of molasses in January just to mess with her. She'd gotten some groceries, wandered the aisles at the craft store (and bought some jewelry supplies), and made an appointment with Junebug Farms, the local animal shelter, to talk to them about what kind of dog she was looking for. That last one made her grin, and she picked up her phone to scroll through the dogs they currently had for adoption. She got so lost in them that when Rebecca pulled the passenger side door open, it made Spencer jump, a little yelp escaping her lips.

"Sorry," Rebecca said, as she sat and closed the door against the chill. "I didn't mean to scare you. Thought you saw me." She leaned over, presumably to see what held Spencer's interest, and her eyes widened. "You're getting a dog?"

"I am. Haven't picked one yet."

"Oh, Spencer, that's awesome. I'm happy for you. When?"

"I have an appointment this weekend to talk to the shelter." Rebecca looked so genuinely happy for her. "Hey, want to come with me?"

Dark eyebrows raised. "Really?"

"Really. In fact, I'd love to have you there." The words came as a surprise to Spencer; this wasn't her plan. But there was something about Rebecca's smile, her sincere happiness, that Spencer wanted to hold on to.

"Then I'd love to go with you."

The car was running. It was warm. It was dark. And Rebecca was sitting next to her. Things couldn't get much better for Spencer in that moment.

And then they did.

Rebecca leaned forward, no preamble, no warning, and captured Spencer's mouth with her own. The kiss was gentle. Tender, but with a heat that left a promise of what was to come. Spencer let herself sink into it, the feeling so incredibly different from the last time they'd kissed. There was nothing in the background, no little voices to battle or silence, no worries, no guilt. Just Rebecca. Rebecca's lips. Rebecca's presence. And this kiss.

It was everything.

When they finally parted, Rebecca stayed close for a moment, stroked Spencer's face. "I had to get that out of the way," she whispered, her expression apologetic. "It was distracting me."

Spencer swallowed, nodded, tried to find her voice.

Rebecca sat back, looking ridiculously radiant in the passenger seat of Spencer's car. "Now take me on a date."

"Whatever you want," Spencer said, knowing by the feel of it just how lit up her face was. She shifted the car into gear. "Whatever you want."

About the Author

Georgia Beers is the award-winning author of twenty lesbian romances. She resides in upstate New York, where she was born and raised. When not writing, she enjoys way too much TV, not nearly enough wine, spin class at the gym, and walks with her dog. She is currently hard at work on her next book. You can visit her and find out more at www.georgiabeers.com.

Books Available From Bold Strokes Books

Captive by Donna K. Ford. To escape a human trafficking ring, Greyson Cooper and Olivia Danner become players in a game of deceit and violence. Will their love stand a chance? (978-1-63555-215-7)

Crossing the Line by CF Frizzell. The Mob discovers a nemesis within its ranks, and in the ultimate retaliation, draws Stick McLaughlin from anonymity by threatening everything she holds dear. (978-1-63555-161-7)

Love's Verdict by Carsen Taite. Attorneys Landon Holt and Carly Pachett want the exact same thing: the only open partnership spot at their prestigious criminal defense firm. But will they compromise their careers for love? (978-1-63555-042-9)

Precipice of Doubt by Mardi Alexander & Laurie Eichler. Can Cole Jameson resist her attraction to her boss, veterinarian Jodi Bowman, or will she risk a workplace romance and her heart? (978-1-63555-128-0)

Savage Horizons by CJ Birch. Captain Jordan Kellow's feelings for Lt. Ali Ash have her past and future colliding, setting in motion a series of events that strands her crew in an unknown galaxy thousands of light years from home. (978-1-63555-250-8)

Secrets of the Last Castle by A. Rose Mathieu. When Elizabeth Campbell represents a young man accused of murdering an elderly woman, her investigation leads to an abandoned plantation that reveals many dark Southern secrets. (978-1-63555-240-9)

Take Your Time by VK Powell. A neurotic parrot brings police officer Grace Booker and temporary veterinarian Dr. Dani Wingate together in the tiny town of Pine Cone, but their unexpected attraction keeps the sparks flying. (978-1-63555-130-3)

The Last Seduction by Ronica Black. When you allow true love to elude you once and you desperately regret it, are you brave enough to grab it when it comes around again? (978-1-63555-211-9)

The Shape of You by Georgia Beers. Rebecca McCall doesn't play it safe, but when sexy Spencer Thompson joins her workout class, their nonstop sparring forces her to face her ultimate challenge—a chance at love. (978-1-63555-217-1)

Exposed by MJ Williamz. The closet is no place to live if you want to find true love. (978-1-62639-989-1)

Force of Fire: Toujours a Vous by Ali Vali. Immortals Kendal and Piper welcome their new child and celebrate the defeat of an old enemy, but another ancient evil is about to awaken deep in the jungles of Costa Rica. (978-1-63555-047-4)

Landing Zone by Erin Dutton. Can a career veteran finally discover a love stronger than even her pride? (978-1-63555-199-0)

Love at Last Call by M. Ullrich. Is balancing business, friendship, and love more than any willing woman can handle? (978-1-63555-197-6)

Pleasure Cruise by Yolanda Wallace. Spencer Collins and Amy Donovan have few things in common, but a Caribbean cruise offers both women an unexpected chance to face one of their greatest fears: falling in love. (978-1-63555-219-5)

Running Off Radar by MB Austin. Maji's plans to win Rose back are interrupted when work intrudes, and duty calls her to help a SEAL team stop a Russian mobster from harvesting gold from the bottom of Sitka Sound. (978-1-63555-152-5)

Shadow of the Phoenix by Rebecca Harwell. In the final battle for the fate of Storm's Quarry, even Nadya's and Shay's powers may not be enough. (978-1-63555-181-5)

Take a Chance by D. Jackson Leigh. There's hardly a woman within fifty miles of Pine Cone that veterinarian Trip Beaumont can't charm, except for the irritating new cop, Jamie Grant, who keeps leaving parking tickets on her truck. (978-1-63555-118-1)

The Outcasts by Alexa Black. Spacebus driver Sue Jones is running from her past. When she crash-lands on a faraway world, the Outcast Kara might be her chance for redemption. (978-1-63555-242-3)

Death in Time by Robyn Nyx. Working in the past is hell on your future. (978-1-63555-053-5)